Cha

You're Nev...

"Freeze! Put your hands in the air!" Bill stood up, covered in red from head to toe, clutching Sandy's purple weapon.

"Leave him to me boys, I'll take him to see the boss and I'll explain to Bill how much trouble he's in on the way," Marvin shouted towards the other men as he secured Bill's wrists into the handcuffs again, only this time much tighter than before. Bill peered around the room for Sandy, but she was nowhere to be seen. As he was led out of a hidden door to the side of the stage, Marvin pointed his finger towards Bill expressively telling him off, before explaining that "what he had just done to Sandy was really bad, and in the state of Texas, it carried a sentence of twenty-five years to life."

Bill was led through a series of doors and corridors, still dressed in his bright red suit with his family treasures poking out for everyone to see, and wondering why his weapon was still primed after being told of the trouble he found himself in. Eventually they came to a door with two large, muscular men either side of it. The door was twice the size of a normal one with a sign above in red

1

letters: 'DO NOT ENTER'. The men acknowledged Marvin with a handshake before the man on the right asked, "Is this the pervert who just assaulted my woman? Look at him standing there like a weasel." He turned to Bill, and with a serious face, told him that for his sake, he should hope and pray that the boss doesn't want to cover this one up. It was his turn to carry out the punishment, and a long prison sentence would be easier than spending his final five minutes alive alone with him. Bill's body was trembling, his heart was beating erratically after listening to what he'd just been told, he just wanted to plead with the man and tell him how it was, a simple misunderstanding. He looked at Marvin and pointed with both hands towards his muzzle, gesturing for him to remove it. "Sorry partner, I can't take it off. If I do, I could get charged with tampering with evidence. It's state law that if we hand you over to the police, then we have to do so with you dressed exactly as the crime was committed." Bill couldn't believe what he was hearing, prison or death? He thought to himself, knowing he'd really messed up this time with his choice of birthday gifts for Shelly. Bill's thoughts were interrupted by the man standing to the left of the door. He told Marvin that he could leave Bill with them, and they would take good care of him until the boss was ready to see him. Marvin looked at Bill who was shaking his head from side to side, pleading for Marvin to stay. He smiled before replying, "It's alright lads, I've got to know this one quite well, so I'll stay and tell the boss what's happened; I'd hate for him to hear an exaggerated third-hand version of events."

The men stared at each other before focusing their attention back towards Marvin again, both saying "OK" at the same time, whilst Bill's mind slipped back to earlier and how he'd got himself into his current predicament in the first place.

One hour, thirty-four minutes and sixteen seconds earlier.

It must be around here somewhere, Bill thought to himself as he navigated the streets amongst the hustle and bustle of fast-paced, inner city life; a life far from his usual one back on his ranch in the middle of Ringgold. Life was so laid back there nothing ever got done. He was proud of himself for having driven the one-hundred-plus miles to arrive in Dallas without getting lost. All he had to do now was find somewhere to park and continue his journey on foot, hoping that the directions Conner had given him were accurate; he'd hate to get lost and rely on asking a complete stranger for directions to the Real Adult Superstore, shaking at the mere thought of the humiliation he'd feel if he had too. Bill picked up the piece of paper that Conner had drawn a map on. Carefully studying it whilst driving, he concluded that if he took the third turn on the left, the entrance to the superstore should be half-way down on the right. Driving along, his mind became distracted by all the bright advertising billboards high on the sides of buildings. He'd never seen anything like them before in his 50 years on this planet. He was amazed at how crystal-clear the images were; images tempting you to buy the advertiser's products portrayed by scantily clad goddess's selling the benefits of using the said advertised goods. Bill laughed to himself, questioning whether anybody could be so stupid to believe the claims of the advertisements. His eyes then focused on the amount of people and cars everywhere. It was chaos; cars suddenly stopping with no warning at all, pedestrians walking out into the road without looking and everyone fighting for whatever little space was available so that they could continue with their journeys. Bill knew that he had to take the next left and somehow barge his way through this heavy traffic in order to make it. He indicated and started to pull over when he heard a prolonged, loud beep from a car horn, followed by an angry man shouting something in an accent that he couldn't quite understand; but sounded like, "fucking wanker." Bill waved apologetically and continued to pull over to the left lane and waited patiently for the traffic lights to turn green. His mind wandered to the reason why he's made the trip to Dallas in the first place: his wife Shelly's upcoming 50th birthday present.

Bill had been racking his brains for ages trying to decide what to get her, until eventually he plucked up the courage to ask what she wanted. He really didn't want to make a balls-up of such an important present like he'd done in most previous years. He was rubbish at choosing gifts. Two Christmases before last he'd seen how Shelly had been struggling while cooking the Christmas

4

vegetables in her small old pans, so he decided to buy her a new bigger set as her present for the following year. But he didn't get his Christmas vegetables cooked in them. Instead, he spent the next two days in bed recovering from the beating that Shelly gave him with the pans. After she'd ripped the wrapping paper off, her excitement turned to anger when she realised what she'd been given. As she flung the largest of the three shiny new pans from her right hand, it made a loud thud as it connected with Bill's left temple and knocked him out cold with the ferocity of her throw. Lying lifeless on the floor, Shelly continued to use him as target practice with the other two pans. He'd hate to think what sort of a punishment he'd get for screwing her 50th present up. The lights changed to green and he checked the road-name on the sign. As he turned in to, 'Main Street', relief came over him, he'd made it and luckily a car was just pulling out of a parking space. Bill grabbed it before anyone else could. He turned his engine off and stayed still for a moment, questioning in his mind if he was going to buy the right thing for Shelly. When he'd asked her what she wanted for her 50th Shelly hadn't given much away, she'd simply said, "Surprise me, use your imagination. I want it to be a birthday where I'll try new things and experiences that awaken my body and mind; things that I'll never forget and if I like them, I'll do them again."

After hearing Shelly say that, Bill came up with the idea of getting her some nice sexy underwear to wear and a collection of toys to experiment with, awakening her body and mind as she'd suggested, and hopefully igniting the spark in their love life at the same time. Decision made, and as he'd come this far, he was going to go through with it, he picked up the map one last time. Studying it, he realised that he needed to look for an old, cast iron arched sign hanging above an alleyway, saying, 'Can We Tempt You,' on it. He got out of his car, put two dollar coins into the parking meter before walking down the road, his eyes focused on finding the sign on the other side. After a five minute walk through the crowds of people, he finally saw it hanging there, in between two huge buildings. He made his way across the road, dodging the cars travelling in both directions, whilst his heartbeat raced at the thought of what he was about to witness in his first ever visit to a sex shop.

Bill found himself staring down a dimly lit alleyway, wondering if he was in the right place. The arched iron sign was above his head, but from where he was standing, it didn't look anything like the Adult Superstore he'd been told about. Surely it should be massive if it's a superstore, with bright signs and offers to tempt you in, he thought to himself. From the back of the alley he spotted a large black man approaching him, waving, and shouting, "I'll be right with you now partner. I was just having a quick pee." Bill waved back and replied, "Don't rush, I'm not sure if I'm in the right place. I don't want to be wasting your time, I'm looking for the Real Adult Superstore. Do you know where it is, please?" By this time, the man had fully emerged from the alleyway, holding his right hand out towards Bill whilst saying, "I certainly do. My name's Marvin and seeing as you haven't been before, I'll be your guide for the day and show you around." Bill reached out to shake Marvin's outstretched hand and instantly noticed how tight his grip was. He didn't really want a guide showing him around, he'd much rather browse at his leisure, unsure as to how he'd feel once inside. Bill explained this to Marvin and asked to be shown the way to the entrance. After a short pause Bill received an answer he wasn't really expecting. "I'm terribly sorry but it's a condition of our trading licence. For us to use real live models to demonstrate our goods, everyone who visits for the first time has to register for membership and must be accompanied at all times. Now let's get you registered. What do we call you?" Feeling nervous, Bill took a deep breath, unsure whether to register and see what awaits him inside or turn around and buy Shelly something different. He exhaled before replying, "I'm Bill from Ringgold." Marvin handed him a clipboard with a form on. He informed Bill that once he'd completed it, he could enter the superstore and have his eyes opened to the delightful pleasures that await. Bill started to complete the form when for some reason he felt scared, uncomfortable, and dirty at the thought of what he was about to witness: real women demonstrating whatever products he wanted. He was also getting quite excited at the thought of seeing somebody other than his wife naked, with their flesh hanging out of sexy silk and lace underwear.

Bill had completed the first two questions of the registration form, but was baffled as to why they needed to know the answer to the next one: "How many people have you had sexual intercourse with?" He looked at Marvin and asked him in a nervous voice, "Do I have to fill this in and why do you need to know?" Marvin chuckled before he replied, "Well, you see, Bill, I'm the lucky person who's going to be your wingman for your first ever experience of The Real Adult Superstore. In order for me to do my job properly and give you the best experience possible, I need to know all about you: who you are; where you come from; what are you looking to gain from your visit today; what makes you tick, etcetera. So, while you're completing the rest of the form, why don't you tell me all about yourself, instead of me having to read it." Bill felt nervous and anxious at this point, he contemplated whether to hand Marvin the uncompleted form, along with the clipboard and pen, before running as fast as he could in the opposite direction. But then he pictured Shelly standing at the top of the stairs, looking sexy in the underwear that he was about to buy, beckoning him to follow her upstairs and play with her new collection of toys. With a smile on his face Bill opened up to Marvin, warts, and all.

He explained how he was a 50-year-old dog loving straight male, an only child who owned a cattle ranch in Ringgold which had been in his family for generations, how he's been married for twenty-seven years to his beautiful wife Shelly, and how unfortunately, despite longing for children, Shelly had never been able to conceive. Bill paused for a minute, staring at Marvin, who had a sympathetic look on his face and was beckoning for him to continue. Bill commenced completing the form again before continuing to tell Marvin some more. He explained that he was in Dallas to buy Shelly a surprise for her upcoming 50th birthday and how he was rubbish at buying presents. And that when he asked his wife what she wanted, she told him to surprise her and use his imagination. She wanted it to be a birthday where she would try new things and experiences that awaken her body and mind, things that she'll never forget and if she liked them, she'd do them again. And so that's when he decided what she was really saying was that she wanted to try and broaden her sexual horizons, with sex toys and sexy lingerie. After a short pause, he continued to tell Marvin how Shelly was the only woman he'd ever kissed, seen naked and made love to. He admitted to Marvin that the 'bedroom department' had been lacking for a couple of years since he bought Shelly pans as a Christmas present, and how he ended up unconscious after Shelly attacked him with them. Marvin laughed out loudly, as did Bill, before adding how he missed the long summer days they used to spend frolicking about in the hay barns naked, experimenting, while making love for hours on end. Bill then finished off by telling Marvin that this was his first trip outside of Ringgold, ever, and his life was a pretty boring country one where the most excitement that he ever got was when a raging bull had escaped its pen and needed capturing. Marvin smiled before telling Bill, in a reassuring manner, how glad he was that he had been so honest with him and hadn't come over all macho, like most other first-timers, and that he could now take great care of him once they were inside. He then asked Bill to tell him all about Shelly, what she looked like? Was she a nice wife? Did she come from a big family? How did they meet? Had she ever slept with anyone else?

Bill had completed the form by this time and handed it back to Marvin. His body was now trembling with excitement at the thought of being one step closer to experiencing the thrill of his life. "Can I tell you all about her as we walk towards the store please, Marvin? I've only paid for a couple of hours parking and I'd hate to get a ticket," Bill asked calmly, unsure how he could do so with all the wicked thoughts going through his mind about Shelly and her toys. "Sure, you can, but it's very important that you carry on being completely honest with me," Marvin replied. He put his right arm around Bill's left shoulder, and they started walking side by side down the dimly-lit alleyway. That was Bill's cue to open up about Shelly, describing how she was a stunningly beautiful 6 ft tall blond with the most amazing figure for a nearly fifty-year-old. She was an only child who lived on the next ranch in the county some ten miles away. He explained that they met when he was 21 after her family had just bought the neighbouring ranch, and how he'd been invited over to her parent's ranch for her 21st birthday party. It was a big event and a huge celebration, attended by cattle farmers and their families from hundreds of miles away. Her father had arranged for lots of competitions to be staged, showing off a wide variety of traditional country skills followed by an amazing hog roast, dancing, and lots of moonshine. Marvin interrupted, asking if Bill won any of the competitions and if that was how he came to marry her. "Sadly not," Bill replied, before explaining that what he was about to tell him he had kept secret for twenty-nine years, and it must stay that way. "Marvin do you agree to keep it a secret and promise not to tell anyone?" He agreed, and Bill started to explain in detail the strange events that unfolded on that summer night all those years ago. "You see, Marvin, after all of the fun and games of the day, Shelly's father was getting a little bit tipsy, along with most of the other parents that were singing around the fire waiting for another hog to be roasted. This left just myself, Shelly, and the other dozen men from the county, all of whom were older than me, sitting on a fence, seizing the opportunity to help ourselves to whatever alcohol we could find, discreetly consuming it and passing it around whenever our parents' beady eyes looked the other way. After a couple of hours Shelly's father suggested that if the men re-stacked some hay bales that had fallen over in one of the fields, then he would give us a crate of moonshine so we could go and have our own party elsewhere on the ranch, leaving the adults to get to know one another better. Everyone accepted and Shelly's dad handed her the crate full of bottles, instructing her to supervise us men, while making sure the job was done before the partying

commenced. Everyone's spirits were high at this point
and as soon as we were out of sight of the adults, Shelly
cracked open the first bottle. She took a big swig before
passing it around for everyone to have some. After about
a ten minute walk and a couple of bottles between us, we
arrived at the field and to our delight, what we had
thought was going to be a big job, turned out to be only
two bales of hay out of place. At this point the other men
were getting a bit tipsy and starting to be a bit boisterous;
their testosterone was probably getting the better of them
as no boy in our county had ever been in the company of
such a stunner before. I was quite shy, still sober, and not
interested in getting involved with their macho games
competing for Shelly's attention by seeing who could
impress her the most. Instead, I offered to restack the
bales alone while they went and found somewhere
suitable to carry on partying. Once I'd finished, I would
catch them up."

Marvin stopped walking at this point, but Bill didn't stop
talking. "All of the others left me alone after thanking me
for restacking the bales, but their thanks soon turned to
jeers when Shelly came over to me and made me get all
embarrassed when she kissed me on the cheek before
leaving. Placing the first bale back in its rightful place in
the stack, I started to daydream about Shelly and how
lovely it would be if I could be the one who won her
affections. I knew that if I were going to succeed my best
chance would be to do the complete opposite to what the
others were doing and hope that she was the kind of girl

who went for brains over brawn. I picked up the second bale but as I lifted it over my head and leaned forward to place it on top of the first one, I lost my balance and it fell on top of me, knocking me out cold for what seemed like a good hour. When I came-to it was starting to get dark. I managed to wriggle free from underneath the bale and restack it properly before making my way back to the buildings to find the others and join the party. As I approached the barn complex, I heard a lot of screaming coming from inside one of them. It was a woman's voice screaming. I'd never heard a woman scream in this way before, it sounded more of a pleasure scream than one of fear. Still unsure what was causing her to scream and not knowing what to expect, I picked up a pitchfork from outside before entering, extremely nervously. I couldn't see anything at first and just followed the screams as they got louder and louder until I froze instantly on the spot. I couldn't believe what I was seeing with my very own eyes."

"Shelly, naked for the first time, her large breasts bouncing up and down, completely out of sync with each other as she was straddling one of the other men and screaming with pleasure each time she squatted down. The other eleven men were all standing close-by to her, naked. A few of them were pleasuring themselves whilst watching, all of them were extremely lively and egging each other on. I was too shy to join in but I could feel myself getting excited at what I was watching, so I slowly moved to my left and positioned myself strategically behind a stack of hay bales, ensuring I had a bird's eye view of the action whilst remaining hidden, safe in the knowledge that no one knew I was there. As soon as one man had satisfied himself Shelly would stand up, walk towards the surrounding group of men whilst looking each of them up and down, deciding who she wanted to satisfy her next. Once she'd made her mind up, she stood in front of him, whispered something in his ear and kneeled before starting to suck his erect penis, sucking it harder each time he moaned out in pleasure. Then she would stop sucking and push him hard backwards so that he fell to the ground, before pleasuring herself on his solid penis. I found myself watching and listening carefully to the different movements and sounds Shelly was making, getting quite excited by the sounds of pleasure when she was really enjoying a particular man, but found myself less excited when her moans and screams seemed fake with others. I'm not sure how long I'd been standing there enjoying my first ever sex education lesson, or how many men Shelly had pleasured, nor how many times, but the partying came to a very abrupt end when Shelly's father appeared from nowhere just as she was about to pleasure two men at once. He was an excessively big man, a good six-foot-six tall with a chest the size of a bull's and hands bigger than shovels; and he was very furious at what he saw. I was extremely glad that I was hidden well out of his sight as he started to batter each boy, one by one, for totally disrespecting his angel of a daughter and taking advantage of her in a drunken state. Within a couple of minutes Shelly had managed to fully cloth herself, and her father had well and truly taught the men a lesson, judging by their blood-soaked, lifeless bodies lying on the floor. All of them were moaning feeble apologies, asking for Shelly's and her father's forgiveness. Her father warned them that what had happened in the barn that night was never to be mentioned ever again, by anyone, to anyone, and if one of them did then he would personally kill them all; as he would if he ever saw any of them anywhere within a mile of his daughter. After he'd made them all promise, he turned towards Shelly. You could see the anger in his face as he shouted at her for her devil-like behaviour, informing her that she would now be a regular at the local church as punishment. Shelly was just about to be whisked away from the barn by her father, who'd instructed the other men to sleep in it for the night and not to set foot outside, as the adults' party was going to continue late into the night, when he asked everyone where the boy from the next ranch was: meaning me. They all told him they hadn't seen me since leaving me to restack the hay bales in the field earlier. Shelly and her father left. I sneaked out quietly as soon as the last boy had fallen asleep, setting off on a long walk home trying to make sense of what I'd just witnessed."

They both started slowly walking down the alley again when Bill paused. He took a deep breath before noticing that Marvin had an intrigued look on his face. Baffled as to whether Bill was being completely honest with him, he asked if he was telling the truth. In his mind the couple didn't seem very well matched; to Marvin it sounded like Bill was the sort of person who wouldn't look out of place as the head of the local church choir, who unfortunately married the village slut. Bill laughed. After navigating what seemed like a maze of alleyways, Bill found himself staring at a sign in the distance, saying, 'Can We Tempt You', before telling Marvin how he'd got Shelly all wrong: all of the other men admitted taking advantage of a drunken situation, and to give them their due, they kept their word and never came anywhere near Shelly until her father died the Christmas before last. That's when a couple of the brothers who played an active part that night in the barn, bought her father's ranch from her. Bill explained that the following Sunday after the barn incident he joined the local church, taking comfort in the knowledge that he'd have no competition for Shelly's affection after the promises of the other men. "Our relationship blossomed from that day on and within a couple of years I got my reward for not getting involved that night in the barn, by marrying the most strikingly beautiful woman in the whole wide world. Aren't I the lucky one?" Marvin agreed, and with that they were now standing in front of a door, under a sign with pictures of people dressed in funny outfits and holding strange contraptions with a slogan saying: 'Welcome to the Real Adult Superstore where one visit really can change your life'. Marvin took one last look at Bill before opening the door and announcing, "Welcome, my friend. I'm here to protect you, so if you need anything, or are unsure, just ask and

I'll see you come to no harm." Bill then took his first step into his future.

Chapter 2

A Brave Man

Looking around the large room Bill had entered; he couldn't understand why it looked completely different to what he'd imagined in his mind. He'd thought a sex shop would be dimly lit, with sex and filth on display, erotic films playing in the background, women screaming out in pleasure and little booths for people to get off in. Instead he found himself being offered a seat on a huge, light brown, leather chesterfield suite; the sort of suite that wouldn't look out of place in the Ritz hotel. Sitting down, the couch gripped him as his body sank into it. Marvin offered him a drink. He declined and found himself staring at the beautiful lady who stood behind what he could only assume was the reception desk. A tall, slim brunette with shoulder length hair, her large breasts bulging out of what seemed to be the smallest top he'd ever seen in his life. She looked at Bill and smiled, showing off her perfect white teeth, before leaning over the reception desk, intentionally showing off her ample cleavage to Bill whilst doing so. Marvin approached the desk, placed Bill's completed registration form on top of it and asked her to process his membership. "I'd be delighted to," she replied, as she walked from behind the desk towards Bill, displaying her stunning, semi-naked figure, from her waist down. "You leave him here with me for now, he'll be in my safe hands and I'll buzz you once I'm done," she informed

Marvin, before holding her right hand out towards Bill and introducing herself as Sandy. Bill couldn't take his eyes off her vagina; he'd only ever seen Shelly's in real life; seeing pictures of others just wasn't the same as seeing the real thing. Then his mind started to wander, he could feel his heart, beat faster. His body was starting to tingle with excitement and his penis started to throb as he imagined Sandy lying next to him on the couch, her legs wide apart, her toes reaching towards the ceiling as he gently licked and tasted her perfectly shaved sex organ. Bill stood up and introduced himself. He latched onto Sandy's outstretched hand, gently shaking it whilst his body trembled with excitement, and he fought hard to resist the temptation to touch. They sat next to each other on the couch as Sandy started to explain the registration process along with the rules of the club and the authorities.

"OK, Bill," she started, "I'm very pleased to meet you and I'm flattered by the thoughts that have probably just been racing through your mind and it does taste as nice as it looks; well, so I'm told anyway. But we have a strict, no-touch rule: once you go through the doors into the store, handshakes only; do you agree to that rule?" Bill was shocked, asking himself how Sandy knew what he'd been thinking, before agreeing to the no-touch rule. Sandy then explained that a photograph was required for his membership card, it was always required by the authorities to be worn and visible whilst on the premises. Bill agreed before he stood up, asking where he should stand for it. Sandy laughed, before inviting him to sit back down next to her, explaining that they had already taken a still from one of the many CCTV cameras installed all over the shop - they just needed his permission to use it. Bill agreed. He'd probably agree to anything at this point. He was starting to sweat heavily, despite the coolness of the air-conditioned room, with all the disgusting thoughts going through his mind. Suddenly the excitement in his body subsided as Shelly came into his mind. He started to feel guilty and unfaithful towards her. It didn't last long. He heard Sandy's voice whispering in his ear, "I'd love to suck you right now and feel you explode in my mouth. Does that make you feel horny?" He looked at her, his penis bulging in his pants as he leaned towards her and gave a little peck on her cheek, before whispering in her ear that, even though he would love her too, she couldn't, as he was a happily married man. Sandy smiled before removing her top, revealing her well-proportioned chest with bullet-like nipples, both of which were pierced, before continuing to explain the rules.

"Our membership fee is 100 dollars a year, however, you get 50 dollars off your first two separate purchases when you spend 100 dollars or more on separate visits to the store." Bill hadn't expected to have to pay a membership fee, he didn't really want to pay one and asked Sandy if there was any way around it as he wasn't planning on coming back for a second time. Sadly, there wasn't. She explained he had to agree to every rule otherwise he wouldn't be allowed to choose birthday presents for Shelly. Sandy whizzed through all of the other rules. She could see Bill was struggling to keep his eyes off her naked body and she was getting quite excited too, as she teased and tempted Bill with subtle body movements, deliberately encouraging his eyes to wander wherever she wanted them to go. Once Sandy had finished explaining the rules, and Bill had signed to say he agreed to them, she stood up from the couch and faced him, her vagina the same height as his eyes. She bent forward towards him, her breasts missing his face by millimetres, and kissed him on his left cheek before congratulating him on becoming the newest member of the 'Real Adult Superstore'. With that done, Marvin appeared out of nowhere, congratulating Bill on his successful membership application as he sat down on the couch next to him, placing Bill's freshly made membership card around his neck. Sandy departed and left the two men alone, wiggling and touching her peachy backside as she walked, knowing that Bill's eyes would be firmly fixated on it.

Marvin inquisitively asked Bill, on a scale of one to ten, how horny he was feeling. Seven was his reply. Marvin laughed before suggesting how he could take it up to ten and beyond if Bill were interested. Bill stared him in the eye before confirming he was, and asked what Marvin had in mind. Marvin reached into his blazer pocket and pulled out a molded piece of plastic, it was black, about nine inches long, three inches wide, cylindrical in shape, smooth and shiny on one half, covered in buttons on the other. Bill was baffled as to what it was, until Marvin pointed it at the wall in front of them. He pressed the big red button on the end and what seemed like half of the ceiling started to lower, revealing the biggest TV screen Bill had seen in his life. "Time to choose your personal assistant to demonstrate our products to you," said Marvin. "Making sure you leave as a well and truly satisfied customer - hopefully, just as satisfied as Shelly will be when she tries them for herself; that's if you want one, of course?" Before Bill could answer the TV screen filled with pictures of all the assistants on duty today. There must have been over three hundred to choose from: petite ladies, large ladies, blonds, brunettes, large chested, small chested, black, white, Asian, long hair, short hair, feminine and butch looking ladies - the choice seemed endless. Marvin explained to Bill he could choose any lady he wanted, and she would demonstrate any products that were on sale in the store, as long as he can control the sexual desires that will rage throughout his body and remembers to abide by the no-touch rule. Bill was unsure what to do. When he thought of the idea of coming to Dallas for some sex toys, he presumed that he'd be able to just pick what he wanted from a shelf and pay for it before his long drive back home. He was already confused by what had happened so far that day, but having a complete stranger doing whatever he asked her to do was simply too good of an offer to refuse. "I'll have a tall blond lady, please. Large chested like Shelly, with lovely long legs," asked Bill. Marvin pushed a few buttons on the strangely shaped TV remote and instantly

22

the three-hundred-plus pictures of personal assistants were replaced by a dozen or so much larger ones, each with features exactly as Bill had asked for. "Take your pick," Marvin encouraged Bill, before continuing, "anyone you want. If you need any help with making your mind up which one you'd like, you can pick out any three and meet them in person before you choose your final one." Bill was spoilt for choice, amazed by the stores commitment to its customers in delivering the ultimate shopping experience. After a few minutes Bill was still undecided, none of the blond-haired ladies were standing out to him. He asked Marvin if he could choose a brunette, instead, as he was still quite taken aback by how stunning and sexy Sandy had been earlier. "No problem, partner," Marvin replied, and before he'd finished speaking all of the blonds on the screen had been replaced by brunettes. Bill's eyes were instantly drawn to one picture, a face that he recognised and already had fond memories of. "I'll have Sandy please, Marvin," Bill asked in a firm manner, satisfied in his mind that he'd made the right choice.

While the two of them were sitting on the couch waiting for Sandy to join them, Marvin pushed the red button on the remote to raise the TV screen back into the ceiling where it had appeared from. He asked Bill if he had any particular style of lingerie or type of toys in mind for Shelly, or if he'd like Sandy to demonstrate a variety for him. Bill was really starting to enjoy himself at this point, and even though he knew exactly what he had in mind for Shelly, he decided it would be more enjoyable to watch Sandy, half naked in high heels, and wearing only white, silk knickers and a waistcoat, with a whip in one hand and a set of handcuffs in the other. He fantasised about her new collection of vibrators proudly strapped to a belt around her waist for everyone to see as she beckoned him to pleasure her. "I'll let Sandy demonstrate," he replied, just as she appeared out of nowhere, wearing nothing but a fluffy, pink bathrobe with matching slippers and a big smile on her face. As Sandy approached, she untied her dressing gown then leant over to kiss him on his cheek, her right breast popping out from behind her bathrobe, brushing against Bill's cheek in the process. Bill's body tingled all over; it was only the second breast he'd touched in his life and he wanted to touch it properly but knew he couldn't. Marvin asked Bill if he would like to go around the store like all of the other customers, or upgrade to a private shop where each separate product type was displayed in its own room. Marvin would stand guard outside the locked room, he advised, ensuring that whatever happened in the room would remain away from prying eyes, letting Bill have a more personal experience whilst letting himself go. Bill pondered what to do about the upgrade, he loved the thought of him and Sandy being alone to enjoy his shopping trip together, but he knew he'd find it hard to resist the temptation to touch Sandy's beautiful body in one way or another. 'In for a dime, in for a dollar,' he thought to himself as he confirmed to Marvin that he'd like to take the upgrade and asked for it to be put on his bill. "Wise choice", Marvin said, smiling and laughing to himself as Sandy started walking towards the door on the left, opening it as Bill approached to reveal a long, narrow corridor with neon signs hanging from the ceiling at regular intervals, each one saying something different. His mind was curious as he read the one closest to him: 'Appetisers and Stimulants'.

The doors closed behind the three of them as they made their way towards the first room. "What's in here?" Bill asked Sandy in an inquisitive manner. "Little things to get you in the mood," she replied, whilst walking through the door inviting him to follow. Marvin remained outside on guard in the corridor. It looked more like a posh pharmacy than a room in a sex shop to Bill, lots of counter space everywhere, all of it crammed with various different boxes and bottles, all displaying similar messages: 'Get hard, stay hard'; 'Last for hours'; 'The ultimate sexual rush'. Sandy asked Bill, in a subtle voice, whether he had ever used a stimulant before. He laughed out loud, "I tried one once. Shelly was really looking forward to a nice, action packed summer's night in one of our barns - as was I. Thirty minutes before we made our way there, I followed the instructions on the packet to the letter and swallowed a little blue pill, only to be disappointed to find out that I'm one of the unlucky bastards it has the opposite effect on. It turns out to be a passion killer for me." Sandy saw the funny side and laughed, too, before asking if he'd like to take a 'Dallas Pill', instead. "It does the reverse of what the little blue pills are supposed to do, and we advise all visitors who are new members to seriously consider taking one if they think they may struggle with the no touch rule." Bill was pondering whether to purchase a 'Dallas Pill' while staring at Sandy and admiring her beautiful features. Sandy slipped out of her dressing gown and stood three feet in front of him, naked. She started to stroke her right breast before clasping it from beneath and moving her hand upwards, her pierced nipple standing proud as she licked it seductively with her tongue, before placing her lips firmly around it as she started to suck. Bill could feel himself getting excited, his penis started to rise. He found himself unbuttoning his jeans and gently pinching his penis, desperately trying to make his erection disappear; all he wanted to do right now was take Sandy up on her earlier offer of exploding in her mouth. Pinching wasn't working. Watching Sandy alternate from one breast to the other was making things worse and Bill couldn't hold on any longer. He gave in and agreed to take a 'Dallas Pill' to help him ensure that he didn't break any rules. Sandy opened a bottle and removed a small, flat, pink tablet from it, about the size of a small watch battery, with the letter 'P' printed in blue on one side, and 'K' on the other. "Here you go, get a 'passion killer' down you, that should do the job." Bill swallowed it in one, hoping it would take effect straight away so that he could continue his first ever trip to a sex shop. It worked, and before long they found themselves in the corridor with Marvin, Bill carefully studied the signs, deciding which room he wanted to enter next.

The next sign that caught his eye read 'Gimp Suits'.
"What's a gimp suit?" Bill asked Marvin with a curious
look on his face, intrigued by the meaning of this new
phrase to his vocabulary. Marvin laughed in disbelief,
questioning him as to whether he was trying to pull his
leg pretending not to know what a gimp suit is. In a
serious tone Bill told him that he honestly didn't know
what one was. On hearing this Marvin knew if he was
going to be the true wingman, he'd said he would be,
then it was his duty to ensure Bill walked through the
door to get the most out of his 'personal shop'. "Allow
me," he told Bill, as he flung open the door, convincing
him that he really needed to go and have a look for
himself. Bill and Sandy walked into the darkened room.
As soon as Bill heard the door close, followed by the
click of the lock, the room lit up to reveal twelve,
realistic life like statues standing at the other side, all
covered from head to toe in smooth, shiny PVC suits,
with similar suits of all different styles and colours
hanging everywhere, each attached to what looked like a
dog muzzle hanging from the collar. Out of the corner of
his eye it looked like Sandy was whispering, but he
dismissed it and presumed that she must have been
muttering something to herself as it was just the two of
them present. Bill turned towards Sandy and asked to
leave the room as he had no interest in what he was
seeing. Sandy walked towards Bill, slipping out of her
bathrobe as she did, before kneeling on the floor in front
of him. She looked up towards his face, staring at him for
a while. What a lovely sight for Bill, her perfect large
breasts clearly on display either side of her cheeks, which

were blocking his view of her ample cleavage. She stood up and whispered in his ear, "I love nothing more than an anonymous man dressed head to toe in a gimp suit, his mouth muzzled with a brightly coloured ball strapped around his head by a leather studded strap, and his rock hard penis and testicles breaking free from his suit with excitement as I unbutton the zip. Will you try one on for me please? I'd love to see what you look like in one." Bill was feeling really horny at the thought of this, and without hesitation he invited Sandy to pick one for him, telling her that he particularly fancied a red one. "That's good, I do have a soft spot for a man in a red, gimp suit," Sandy commented, just as she invited Bill to remove all of his clothes while she looked for a suitable fitting one for him. "What, you want me to get naked, right here and right now?" Bill replied in a worried manner before confessing that only Shelly had seen him with no clothes on before, and she wouldn't get turned on by seeing him dressed in a red gimp suit. Sandy paused rummaging through the suits and turned around to face Bill, giving her breasts a wiggle as she did. She pointed to a red suit hanging alone on the wall by itself, saying in a seductive voice, "Please try that one on for me - I'll make it worth your while," as she gave him a wink. Before Sandy had chance to remove it from the wall and hand it to him, Bill had stripped naked and was standing in the middle of the room, feeling vulnerable, desperate to protect his modesty by wearing a gimp suit. Sandy walked towards him and invited Bill to hold up his right foot as she helped him get dressed. He did, so Sandy knelt in front of him as she helped secure his right foot in place. She asked for his left foot, explaining that once both feet are in, he'll find it much easier to do the rest himself. Bill did as Sandy asked and as he did, she moved her head towards Bill's left leg, brushing past his penis, almost touching it by a fraction of an inch as she helped with his other foot. She then walked behind him and grabbed the hood of the suit in her hands. As he slowly struggled getting both of his arms in it, Sandy placed the hood over his head and zipped up the neck and back. She then picked up a bright-green muzzle and asked Bill to open his mouth as she placed the ball in the mouth-hole of the suit, before buckling the leather-studded strap up at the back of his head and locking it with a padlock. Finally, she placed his membership card around his neck before stepping back, admiring, and complimenting him on how nice he looked in his gimp suit. She started to gently stroke her inner left thigh, before moving to her right one, stopping to say hello to her perfect vagina on the way. He felt a twitch in his penis and looked down towards it, as did Sandy, who smiled inviting him to remove it from hiding so that she could keep her word that trying on the suit would be worth his while. What Sandy was asking him to do was totally out of character for Bill and this was the last thing he expected to be asked to do when he woke up this morning, or any morning in fact, but he couldn't help himself and without hesitation he did as he was invited to do.

Bill was hot and sweaty by now, partly due to the excitement of being alone in the presence of a beautiful, naked brunette, partly due to the clamminess he felt being trapped inside a tight-fitting, bright-red PVC gimp suit. Unable to speak, he was desperate to get out of it and get back to a sense of normality in his own clothes. Sandy approached Bill, looking him up and down and smiling as she did, Bill's heart started pounding fast as she whispered in his ear, "You're making me really wet and horny standing there dressed like that. If you stay in your gimp suit and muzzle for the rest of the shop, at the end I'll take you to a special room for your treat, where the security cameras haven't been working for ages. Now I'll unmuzzle you while you tell me what you have in mind for Shelly's presents before I muzzle you back-up. Nod your head if you agree." Bill thought long and hard about what Sandy had just said. He was feeling uncomfortable about walking around dressed like he was, unable to speak with his family jewels hanging out for everyone to see, but he was intrigued by the treat that Sandy had in store for him, so he nodded his head and before long she had unmuzzled him. "I'm hot and sweaty," Bill informed Sandy. She laughed before replying, "Me too. Now tell me your shopping list for Shelly - I'll choose some nice presents for her." Bill started by telling Sandy that he'd like to see Shelly half naked, in high heels and white, silky knickers, along with a waistcoat and a whip in one hand and a set of handcuffs in the other. Bill paused. Once again, he could feel his penis coming alive, stirred by the vivid images in his mind of Shelly's face after being satisfied with his choice of gifts. He could feel his penis growing and he didn't know if he'd be able to withstand the embarrassment of getting 'proud' in front of a total stranger. He continued to tell Sandy about how he'd also like for Shelly to be wearing a belt with lots of sex toys strapped to it. The thought of this made him tremble all over. He was powerless to stop what happened next. Sandy looked in disbelief as Bill's penis started to point towards the ceiling instead of the floor. Gradually it grew until it was throbbing, and Bill couldn't help himself as he wrapped his right hand around it and started to give it a stroke. "STOP, right there," Sandy shouted, as Bill heard the lock on the door click again. The door opened and in walked Marvin, asking if everything was all right. "He's just started to play with himself in front of me. He's had a passion killer, but it seems to be wearing off. I think we need to restrain him - I'm afraid that he's going to break the no-touch rule and that's the last thing we want." Sandy replied.

Marvin looked towards Bill and smiled, before reassuring him that although he'd have to be handcuffed for the rest of the shop, he was not to worry as they wouldn't be tight - he'd easily get out of them if he really wanted to. Bill looked at Sandy, who by now had slipped back into her bathing robe, and apologised for upsetting her by his actions. Sandy told him that she wasn't upset but scared as she was getting turned-on by seeing Bill's penis in his hand dressed like he was, and she was struggling to resist pleasuring him. Bill smiled to himself at the thought of turning on a stunner like Sandy. Marvin advised that it might be best if Sandy went shopping alone for the rest of Bill's list while he waited in the special room at the end of the corridor. The three of them agreed it was probably the best plan, so, as Sandy put Bill's muzzle back on, then gave Marvin the key, he pulled a padded set of handcuffs from his back pocket and placed them loosely around Bill's wrists. Before leaving with Bill's list, Sandy whispered in Bill's ear, "I'll choose wisely. Let's hope the cameras are still broken - I can't wait to demonstrate what I've got in mind for you and Shelly." This left Marvin and Bill alone in the presence of the twelve life like statues, Bill swore he'd seen one of them move and got spooked. Unable to say anything, he walked to the door and luckily for Bill, Marvin followed, and they were both standing outside again in the corridor. Bill fixed his eyes on to the next sign: BDSM.

Marvin approached Bill and put his left arm around his right shoulder as they started to walk down the corridor. Bill wondered what pleasures he was missing by being denied the opportunity to experience rooms such as, 'Whips and floggers', 'Fucking machines', 'Fetish', 'Dress to impress' and 'Not for the faint hearted', to name a few. Halfway down the corridor Marvin started to give Bill some reassurance that he'd done nothing wrong with his actions in the gimp suit room, telling him it was common for first-time visitors' testosterone levels to go through the roof and not to feel guilty about it; after all he was just a normal man with a decent sex drive. Bill muttered a grunt back just as they arrived at another door with no sign above it; there was just a big, yellow, glittering star covering two-thirds of the door with the words, 'Have you been good enough to enter?' printed in red letters. Marvin looked at Bill as he opened the door for him. "Enter my friend, grab a seat and Sandy will join you as soon as she's finished your shopping. This is the end of the line for us, partner; it's been a pleasure. I'll make sure your clothes are taken to the changing room, which Sandy will take you to. I hope Shelly likes her presents and you get your sex life back." Marvin held out his right hand, and Bill, restricted by his handcuffs, took hold of it with both of his, before shaking it as best as he could, his mind wondering what pleasures the room he was about to enter would have in store for him.

Chapter 3

You really didn't want to do that

Bill turned from Marvin and took his second massive step of the day by entering the special room. Marvin shut the door behind him, saying "Bless ya heart," as he did. Bill found himself standing in a small room, probably 10 x 10, with bare walls, extraordinarily little lighting, and a solitary chair in one corner. He was excited at the thought of being alone with Sandy again, only this time she'd be dressed just as he wanted her. He desperately hoped the security cameras were still broken. In his mind, if he was reading between the lines of what Sandy had been saying to him right, then all of her hints, suggestions and body language throughout the day amounted to only one thing: he was in for a good time in the special room. He'd been standing in the middle of the room for about five minutes, with various thoughts racing around his mind; some clean and sensible, some vulgar and filthy. He glanced down at his penis, shocked at how big it looked hanging from the hole of his gimp suit and struggled to comprehend how it remained so solid for such a long time; even after taking a Dallas pill.

Suddenly the lights went out and Bill could hear sounds coming from the walls. They weren't voices, they sounded like electric motors. After thirty seconds or so, and after the noises had stopped, the room was illuminated by a single spotlight beaming down from the ceiling behind him, only this time it was much bigger. Bill's penis started throbbing hard with the sight of what he could see: a raised stage area with three steps leading up to it. Standing at the top was Sandy, her shiny-red, high heel shoes reflecting in the bright light, her modesty protected by a pair of white, see-through silky lace knickers, complete with a slit in the front, left nothing to Bill's imagination. Her large breasts were hiding behind an unbuttoned, shiny-black, waistcoat covered in diamonds that glistened in the light. Her hair was now blond, exceptionally long and dangled over the front of it. To Bill, she looked just like he'd envisioned Shelly would. Bill's penis hardened as he caught sight of the matching purple and pink whip and handcuffs Sandy was holding, her belt containing no less than five new sex toys of various shapes and sizes.

Sandy started to make her way from the stage towards Bill, her pierced nipples occasionally popping out from behind her waistcoat. He could feel his blood pressure rising as she whispered in his ear, "I told you that I would treat you. Nod your head if you like what you see." Without hesitation, Bill nodded. Sandy raised his blood pressure further by removing a glass, penis-shaped ornament from her belt. She licked it before stroking it against the slit in the front of her crotchless knickers. "This feels lovely and cool rubbing against my moist clitoris, it's sending shivers up my spine. How I wish it were your real penis rubbing against me instead," Sandy whispered in a seductive manner, before removing her waistcoat to reveal her naked breasts. Bill raised his hands to touch them, but Sandy clocked what was about to happen and moved back towards the stage, climbing up the first two steps before turning around and sitting down on the third. Bill remained where he was, scared by the thought that he couldn't resist Sandy anymore. He wanted to take up her earlier offer of letting him explode in her mouth. Sandy looked at Bill standing proud a short distance away and beckoned him to come over and join her. When he didn't, Sandy stood up and removed her white knickers, before taking a large, cone-shaped object, with a flat round handle attached to the base, from her belt. She sat back down and opened her legs to reveal her perfect vagina to Bill. Sandy placed the cone-shaped object in her right hand and moved the narrow end towards her vagina. Bill watched enthusiastically as she inserted it into her vagina, her cries getting louder with each deeper thrust.

Bill was soon standing at the bottom step, his penis feeling like it was about to explode watching Sandy bring herself to orgasm, as apart from the base, the whole cone disappeared inside her. Sandy smiled at Bill as the cone reappeared, licking it all over before placing it back on her belt. Her hand then pulled out another strange looking object. It was purple and looked like a misshaped penis to him, with something resembling what could only be described as a snake's mouth on the end of it. Sandy rotated the base and it started to buzz and vibrate. Her eyes lit up as she moved it towards her vagina, letting out a solitary cry of joy as it made contact for the first time. She started to shout, "Fuck me," in between every cry of passion as the sex toy disappeared and reappeared. Her legs started to shake as she twisted the base and the buzzing got faster and louder. Bill hadn't been this excited in a long time and was struggling to contain himself when, in between Sandy's moans and shouting, he heard her whisper, "The cameras are broken still." Bill took that as his cue. He frantically released one of his hands from his handcuffs, stood over Sandy, and gently replaced her hands on the sex toy with his and replicated her actions. Bill's excitement quickly turned to fear when alarms started sounding and the whole room brightened when several large-looking men, including Marvin, stormed in shouting for Bill to freeze and put his hands in the air.

It was back to reality for Bill when he heard a click from the door and the sign above it changed to green, the letters now read: 'ENTER'. The man on the left opened the door while the man on the right whispered in Bill's ear, "I'll be waiting," as he walked through, laughing after he said it. Bill didn't know what to expect next as he entered a large, lavishly carpeted, and furnished room. At one side of it he noticed a couch, it was twice the size of the one he'd sat on earlier at the beginning of this nightmare journey. There was a grand piano to its right, black in colour with a white lid, which was in the raised position. Next to it was a small, curved bar, big enough for four people to sit at. The wall behind it was covered in bottles of spirits suspended upside-down, with their optics at the bottom. To the right was a mirrored section of wall, complete with a tiled floor and a fireman's pole stretching from the floor to the ceiling. Bill's eyes moved to the far-right corner of the room, amazed at what he could see: a full size 'Bucking Bronco' rodeo bull with lots of cowboy gear hanging next to it. The walls were covered with paintings of naked men and women, each of them with a name-plaque beneath.

Bill looked towards the ceiling as if he was asking for help from above, then his heart stopped as he noticed a rope hanging next to a beautiful, crystal chandelier. Marvin walked towards him with a look of sadness in his eyes. He grabbed Bill's handcuffed hands, avoiding the purple sex toy he was still holding, and apologised for letting him down as his wingman and promised him that he'd do his utmost to try and help him find a way out of the current mess. Marvin then led Bill towards a door that was partially obstructed behind the Bucking Bronco. He knocked three times then paused for a while, before knocking one final time. The door opened and Marvin gestured for Bill to enter. He did and was greeted with the sight of a well-groomed man sitting behind a large, leather bound desk. It was clutter-free apart from four trophies to the right, and a solitary wooden chair positioned in front.

Bill walked further into the room, when, to the left, he noticed another door. It was open and through it, he saw four men sitting around a table playing cards. To the right was a similar situation but, in this room, there were four oriental women sitting around a table counting money, with lots more stacked in neat piles all over the floor. The man sitting behind the desk told Bill to stop before telling Marvin to close the door behind him and to go and play a game of cards with the others while he had a little chat in private with Bill. Marvin was uncomfortable having to leave Bill alone with the boss, frightened that his temper might get the better of him and he'd finish Bill off with a bullet, but he knew he had no choice otherwise he'd end up like everybody else who'd ever disobeyed: unemployed, and unemployable, so he did as he was told.

"Do you realise the amount of trouble you've caused for me?" said the boss to Bill firmly. Unable to respond Bill shook his head before the boss shouted angrily, "Don't shake your head at me you fucking pervert, standing there looking like you've just come from a fetish party, what you've just done is going to cost me and my nine partners a lot of money and could even see this place losing its licence. You're the fourth one who's been in this situation already this year, the other three I've managed to sort out by making them disappear, along with the security camera footage and paying a hefty fine, however, after the last incident the authority's told us, in no uncertain terms, that if any more security camera footage disappears, then so will our licence-to-trade, and a good portion of our bank accounts too. Now sit down while I think about what I'm going to do with you." Bill sat down with the thought of never being able to see his good-looking wife Shelly again, no matter what option the boss decided to choose, if he's lucky and gets passed over to the authority's then Shelly would never come and visit him in prison; knowing that he'd probably die while inside he'd never get to say a proper goodbye. A tear ran down his cheek from the corner of his right eye, but he knew he was powerless to do anything to make his current situation better. He hoped and prayed to himself that somehow, he could find a way to get out of this mess and return to his normal, peaceful life back on his ranch in Ringgold.

The room was silent with just the two of them sitting there, Bill was staring at the boss, watching him looking down towards the desk, his hands grasping either side of it, his mind playing God with Bill's life. The silence was broken by Marvin's voice, "I've got it," he shouted from the room where he was situated. "You'll fucking get the end of my fist, Marvin, if you shout out like that again and disturb my thinking," the boss shouted angrily to Marvin, who appeared from the room, apologising, and explaining how he thinks he may have come up with a way of making the events of the day disappear whilst protecting the store's licence along with Bill's liberty and life. "Go on Marvin, you have my full attention; and it better be good otherwise you'll be unemployable by the time it's dark," the boss said inflexibly. Marvin approached and asked for permission to whisper in his ear. Permission granted, Marvin whispered softly, "If my plan's going to work then please unmuzzle Bill so that he can have a drink and I'll explain it in full to you both. It involves doing a deal with the chief of police, but it relies heavily on Bill's cooperation, and the best way of getting that is for the one person whom he can trust convinces him to cooperate." The boss looked at Marvin with a smile on his face before ordering him to unmuzzle Bill and to get all three of them a drink of iced, cold water.

The boss ordered the four men and women out of their respective rooms to go and get some fresh air, leaving just Marvin and Bill in the boss's company. Marvin made his way to the fridge in the room where the game of cards had been played and returned with three bottles that he placed on top of the boss's desk. Marvin then put his hand in his right, trouser pocket and removed the key to Bill's muzzle. Bill's eyes lit up, he was desperate to say sorry for what he had done and hopefully talk his way out of it. Marvin unlocked the muzzle, removed the purple sex-toy from Bill's right hand and replaced it with a bottle of water while covering his lips with a single finger, encouraging Bill to remain quiet. Bill took a long drink from the bottle; his mouth was dry from walking around for what seemed like hours with a ball firmly in his mouth. His jaw was aching and to him it seemed like it was stuck in the open position. He took another long drink, his tongue now moist as he started to exercise his jaw up and down, desperate for the aching to stop. As

41

Bill was exercising his jaw he was repeatedly saying "I'm sorry" in his head when suddenly he said it out aloud and once he'd said those magic two words he just couldn't stop talking. "It's all a big mistake, I'm a happily married man, I've only come here for some presents for my wife to spice up our sex life. I didn't touch Sandy on purpose I was just doing as she asked, I'm sure the police will understand and let me off with a fine if I plead guilty. I'm only a country boy who's not used to big city life, I'm too young to die and I couldn't handle prison. Please help me Marvin, you promised to be my wingman and protect me, it's your duty to help me." Marvin disappeared into the other room again before appearing with a chair, he placed it next to Bill and sat upon it.

Marvin started by saying, "Please don't interrupt me until I'm finished Bill, as I promised you that I'd do my utmost to try and find a way to get you out of this mess and I think I may have found one. It's a little bit of a bizarre way, but if you promise to cooperate and go along with it, and trust me, then I think it'll probably work. Then, you'll be free to go back to your lovely wife and simple life back in the country." Marvin paused for a deep breath before resuming, "Before I tell you all about my plan let's study the other two options on the table: death and prison. Option one, death, this is usually the boss's preferred method of dealing with sex offenders like you. One of the boys takes you to a secluded spot somewhere out in the country, puts a bullet in the back of your head and leaves you there as food for the wildlife. By the time your body's found, it's nothing but your skeletal remains. Your family will report you as a missing person, but your case will get lost in the system, along with the thousands of other missing persons whose disappearances remain unsolved each year. If the authority's ever come knocking on our door enquiring about a missing person, we'll cooperate fully and let them examine our CCTV footage, and if they discover that any footage is missing, they put it down to a technical fault and we get away with a hefty fine and a slap on the wrists. However, choosing option one in your case would be a bit trickier for us as we've already had to use this option three times this year; the state wouldn't take very kindly to our security cameras being faulty for a fourth time and the minimum penalty for this offence is a six-month suspension of our licence-to-trade. That would cost my boss and his partners a lot of money, and they would probably have to try and recover their losses from your family." Marvin paused and took a drink of iced, cold water from his bottle. He looked at Bill and could see the fear in his eyes after listening to option one. "We don't want that option happening now, do we, Bill?" Marvin asked in a calm voice. Bill shook his head from side to side agreeing with him. Marvin resumed speaking, "Let's look at option two then, shall we. We report you as a sex offender to the police."

Bill started shaking his head rapidly from side to side, pleading for this option not to happen. He couldn't bear the thought of being locked behind bars with real criminals, he'd be easy pickings for them, and he knew his destiny inside would be to become some big macho-man's bitch. Marvin acknowledged Bill's disapproval of option two but commented how they still needed to study it in depth and look at the incident from both sides. Marvin took another drink from his bottle before resuming. "We call the police and tell them that one of our staff has just been sexually assaulted with a sex-toy and we've got the offender in our custody. They'll be here, in force, within a couple of minutes, by which time we'll have put your muzzle back on, they'll walk through that door to find you sitting there, dressed in your bright-red, PVC gimp suit, your mouth muzzled, your hands in handcuffs holding a purple sex-toy and your erect penis exposed for everyone to see. They'll all burst into laughter when they see you, then when they unmuzzle you, you'll plead your innocence with them, tell them how it's all been a big mistake and how Sandy was demonstrating one of our sex-toys when she shouted for you to fuck her. You'll continue to tell them how you were conscious of the no-touch rule, so you used a sex-toy instead, oblivious to the fact that you were committing an offence. Sandy will then be asked to give her side of the story. She'll tell them how, at the very start of your personal shop, you went into the 'Appetisers and Stimulants' room and took a pill before purchasing a gimp suit and muzzle from the next one, and how you couldn't wait to try it on as she found you standing in the middle of the room, naked, before she'd even had a chance to pick out a suitable one for you. Sandy will

44

confirm that she helped you get dressed into it, and how once you were 'in costume', so to speak, you made a pass at her. I'll confirm this by telling them how I had to enter the room and it was decided that it would be in the best interest of all parties if Sandy finished your shopping alone after I took the precaution of handcuffing you to prevent any breach of the no-touch rule." Marvin took another drink from his bottle, as did Bill.

After an extended pause he finished his summing-up of option two. "I'll then tell the police how I took you to the special room for you to confirm that you were satisfied with your day's purchases and how I left you there alone, dressed exactly as you are now, apart from the purple sex-toy, waiting for Sandy to enter. Whilst Sandy was demonstrating your purchases you finally gave into your sexual desires and broke free from your handcuffs, before allegedly committing the sex-act that you'll stand accused of. The police will then go to our security room and watch the CCTV recordings to help them decide which side of the story to believe, before coming back and putting you in proper handcuffs after the CCTV confirms that you were stood over Sandy repeatedly probing her with a purple sex-toy dressed exactly as you are now. They'll throw the book at you and lock away the key." Bill hadn't thought about any of what Marvin had just said and it brought his world crashing down around him. Now he realised how the day's events would look to the police. Marvin went to take another drink from his bottle, but it was empty. He stood up and made his way to the fridge to replenish it along with a fresh one for both Bill and the boss. While Marvin was out of the room the boss stood from behind the desk and approached Bill. He smiled as he whispered in his ear, "I've made my mind up. If I don't like Marvin's plan then I'm prepared to take the chance of closure and that means a bullet for you," before he calmly walked behind his desk and sat down again. Bill's heart fell to his feet, hoping that Marvin's plan was a good one, knowing it was the only thing in the world right now that could keep him alive, he was desperate for Marvin to return and say it was a good plan.

After what seemed an eternity to Bill, Marvin appeared carrying another three bottles of ice-cold water, distributing them amongst the three people present. Marvin sat down and before commencing to tell Bill all about his plan, he told him that it would only work if he cooperated one hundred percent and put his full trust in him - Marvin, his wingman. Bill shook his head in agreement. He'd try anything to avoid the other option that was staring down at him. Confident Bill understood the danger his life was in, Marvin started to tell his plan, in detail, to both his boss and Bill. "Now boss, I'm not sure if you're aware of this, but our local chief of police is a very senior member of a secretive sexual cult, as are a lot of other high-ranking city officials. Now, this weekend is their annual get-together in Vegas, where they hire a whole casino and hotel complex exclusively for their own use. Their motto is 'what happens behind our closed doors stays behind our closed doors', and they abide by the punishment of death for anybody who breaks their motto." Marvin paused and had another drink before continuing, "I'm not a member of the cult, but a late friend of mine was, and as he was lying on his deathbed he told me lots of stories about the wild things that happen at the annual bash on the first weekend of August every year. That's this weekend, and I will always remember how he told me that on the Saturday night, the main event was when a member of the cult would be chosen at random to play a game of Wheel of Fortune, for a chance to win sixty-four million dollars. All that the contestant had to do to win the money is complete the seven sexual challenges that had been chosen by a spin of the wheel. He also told me how every now and then, the contestant would be a non-member; someone who volunteered to play after having confirmed that they met all of the unusual requirements to qualify." Marvin took a deep breath before continuing, "The volunteer must have only ever slept with one sexual partner. They must be married, have no children, their spouse must be present when they play the game, and they must be the sort of person who wouldn't be missed if they were to simply disappear into thin air. Now they like this sort of person because it gives them an extra kick knowing that a complete innocent could win themselves a lot of money while providing great entertainment watching all of the random sexual challenges the volunteer must complete to win big money. However, apparently the time they get excited most is when the wheel stops with the arrow pointing towards the challenge of surviving fifteen minutes with the queen of the cult as nobody ever has. Now, seeing as Bill meets all of the requirements, I propose that we go to the chief of police and try to do a deal of clemency in exchange for Bill volunteering to be a contestant for the Saturday night's main event. What do you think, boss?" The boss looked at Marvin with a big smile on his face, before telling him that he liked what he'd heard but was going for a pee, and if Marvin could convince him of a good plan for making it work, especially how they'd get Bill's wife to Vegas, then he would approach the chief of police and try to make a deal.

Chapter 4

The deal

The boss vacated leaving Marvin and Bill alone, Marvin looked at Bill and burst into laughter from seeing him sitting there standing proud in his Gimp suit, whilst thinking how silly he looked. "What are you laughing at?" Bill uttered inquisitively. "You" he responded, then after a slight pause, he continued. "You don't half look ridiculous sitting there; can't you at least try to put your meat and two veg away. If the boss does decide to call the police, it will be better for you if you're covered up." Bill looked him in the eye with a petrified look on his face, while he unsuccessfully tried to tell Marvin what the boss had stated. After taking a sip of his water which moistened his mouth he tried again, gratefully this time he could. "The boss isn't going to call the police, when you left for the drinks, he told me he'd made his mind up to kill me if he didn't like your plan." The room fell silent for a short time before Marvin broke the calm. "Oh dear that's not good, let's hope he likes my plan but for it to work, you have to place your complete trust in me, and I'll unquestionably need your help in executing it. While I'm explaining it to you both, if there's any part that you don't think you can pull off, then you must say something straight away because we've only got one chance to save your life. Do you understand?" Before Bill could answer back the boss re-entered and as he walked towards his desk, Bill gave his response, "yes."

The boss frowned at Bill whilst inquiring what he was agreeing to. Bill stared at Marvin whilst unsure what to say, hence when Marvin nodded, Bill assured the boss he was agreeing to cooperate FULLY with Marvin's plan and if he thought any part would fail, he'd say so now. The boss then educated the worried pair about how he was beginning to like Bill now that he'd made the sensible choice of cooperation, prior to telling Marvin to hurry up with his plan, since he was away on a short vacation this weekend and needed this horrible business fixing before he left.

Marvin did exactly as instructed when he began unwinding his plot. "I think convincing the chief of police to allow Bill too volunteer will be quite easy as long as when he meets Bill he's dressed exactly as he is now, only muzzled to prevent him from putting his foot in it. It's probably best if you do the talking at the meeting boss, I'm sure he'll respect you more than us." A nod of his head confirmed his approval then Marvin continued. "The hard part of my proposal is how we'll get Bill and his wife, Shelly to Vegas without her suspecting anything or Bill slipping up and giving the game away." Marvin paused, took a drink from his bottle, then turned towards Bill and asked where Shelly thinks he's gone today?

Bill explained how she knew he had come to Dallas for her presents, but how she had no idea what he'd come for, so Marvin resumed describing his plan. "Good. We tell her that you really came to Dallas because you won a competition which you'd entered for an all-expenses paid weekend away for two in Vegas. You didn't want to tell her and build her hopes up as you were unsure whether it was a wind up or not. After arriving in Dallas to collect your prize and you found it to be true, you couldn't wait to tell her the good news, therefore you called her. Would she believe that?" You could hear Bill's brain working overtime processing what Marvin had just suggested, thinking Shelly would probably be apprehensive since he would have normally mentioned something like a competition entry to her. He voiced this to Marvin who took a while to think before responding. "OK so you tell her that you keep it a secret because you still feel guilty about the 'pan' gift, and for her 50th you wanted to get her something really special, which you would have got while in Dallas, if the competition win had turned out to be a wind up. Would she believe that?" Bill laughed before replying, "Yes, she hated that gift and always threatens me with divorce if I ever get her present choice that wrong again." The boss pitched in without looking up from his desk, "How do know all this Marvin?" "Bill told me earlier, the funny part is, he spent two days unconscious once she'd opened them and used them to knock him out cold!" The boss hooted uncontrollably after hearing this, followed by Marvin and then finally Bill. The three men must have been laughing for two minutes solid prior to the room falling silent again, once the boss had stopped laughing. Marvin then broke the silence. "That's how we explain the weekend away in

Vegas to her, now the next part of my proposal is going to have to be sponsored by you, boss. I'm sorry and I'll understand if you don't agree to fund it, but I'm sure Bill will more than compensate you for your losses out of his winnings, won't you Bill?" Bill bowed his head before the boss peered towards Marvin and nodded, urging him to carry on. "Before I continue there's just a couple of questions that I need you to answer please Bill. Does your ranch have an airstrip where a private jet could land, and does Shelly have appropriate clothes to wear for a posh bash?" Bill couldn't answer due to a series of knocks on the door, three consecutive ones, then a short pause, followed by a final one, and the boss shouting "Come in" from behind his desk. Bill glanced towards the door and as it opened his heart sank to his feet, when in walked the man from earlier who'd said that it was his turn to carry out any punishment stating, "You wanted me boss?" The boss gazed towards Marvin whilst ordering him to go and get some fresh air with Bill, for fifteen minutes and not to be late back. Bill's body started to shudder, he didn't know what to expect next, Marvin hadn't finished explaining his plan and the boss had called for Sandy's man. In Bill's mind this meant that the boss didn't approve of Marvin's strategy and he was about to meet his bullet, after Sandy's man had pulled the trigger. Marvin stood up and walked towards the door, initially alone while Bill remained seated, until he stared back and gestured for him to follow. Mercifully, Bill saw sense and did.

With Marvin and Bill now out of the room both the boss and Sandy's man erupted into laughter, Sandy's man even commented on "how fucking gullible Bill was." The boss agreed whilst he pulled two brown envelopes from a drawer. He handed the first one to Sandy's man and educated him about there being a little bit extra in it for Sandy following her remarkable assignment with Bill. As he handed over the second, Sandy's man notified the boss that he didn't need to pay for a scout this time, seeing as Bill wasn't found via their normal scout network, but by an ex cult member who'd pulled in a favour, as he wanted Bill out of the way permanently. The boss looked towards Sandy's man and described how intrigued he had suddenly become with this mystery man who refused money, and he ordered him to go and fetch this non-member to explain his real reason for wanting Bill out of the way. Before Sandy's man departed, he asked the boss how Marvin's plan was coming along, the boss updated him about it being quite good and plausible so far. Then queried whether he was sure Marvin had no idea about any of the seedy activities that his staff get up to, as active members the cult? Sandy's man smiled before enlightening him how it's a standing joke between most of the staff and they quite often wonder whether he does but chooses to turn a blind eye because he's never experienced such a well-paid job like this before. "What's the plan now then boss?" Sandy's man requested, the boss looked at him, and while grinning like a horny bull, he retorted. "Marvin's doing a really good job of getting Bill to cooperate, so he'll finish off his plan, then after I agree to it, we'll go and have a meeting with the chief of police, and I'll endorse the deal. All being well, tomorrow night Bill will be the main entertainment, and hopefully he'll face the queen just like all of the others have when we've taken the show on the road; demonstrating how much fun it is to our sisters. That way it'll save you from having to take 'gimp boy' on a one-way ticket to the country. Now Bill cooperating still isn't a done deal so, go back and stand by the door and when you see him, make sure you say something that makes him think he's still got a terrific chance of taking a bullet to the brain. Then go and bring me the mystery man! When you find him fetch him straight to me, even if I'm at my hotel in Vegas, and you can use one of the private jets if you desire." Sandy's man exited, and the boss pulled his mobile from his pocket to make a call, however his conversation was interrupted by the sequence of knocks sounding on the door, thus after ending his chat, he bellowed "Come in."

It was Marvin and Bill re-entering exactly fifteen minutes after they disappeared. Bill went straight towards his seat and sat down fearfully waiting to find out his fate, wishing what Sandy's man had just told him was untrue. Marvin took a slight detour via the fridge and passed everybody present another iced cold bottle, before retaking his seat and continuing to talk through his proposal. "Bill you didn't get chance to answer my questions from earlier, so I'll repeat them now you've had some thinking time. Does your ranch have an airstrip where a jet could land, and does Shelly have suitable clothes to wear for a posh bash?" Bill took a sip of his water and then muttered, "yes and no. Yes there's a field suitable for landing a private jet and no, the only nice clothes she owns are her flowery dress for weddings and plain one for funerals." Marvin fell completely hushed after hearing what Bill had just said, he wasn't expecting Shelly not to have appropriate clothes and thought, 'She's a woman for Christ sake, all the women who I know have far too many clothes and shoes for every occasion. Some even have outfits for the 'just in case I get invited to ones'. Breaking the silence he stated. "Never mind, I'll think of a way around that obstacle while I tell you the rest of my plan. Now, for the next piece to work, I'm going to need a few things from you please boss. The use of your private jets, somewhere suitable for Bill and me to sleep tonight and for you to ask the chief of police if I can have special dispensation from him; by being granted membership to his cult for one night only. I'll need this so I can be Bill's wingman and keep a beady eye on him to make sure he pulls it off, then we can all go back to our normal lives. I promise to abide by the cults motto but please don't give me your answer until I've explained the rest of my plan."

Marvin scrutinised the boss as his head dipped, inspiring him to continue. "Bill calls Shelly and enthusiastically tells her about his stroke of good fortune, and how she'll be getting picked up by a private jet from her ranch at 2 PM tomorrow to join him, so she's to make sure the airstrip field is empty of cattle. He'll then explain, that as well as winning the competition, he's got a lovely present in mind for her that does exactly what she wanted." Marvin abruptly stopped. You could see his mind remained in deep thought and he lingered for a couple of minutes while his body and hands occasionally twitched, before he excitedly shouted, "I've got it." He took a short breather and the others stared at him during this time, eagerly awaiting to hear what it is he's got. Marvin put them out of their misery when he resumed speaking in his normal tone. "You also tell Shelly part of the prize, is too choose lots of clothes from the company who held the competitions new formal wear range. We pack the jet with a wide collection of garments and shoe's from our 'Dress to impress' for her to pick from. That then solves the suitable attire issue." Marvin snatched another drink then persisted. "We make clear to Shelly, that one of the conditions of the prize, is for Bill to be a judge for a fashion contest which the competition organisers have arranged for tonight. A low-key event attended by only a few select individuals. This will keep Bill absent from Shelly and eliminate the possibility of him opening his mouth and fowling up. Bill will be with me all night, so I'll prevent any slip ups happening this end. At 2 PM tomorrow one of your jets will land at Bill's ranch full of clothes and fly Shelly to Vegas. This will give her ample time to try on stacks of outfits and if she's anything like my wife, she'll probably end up eventually picking the first one which she tried. One of your stretched limousine's will wait at the airport to pick her up and deliver her to the venue, thus enabling her to get ready while she waits for Bill to arrive."

"At 4 PM a jet will depart from Dallas airport with Bill and I on it. We'll also need a limousine waiting when we land. When we arrive Bill will call Shelly and tell her he's still on official competition winners business, and he'll call once he's finished, so she can meet him in the main bar when she's ready. Bill will be waiting, along with myself as the organiser of the competition and a business associate of mine, who's had a few too many. I'll need you to provide the business associate for this please boss. I thought Sandy's man might be a suitable candidate if that's OK boss?" He wet his lips with a drink from his bottle, before confirming that using him was fine, as long as his current errand had been completed first, and if not, then he would gladly provide somebody else. Satisfied with the bosses backing so far, Marvin resumed, "Thanks boss. Now as Shelly enters the bar my drunken business associate will take a shining and produce a lewd comment aimed at her. Bill won't enjoy this and will demand an apology. My associate refuses, leaving Bill with no alternative but to teach the man a lesson with his best right hook; sparking my business colleague clean out. Witnessing this I'm appalled with his behaviour; therefore I invite Shelly and Bill to my table as an apology. While we're sitting down the police enter and tackle Bill, then they arrest him for assault and take him away for questioning. This will leave Shelly in my safe hands to make sure she doesn't spoil our plot, and more importantly, it will get Bill safely out of the way to change into his gimp suit, ready to play the game. Once completed, he re-joins us clarifying that my business associate has now sobered up and dropped the charges once he'd realised how crude he was. Then if all goes to plan it will leave us to enjoy the rest of the evening. What do you think to that boss? Can you supply all of the effects that we need on time? Bill do you think you can pull it off?"

Marvin sat staring at the boss, whilst waiting in anticipation for his approval. The boss glared back while he took a minute to mull it over, so Marvin turned to Bill and quizzed him again whether he thought he could succeed, hesitantly Bill reacted. "I think I'll be able to do it as long as I'm in your company at all times. The only thing I'm unsure about is the 'encounters', what sort of things will I have to do?" Marvin couldn't solve this question, his friend had died before he'd managed to go into detail about each individual game and knew he couldn't tell Bill this as it would unnerve him, therefore he decided to paint the best possible picture he could. "It'll probably just be a few silly little things like, pleasure a woman, conduct a ceremonial ritual, get pleasured by an ugly and similar. Your actions will then entertain the cult for the night and make them giggle, but don't worry about them clocking on that it was you when you return, just make sure you keep your gimp suit on at all times." Bill took a moment while his brain absorbed what Marvin had just told; he'd have to be unfaithful to Shelly and wasn't feeling very comfortable about it, but knew it was his only chance of staying alive. "I'll be fine as long as we stick to the plan, and Marvin promises that he'll always have my back." Marvin smiled and felt a sense of relief, knowing that Bill was comfortable with the proposal, so he reassuringly shouted "I promise" prior to facing the boss to await his decision. "OK I'll give you everything you need to make it happen, but I'm warning you that if either of you mess any part up, then you'll both face a very nasty death." Bill felt relieved as did Marvin, safe in the knowledge that they'd successfully passed the first hurdle in keeping Bill active. All they needed to do now was convince the chief of police to let Bill volunteer, and for Marvin to be granted affiliation for a single night.

Marvin respectfully questioned his boss "When would you be able to call the chief please boss? so that we can obtain his consent." Once finished, he fell silent whilst he awaited his reply and thankfully, he didn't have to wait too long before it came. "Marvin, I like you, and Bill I'm really starting to adore you. It's a pity that we didn't meet under different circumstances, as I'm sure I'd of fleeced a lot of money from you over the years, once you'd become a frequent follower of mine. Therefore let's hope you survive this by keeping to your part of the deal. Now Marvin you've worked below me for nearly four years now and I trust you. You're keen, respectable, courteous, and good with the customers. However, I need to know I can really trust you because I have a special job lined up for you if your projects a success. I'm about to tell you something regarding me that very few people know, and I'd like to keep it that way, so you both have to promise that what I'm about to tell, will never be repeated again, not even to each other once you've left this room. Do you both promise?" They both vowed at the same time, thus permitting the boss to resume. "Marvin there's no need to call the chief and ask for clemency in exchange for Bill volunteering, he's purely a puppet in a uniform who'd need to request the head of the cults permission, along with the owner of the venue's to make sure he'll permit a non-member access. Now it just happens that you're in luck as both the head of the cult and the proprietor of the location like your plan and have given it full approval." Marvin gawked at the boss, intrigued as to how both of them could have granted their endorsement so rapidly, when in reality, less than five minutes had elapsed since he'd fully enlightened it. Baffled, he questioned the boss. "Sorry for being rude boss and I know you're a very resourceful and connected man, but how can you be sure we've got their approval when they don't know the plan?" Marvin remained a little bit jumpy after raising such a query to his boss, a man with a reputation of showing violence when questioned and he didn't know what to assume when his boss gave his response. "Marvin you interrupted me before I'd finished speaking, I'd only hesitated as my lungs needed some air and I still had something important to say. But I warn you it must never be mentioned again. Now Marvin if you can keep it to yourself, then you'll prove how I can trust you, and you'll get the special job that's waiting. The owner of the venue and the head of the cult approve of your plan since they are both the same person. Me!"

Chapter 5

Executing the plan, part one

It fell mute following the boss's confession, both Marvin and Bill where unsure whether it was a wind up and were too scared to comment. The silence came to be broken, by the boss clarifying how they needed the comperes help on the night and how his dead friend had failed to tell him a couple of crucial particulars regarding the game. The first aspect Marvin didn't know, was to make it more entertaining for the audience, tradition dictated that it must be the companion of the contender who span the wheel. The second, the audience got great pleasure from, when the contestants antics get broadcast to our fellow cults. Worldwide. It's also exhibited on enormous screens peppered all over the place for our invitees to view, along with the participants partner. Marvin and Bill gawked at each other; Bill shuddered his head in disbelief with what he'd just discovered. Marvin twisted towards the boss and requested his help in recruiting the compere, then with a smirk all over his chops, he reacted. "You leave that to me, since it's my cult, at my venue, I think it's only fair that I do the compering. You see, I like to be centre stage, unrecognisable in my attire directing the twilight's enjoyment, whilst guaranteeing things go to plan and all of my customers leave with a smile on their face. By the way what did you say your dead friend who told you about the cults name was?" Marvin stuttered before divulging, "Fred Jones." Bill disrupted Marvin's words, when he updated the boss regarding his grave concerns concerning the game. The thought of him being watched by potentially millions sent shivers through his spine, and he confessed about being sceptical as to whether he could perform as expected. "Don't worry about that, I've got something downstairs in one of my rooms that will help, so I'll throw a couple in on the house for you, seeing as I'm really looking forward to witnessing you perform in your bright red suit. Now listen you two leave everything to me, since this is what's going to happen. Go from here and get Bill dressed normally, his clothes are already in the next room waiting. Then give his membership card to the bartender before coming back in here so Bill can make the most important call of his life, and if he persuades Shelly to have faith in him, you'll both live." Marvin thought he'd misheard the bosses comment and questioned whether he had. The boss clarified that he hadn't. "Yes Marvin if Bill doesn't influence Shelly then you'll both disappear. I did say earlier that if you messed up any part of the plot, you'd both get a bullet. Now for your wife's sake you better hope he doesn't, now get out and knock on the door when he's changed."

Marvin and Bill escaped the room, both now feeling the added pressure of being accountable for someone else's life. Bill then observed his clothes piled on the couch next to the grand piano, and a man standing behind the bar wobbling a cocktail shaker. Marvin removed Bill's card from around his neck, then sat at the bar and handed it to the bartender, while Bill picked up his clothes and travelled towards the nearest corner. "Any chance of a drink please bartender?" Marvin inquired but didn't take kindly to his reply. "Sorry you'll have to wait until after you reappear from the bosses office. It's pointless wasting a great bourbon in case things don't go to plan. If they do, you can have one and your friend can have this lovely concoction which I'm preparing now to send him off to sleep." It was at this point that the penny finally dropped, and Marvin grasped how he was probably the only member of staff who was a non-member. He thought how stupid he'd been by not twigging on to all the strange behaviour and coincidences that he'd witnessed throughout his employment. His mind pondered towards the three other people who'd faced the bullet instead of justice already this year, and he questioned himself whether they'd faced the same fate as Bill and to his boss, this was all just a big pantomime. Whilst approaching the bar, Bill interjected Marvin's thoughts when he shouted out "that's better, I'm glad I'm out of that bloody red thing," Marvin responded by enquiring as to how he was feeling, but Bill didn't have the opportunity to reply; the bartender had pitched in instead. "Go back and see the boss and be fast about it, you're keeping him from his fun weekend away and he's eager to enjoy it. You don't want to put him in a mood now do you?" With that, Bill followed Marvin back in the direction of the bosses office before he executed the required pattern of knocks and waited patiently to be welcomed in.

When they entered, Bill noticed the room appeared just like before, apart from the boss being accompanied by a man sat beside him, along with a big yellow phone located on the desk. Bill prayed he wasn't going to be invited to use it; Shelly had a habit of buttoning un-recognised numbers. Instead she'd wait for a voicemail and after a couple of days listen to it before opting whether to return the call. "Sit down," yelled the boss, "this little business is keeping me from my unexpected important engagement which I'm to attend, prior to my Vegas retreat. So listen carefully, I'm only going to say this once! Make the call, go outside, Bill drink the drink then go and have a terrific night's snooze. Now the only space I've got spare for the night is the orgy room, therefore you can both sleep there. Marvin you're on guard duty so make sure he speaks to nobody! You'll both stay present in the room and the only humans you're to have contact with, are my staff members when they bring in your refreshments during your memorable stay. Tomorrow morning a selection of formal wear and a new gimp suit for Bill will be delivered, then at precisely 3.15 PM make sure you're both prepared, because that's when you'll get picked up. Do you both understand?" They both screamed "Yes" concurrently, before the boss stood up, and whilst gazing towards the man sitting next to him, he handed over his weapon and ordered its use if things didn't go as expected. The boss then strolled towards the door and exited, leaving Marvin and Bill in the company of the other man.

Once the door had shut Marvin encouraged Bill to make the call, thus enabling them to have a break from the days crap until tomorrow. Bill duly obliged and pulled his phone from his shirt pocket. When he unlocked it, he noticed seven missed calls from Shelly. These alarmed him and based on the knowledge of how mad she'll be with him for not answering, he started to doubt his ability to succeed. He dialled her number and before long he was greeted with Shelly shouting down his ear. "Where the hell have you been, I've been worried, thinking that something horrible had happened. Conner's here, helping me calm down an out of control rampant bull. I'm just making us dinner then he'll go and secure the fence. What time will you be back?" Bill didn't like his thoughts of Shelly being at home alone with Conner, all he could picture in his mind was the scene from the barn. Bill took a deep breath, nervous with the thought that what he was about to say was the difference between life and death, he reacted. "I'm fine thanks honey, please thank Conner for backing you with the bull and tell him I owe him. Now baby I've got some exciting news regarding your present." Bill paused allowing an impatient Shelly to speak. "What have you got me? Is it something nice? You know if it's pans, you'll be a single man." Bill giggled before responding. "I know sweetie, this year I've managed to come up with something special that I know you'll appreciate and recollect for years to come, but first I need to apologise." Shelly unsuccessfully tried to interrupt Bill, who whispered, "shush, please let me finish and ask any questions at the end. I've had a roller coaster of a day and I've got some thrilling news." Shelly agreed and Bill persisted, unbroken, to educate her regarding her present. "I've been keeping something from you, nothing serious just something rather small and insignificant, but it's really relevant now. I received a letter earlier in the week from a company whose competition I'd entered, and it said that I'd won first prize, but to claim it, I had to visit their store in Dallas no later than midday today. I'm sorry I kept it from you honey. However it's an extraordinary prize, and I didn't want to tell you and build your hopes up, just in case it was somebody performing a practical joke. I used the excuse of coming to Dallas for your gifts as a cover story, so if the competition had been an untruth, I'd have still been able to acquire you something nice whilst I was here. Honey Bunch we've won an all-expenses paid trip to Vegas and it's this weekend. What do you think to that babe?"

Bill knew instantly that Shelly wasn't impressed, just by the silence on the other end of the line. She'd hung up. When he redialled it rang endlessly and his spirits sank deeper and deeper with each one, with knowing that if she didn't answer, he'd never listen to her tone again. Mercifully for Bill, she eventually picked up. "I don't want to go to Vegas! I want a quiet celebration! Just the two of us relishing each other's company whilst observing the sun go down and the moon come up while gazing at the stars. I even thought, how nice it would be for you to name one after me. Don't worry about the competition, tell them you don't want the prize. Then go and get me some nice treats and get back here rapidly so you can help Conner mend the fence." Bill's heart stopped beating for a second or two when he realized he'd have to come up with something good and fast to convince Shelly to reconsider. "OK baby I understand, there's nothing more in the world I'd rather be doing right now than that, but the prize isn't just a weekend away in Vegas. You will be picked up from our ranch by a private jet, which will be packed full of the company's new formal wear range and you get to select and keep anything you like. Then on the Saturday night we get to play a competition for the chance to win sixty-four million dollars. Imagine how that much money would change our life. Do you like the sound of that sweetie?" Bill knew how slipping the prize money into the conversation should do the trick. Shelly had always dreamed of being a multi-millionaire and having the lifestyle which it brought. After a pause she responded. "You're the best husband that a woman could ever desire, what time will you be home?" With a sense of relief in his voice, Bill clarified the rest of the proceedings. "OK sugar, I'm really looking forward to our wonderful weekend away, just think of all the fun and frills we're going to have. But I'm sorry sweetie, as part of my winners duty's I've got to stay in Dallas tonight and judge a fashion contest for the company, so we'll catch up with each other in Vegas tomorrow teatime. Now, a private jet will land in our big field at 2 PM tomorrow to collect you. Honey Bunch are you OK with that?" Bill grasped how excited she was from the sound of her feet reverberating around the room, and while she jumped for joy upon the floorboards at the prospect of becoming a multi-millionaire, Shelly retorted "Yes," Then they said their goodbyes with an effortless "I love you."

Marvin commended Bill by offering him a 'well done' pat on the back, Bill responded with a begrudged "thanks." The other man present picked up the big yellow handset, he waited a few seconds then muttered, "it's done," before standing and departing, thus leaving Marvin and Bill alone. Hesitant with what they were intended to do next; sit there and wait for someone to escort them or make their own way whilst taking a detour via the bar. They stared at each other, then Marvin remarked to Bill how he didn't think he could pull it off when Shelly folded, and how for the first time in his life, he said a prayer whilst he redialled. Upon concluding, he stood up and gestured for Bill to do the same before they exited the room and proceeded straight for the bar.

"You're still alive then?" the bartender inquired towards them and after smiling and laughing for a twinkling, he gave some directives. "Come and have a seat, I've got a lovely bourbon for you Marvin and something that will help you sleep." Pointing his finger towards Bill as he said 'You'. Bill wasn't enthusiastic with what the bartender had alleged. After the days strange events he was exhausted and scared with the thought of what may happen whilst having a nap. However by the sounds of it, the ruling had already been taken out of his hands and he knew he was powerless to prevent it. So while he slept, he'd have to put his life in the hands of a man who he'd met only a few hours earlier. "What's in it?" Bill queried the bartender, who smiled before enlightening how it was a wonderful blend of the world's finest ingredients, with each one being specifically chosen for its unique ability to help calm and relax the body and mind. Thus allowing you to slowly drift into the best night's sleep you'll ever have, and with it the most life-like dreams that anybody could ever wish for, dreams that feel so real, you'll question whether they were. The bartender handed Bill the cocktail, who glanced at it, then circled to Marvin, who was sitting smugly with his glass in hand, before swallowing. Once finished, he sounded a huge burp. This put a smile on the barman's face prior to his next comments. "Christ you must have been thirsty, now go to your bed and get yourself comfy within thirty minutes, otherwise you'll collapse on the spot and have the most horrible night's sleep ever, along with some terrible nightmares. There's some cuisine in the room waiting, so upon arrival, make sure you have a nibble before the drink kicks in." Once the bartender had finished speaking the door opened, and in walked their chaperones. Then following a brief introduction, one of the escorts guided them back into the corridor, while the other brought up the rear, and all four walked down the corridor towards the special room's secret door, prior to ascending a set of stairs, which were situated further along on the opposite side. This set led to a small landing, then another aided their rise in the opposite direction, and once at the top, they walked through a huge set of double doors where Marvin and Bill received their strict instructions to remain in the orgy room alone.

When the doors closed behind them, they found themselves stood in a very large wooden floored room, with a huge stripy patterned couch positioned along one wall. It was massive and seemed like it would easily seat twenty. A group of six tables were arranged on the opposite side of the room, with each one having four chairs arranged neatly around, and two of them were covered by overflowing plates of food. A single plain door was also stationed in the wall behind them. Located in front of the two men and towards the left-hand side of the room, were three large beds which had been shoved next to each other to construct a vast sleeping spot. A short distance away towards the right, was something that seemed to be like a large gym mat covering a sizeable portion of the floor. Bill couldn't help but question himself why the bed area was cluttered with camera's on tripods. However, now feeling sleepy, he managed to brush his thoughts away while he travelled in the direction of the beds, and when he'd reached his destination, he lay down and warned Marvin that, seeing how it might be his last night alive, the bed was all his. Bill was enthusiastic to see if the drink pusher had been truthful, he knew the dreams he'd like; sweet ones about him and his lovely wife Shelly. Marvin didn't object to Bill having the beds, but he did object to him lying down without having anything to eat. He reminded him and whilst walking across the room with a plate in his hand, he advised him to "get some of this inside you." Bill was very sleepy by now and no sooner than he'd finished his second sandwich, he'd drifted off into his own little world for some much-needed pleasantness.

Chapter 6

The longest night

Marvin appeared to be startled by a knock on the door, so he marched towards it but never got a chance to open it; in walked Sandy wielding a champagne flute in each hand. Marvin didn't recognise her after having never viewed her fully clothed before. They walked towards the massive couch and sat next to each other and whilst glancing in Marvin's eyes she urged him to have a drink, thus permitting them to become properly acquainted. Marvin agreed, as long as she wasn't expecting any weird business, and seeing how he was a happily married man, he told her so. Sandy tittered whilst clarifying how he wasn't her type; she's just curious why Bill was spending the night in front of the camera's. Marvin didn't know how to respond, sceptical whether Sandy knew the real reason and unsure that perhaps his boss had sent her as a test, so he thought quickly on his feet and stalled fulfilling Sandy's curiosity, with an issue of his own. "Why's this big long couch here?" Sandy then chuckled while she reacted. "You really don't know? and I suppose you don't know what materializes in this chamber either!" Marvin observed her features with a strange look in his eyes, now even more intrigued concerning its true function. Curiously, he asked again, prior to denying any knowledge as to what events occur, but he clarified how he'd love to find out. "Have a sip of your drink, get comfortable and I'll tell you all about it,"

Sandy advised in a heart-warming tone, then she persisted.

"This room is where the DVD's are created for the store, and through the door behind the tables you'll find outfits, scenery, accessories and everything else that you need to transform this area into virtually anywhere. Then on a filming day the models appear dressed appropriately for whatever scene they're shooting, and the location will be packed full of people. Some will be starring in the DVD, others like camera men, sound men, runners, fluffers and the director are here to manufacture it." Marvin interfered, "what's a fluffer?" Sandy sniggered and glared when she gave her reply. "I'll come to that in a minute. The main action materialises on the beds and the mat. Sometimes they're filming straight sex amongst a man and a women, whilst other's it's gay sex featuring men or women, however most of the time it's orgy's, hence the name. But it doesn't matter what they're filming, this couch continually gets in on the action." Marvin stood in disgust whilst shouting, "you mean people have sex on this couch and I could have been resting in a somebody's love juice." Sandy commanded him to sit and stop being childish before she informed him how the couch is made of a special material which gets thoroughly scrubbed after each shoot. Marvin did as instructed, and Sandy resumed. "People do have orgasms on this settee, typically when they do it's 'group action', but it's main purpose is where it gets its nickname, 'fluffers couch'. A 'fluffer' is a person, man or woman, whose sole objective is to do whatever it takes to make sure the man's warhead is primed at precisely the moment it's required. That was my first position in the store, I adored it, getting rewarded generously for doing something I enjoy. Then I progressed to play the lead prior to gaining an additional offer. You look sleepy Marvin, are you?" He eyeballed her, nodded his head then completed his fizz, so Sandy sustained. "Why don't you take your shoes off, put your feet up and get a few hours' sleep. I don't mind residing here for a bit to keep an eye on Bill and I'll knock you up when I'm done." Marvin didn't listen to all of what Sandy had to say, he was lying comfortably on the couch, slowly snoring away.

Sandy detached the flute from Marvin's hand and placed it on the table while she ambled in the direction of Bill lying asleep on his side, and once next to him, she began gently stroking his mane. Shocked by her touch he changed position, his body now lying on his back, and while focussing her fondling upon his chest, she murmured into his ear. "I'm so regretful Bill for this mess I've gotten you in, I didn't mean to tease you so much, I just fell in love the moment you grabbed my attention. Please don't say anything and let me do all of the talking, then if you manage to remain silent, I'm going to complete what I commenced earlier. Don't worry about Marvin disturbing us, I've slipped a little something into his beverage, and as a result we can have us a little bit of private time. You're in grave danger,

Marvin isn't who he appears to be. Don't trust him, in fact from this moment on don't trust anybody but me, and if you get out of this mess alive, then I want you to rescue me from this seedy life of mine, by taking me back to Ringgold as your mistress. Just picture the naughty times we can have rolling around in the hay. Tomorrow they're going to humiliate you, and the wheel is rigged with a device which allows the boss to stop it on whatever task he wishes. He'll normally kick off with easy things like one on one sex or foreplay, but each mission gradually gets worse with each spin. However, there's only two encounters which you need be afraid of, having sex with a man and enduring fifteen minutes with the queen. The boss doesn't usually stop the circle on having sex with a man, being straight he despises the thought of viewing two men experiencing masculinity, therefore this is normally only used as a severe punishment. Now, if a contestant makes the seventh and final task then they're in line for a big win, so the boss will always have them confront the queen. The only way of triumphing is to kill her sooner than she kills you. No one has ever succeeded, so please be careful and ensure that you kill her, otherwise I'll be entombed in this sleazy lifestyle that I'm so desperate to escape." Sandy's hand shifted towards Bill's trousers, before she released his belt and button ahead of lowering the zip. He didn't move an inch, so Sandy continued. "Shelly's a slag, she's been having it away with Conner ever since he secured her father's ranch, and she's had his brother two. That didn't last long though because he got guilty with the thought of her cheating on you, and since having had it performed upon him, he recalls how soul-breaking it is. Now what I'm about to state, please don't repeat to another person, otherwise it will jeopardise my existence. All that's happened today is not an unlucky set of flukes, you've undoubtedly been set up and I'm sorry for being the bait, but I promise to make amends if you can discover it in your soul to exonerate me. Currently, I don't know who or why, although I understand the boss suspects that you have and he's striving to learn by who. Please be vigilant tomorrow, you'll need to be quick-thinking to survive. Now let me finish off what I opened earlier."

Sandy stood from the bed, and whilst eliminating her lace top, she exposed her ample cleavage for the whole world to see. Then she removed her skirt and divulged her freshly shaved, delightfully looking, perfect sex organ. After joining Bill on the bed, she straddled him, prior to unbuttoning her bra and freeing her large glands, to expose her projectile like speared nipples. Unpredictably Bill's eyes opened, and he became alarmed with the spectacle of Sandy confining him. Reacting responsively, she positioned her finger across his lips, and gestured for him to say nothing whilst placing her right bullet in his mouth. Bill reacted and gently started to rotate his tongue, however, every now and then he'd sporadically stop for a quick nibble and taste. This awakened Sandy and her nipple grew significantly in size after each fresh suck, so she withdrew her projectile and substituted it with her

Vagina, and whilst rubbing gently against Bill's moist lips, she grumbled out with pleasure whenever his tongue connected, thus encouraging Bill to venture deeper inside with each new lick. Sandy then rotated, with her face now peered towards Bill's feet, and while bending over she wiggled his trousers over his hips and became astonished by how promptly his penis reached for the stars. Bill must have been playing a sad tune on Sandy's organ, she was weeping, and the more vigorously he played, the harder she wept. Sandy placed her right hand around Bill's love organ and gripped with all her might while she started to stroke, and she could feel it pulsating when the throbbing intensified with each stroke. Consequently, she leant over a little more prior to placing it in her mouth then she licked and sucked with pleasure. The two remained in this spot for a good while and Sandy's moans became louder with each fresh orgasm. Bill remained silent, he was still unsure whether it was a dream, however when he couldn't take it anymore, and with perfect timing, he exploded just as Sandy craved for her cream.

Satisfied, Bill lingered horizontal on the bed, but Sandy was rampant and there was no way she was stopping, so she trapped his dagger amongst her breasts and attempted to transform it into a sword. Enjoying this, Bill's blade grew in length with every stroke, then once Sandy remained convinced it was of the mandatory size, she removed her organ from his face and repositioned it over his weapon prior to taking a squat. An almighty screech resonated around the chamber when it wounded her for the first time, and Bill still couldn't believe he wasn't fantasizing about making love to a beautiful woman like Sandy. Either way he was determined to enjoy it. Every time Sandy crouched; Bill thrust his pelvis skywards, ensuring he gained maximum velocity whilst guaranteeing precision prodding when she was at her lowest, thus resulting with Sandy letting out a pulse intensifying scream every time. When Bill felt like he was nearly ready to detonate again, Sandy sensed his enthusiasm and after disembarking, she accurately located her mouth just in time to thwart his love juice from contaminating the covers. Then Sandy span around and blocked his view with her large beasts hovering whilst she inserted his warhead, so in return Bill ogled her monsters whilst they bounced uncontrollably and uncoordinated with every new squat. The more they bounced, the more thrilled Bill got, the more excited Bill got the more Sandy provoked, while frequently blaspheming whenever she peaked. The cycle of each other's actions persisted to make the other one hornier until, without warning Bill castigated and Sandy grinned whilst mouthing in his ear, "I hope you haven't just cum inside me, I'm not on the pill and the last thing you need right now is the shame of getting your mistress pregnant?" Still unfulfilled, she exposed Bill and ordered him to remain still while she went for some extraordinary items. He smirked, hopeful that it was sex toys; permitting them to complete their earlier unfinished business.

Bill was mystified when she returned holding a bag in one hand and a whip in the other. He was curious with what treats it contained, but when she placed the bag on the floor and stroked his limp sex organ with the whip, his dagger disappointedly transformed into a small blade. Once Sandy had sadly watched his weapon shrink, she whipped it and he winced in pain prior to Sandy repeating her actions again and again and again. She continued until it regained its rigidity, then deposited the whip on the bed and started to rummage through her bag to divulge some of its contents. When she pulled out an aerosol and some strawberries, Bill couldn't help but think how this wasn't a fitting time to have dessert. However, he grasped her intentions when she completely covered his right nipple with cream, prior to placing a strawberry on top for good measure. Sandy then seductively licked the cream from around the edges, whilst taking her time to ensure that Bill was gaining equal pleasure. When the cream disappeared and left the big red juicy berry, Sandy picked it up in her mouth, squashed it, then spat the juices all over Bill's joystick. Sandy then took great pleasure from doing an extraordinarily splendid job of cleaning up the mess. Once finished she lay next to Bill and replicated the covering of her nipple, whilst indicating for him to return the compliment. In doing so his hand became drawn towards Sandy's perfect vagina. Bill found himself in heaven when he got to the strawberry and Sandy let out an almighty scream when his fingers began to walk. The more his digits discovered, the more awakened Sandy became, and her body shuddered stiffer with each fresh peak. Bill's bits had finished marvelling and were supplanted by his tongue. Beginning at no- man's- land, he gently licked whilst slowly working his way aloft until ultimately landing at her clitoris, were he had a long stay. Constantly carping at this point, Sandy was incapable of controlling herself and she grabbed the back of Bill's head whilst pushing down fiercely. Bill managed to free himself from her control and developed excitement with the sight of her lying in front of him with her legs spread eagled, while waiting to be taken to heaven and back. Bill moved his head towards hers and pecked her lips as his thrust his warhead. Sandy's hands grasped his backside, thus enabling her to pull back each time he yanked away. The harder Bill jabbed the more provoked he became from viewing Sandy's beast's bounce in rhythm with every prod. They remained in this position for what seemed an eternity, while Sandy squealed relentlessly from the multiple orgasms Bill was distributing. Bill's weapon was excruciating and felt like it needed to discharge, then when Sandy hollered "harder" and he did, he couldn't contain himself, and prior to rolling over exhausted whilst in disbelief at what he'd achieved. He detonated. They then both lay still for a while allowing time for their bodies to recover. Once reenergised, Sandy rose and began to dress whilst advising Bill not to reveal what had just transpired to a sole, otherwise they'll both be in a lot of trouble. Sandy kissed him goodnight and then departed the room, not forgetting to take her bag and whip.

Once she'd departed Bill's mind floated towards Sandy's comments about Marvin being untrustworthy. To him he appeared a respectable bloke and had managed to come up with the concept of how to save his life, and what did she mean when she said Marvin's not who he appears to be? His thoughts then coasted to Shelly and Conner, knowing that if what Sandy had said was true, then it confirmed an idea which he's had since his bedroom department went west. Bill had presumed it was just a fluke that the 'pan' present incident and Conner shifting so close happened around the same time, and he depicted Conner lying in his bed, nude next to Shelly, while both fatigued following some frantic frolicking. Bill's visions were brought to an abrupt end by the sound of a voice in his ear. "Wake up Bill, today's your big day, I hope you slept well, and you've got lots of energy, because somehow I think you're going to need it." Bill opened his eyes to see Marvin standing above, smiling as he offered him a jug of powerful coffee.

Chapter 7

Executing the plan, part two

Bill stared curiously towards Marvin; he was anxious discovering a man; who he's been warned not to trust, talking whilst handing him a mug. Fearing its contents might be drugged he questioned himself whether he should accept it. "Go on you must be thirsty, you've been asleep in the same position for hours. I've been guarding you all night ensuring you came to no harm. The coffee here's lovely." Bill thought Sandy's visit must have been a dream after hearing Marvin's words, consequently he accepted the hot drink. "What time is it?" He queried whilst scraping the sleep from his eyes. "11 AM, not long to go now. How are you feeling? I bet you're nervous. Did you sleep well?" Marvin retorted. Bill's interest shifted to the delightful smell of freshly baked bread in the distance, and whilst glancing towards the tables, he spotted the vast selection of formal wear hanging near the one which was completely covered in food. Then Bill responded to Marvin's series of questions. "Shitting myself, but I had a lovely dream thanks just like the bartender promised. It was so real; the memories will stay in my mind forever concerning how Sandy and I got to complete our romance." Marvin gazed at Bill well calling him a dirty bastard and instructed him to get some breakfast inside him; seeing as he'd need all the energy he could muster. Before Bill could get off the bed a man threw open one of the doors, and whilst waving Bill's mobile in his left hand he yelled. "The boss says answer it now. See what she wants and whatever you do make sure she gets on that plane." It stopped ringing and when Bill grabbed it, he noticed twelve missed calls from Shelly, now extremely concerned for her wellbeing he didn't hesitate in calling her back.

Shelly answered immediately, "Honey I'm so glad you're OK, I was worried that something bad might have happened to you while in the big city. You hear on the news about gang's and cults fighting with each other along with kidnapping innocent victims." Shelly rested, giving Bill time to reply. "It's OK baby I'm fine, happy birthday by the way. I was just having a lie in; I had a late-night fuelled by a few drinks to celebrate our good fortune. Are you ready for the jet at 2?" There was a short silence before Shelly reacted. "Yes sweetie, some men visited late last night, they scared me at first, but luckily Conner was here so he dealt with them for me. They said that they'd been sent to check out the suitability of the landing strip prior to the aircraft arriving. Luckily, Conner was just leaving and didn't mind showing them the field on his way home." Bill's heart sank, upon hearing how Conner had been with his wife for most of yesterday, and he wanted to question Shelly's conduct with him, but knew it would have to wait until another day. Otherwise today would very probably be his last. He thought for a moment before giving his well-executed reply. "Sorry sweetheart that's my fault, with all of yesterday's excitement I forgot to mention somebody would be calling round to check it. I'll have to take Conner for a night out when we get back from Vegas, seeing as he's certainly been there for you whilst I've been absent. Now I've got to go Honey. I've some more official business to do for the competition and I'll be un-contactable for the rest of the day. When you get to the resort stay in your room, and I'll be in touch the moment I'm sat in the bar. Then you can join me, and I'll be all yours for the night. Pick several outfits whilst on the plane and have a safe flight. I love you." Shelly agreed prior to closing the call by declaring how much she adored him and couldn't wait for her present.

Bill wiped the sweat off his forehead with his shirt sleeve, which was now dripping after having to control all of the various emotions which his body had suffered in such a short space of time. His attention stayed firmly on Shelly and Conner, and whilst recalling how Sandy educated him about their misdemeanours prior to describing her as a slag, he questioned himself whether Sandy's visit actually occurred. Then he considered Sandy's accusations for a second, before speedily discharging them after subsequently feeling guilty following his activities of the previous day. Bill decided to forgive her if she was, as long as it stopped; after all it was only a dream. Marvin encouraged Bill to eat whilst everything was sizzling, then clarified whether his 'partner' was OK, before explaining that since the call had ended, he seemed a little pale. Bill notified Marvin that he was fine, just hot, and hungry, so he made his way to the grub and helped himself to a breakfast fit for a king. Hopeful this wouldn't be his last. While Bill ate Marvin talked. "You need to select something fitting for tonight once you've finished. The men who dropped everything off said too travel lightly in the clobber that we're dressed in and whatever we pick, we're to put aside and they'll be collected at 12 noon along with the leftovers. We don't need to worry about freshening up, we'll have chance to do that on the aircraft. I've already picked my outfit, something stylish and luxurious in view of the fact that I've got to look the part. Have you anything in mind?" Bill didn't want to speak with his mouth full, so he waited until he'd polished his plate prior to responding. "I'm not really bothered. I don't think I'll be in mine for long, seeing as I've got a funny feeling that I'm going to spend most of the evening in my red suit." Marvin giggled whilst agreeing and reminded Bill that due to the time, he only had ten minutes to pick and choose. Bill stood up and proceeded for the first suit that came into sight and grabbed it, then he examined the label, before bending over and picking up a matching pair of shoes. Once decided, he communicated how he'd made his choice whilst handing them to Marvin, who placed his new attire to one side. Clothing selected, they then walked to the other side of the room were a place on the fluffers couch awaited.

Bill queried Marvin with a sarcastic tone in his voice. "So, what do you fancy doing for the next few hours? I don't want to sit here mulling over tonight and get

myself all worked up speculating what it might bring."
Bill's question received silence at first, Marvin was
powerless to think of a suitable reply. Then the door
opened and in walked two men exactly on time. Bill
inquired whether they could suggest anything to help
alleviate his boredom; desperate to hear any kind of
suggestion, one of them replied. "Why don't you have a
game of cards that'll kill some time, I'll go and get you a
pack from below if you'd like; there's some with
delightfully naughty images on." Bill observed Marvin
nodding whilst signalling to Bill that he was up for a
game, so he decided to take the man up on his gesture.
After the two men departed the room fell silent, and Bill
was hesitant about entering into a conversation with
Marvin whilst still trying to make sense of last night's
dream. To him, Marvin seemed like a decent bloke, a big
man who didn't let his size intimidate you, unlike the
other members of staff, and if anything, Marvin came
across as the type of man who would more likely kill you
with kindness rather than a bullet. A perplexed Bill
sought some answers, he wanted to understand whether
Sandy's visit really occurred and whether what she said
was true. Bill deduced that if he used the cards wisely
and convinced Marvin to have a game of honesty or risk,
then he could try and find the real Marvin out. Bill
inquired. "Fancy a game of truth or dare when the cards
arrive?" Marvin immediately retorted. "how do you play
that? I've never heard of that game before. Is it a country
thing?" Bill laughed prior to giving his reply. "It
probably is, and I've been led to believe that when
partying a group of people will use a bottle instead of

cards. The bottle gets span and whoever the top points towards when it stops, has to either tell the truth or opt to take a dare. We can have a game of twenty one's and whoever loses will face the others question. The dare element is going to be pretty hard under our current circumstances, but if all goes well, we can save them for when this horrible mess is in our past. Are you in?" Marvin glared and nodded his head, and bang on cue, the man re-entered with an oversize deck, while informing them how he'd selected the double sized pack with the more graphic images on. Bill took the cards, and now desperate for a pee, he inquired as to the loo's whereabouts. The man reacted with a lift of his arm and pointed towards the solitary door positioned behind the tables. "Through that door there, and don't touch anything. Straight to the loo and back. Do you hear me?" Whilst standing up, Bill bowed his head in acknowledgement prior to walking in the direction of the door; placing the cards on one of the tables while en-route, he expressed how he wouldn't be long if Marvin wanted to give them a quick shuffle whilst waiting. Marvin appropriately obliged and stood up off the fluffers couch just as the man exited the area whilst confirming he'd be back at 3.15 PM precisely. Bill then pushed open the door leading to the toilet.

As it opened, the room automatically illuminated with hundreds of tiny lights shining brightly down, and Bill found himself stood still after having been taken aback by the size and number of strange items contained within. He couldn't see the toilet from his position, his view was obstructed from the immense collection of sex toys, whips, outfits, and scenery. It resembled an Aladdin's cave for the sex industry. Bill entered, careful not to touch anything like he'd been warned, and while making his way towards the back, he noticed a bag tucked away behind a bench. After recognising it straight away as Sandy's bag which she'd been holding in his dream, he continued strolling and found himself deep inside, once he'd passed a selection of machinery which had penis shapes attached to the end of a protruding rod. Next, he came across a selection of very large posters with each one depicting a different surrounding, before he eventually found what he'd been looking for and commenced having a very long pee. Whilst stood weeing away, his focus switched back to the bag and he quizzed himself with what it was doing there and what did it contain? He thought how it wouldn't do any harm to take a peek on his return, and if it were empty then it would completely rule out Sandy's visit. After finishing, Bill's heartbeat raced while he hurriedly made his way back, and once he'd reached his destination, he checked the surroundings to verify that he was alone. Once satisfied, he knelt on one knee and unzipped it. His face grinned when he pulled out an empty aerosol can, but when his hand entered for a second time, he couldn't wait to put back what he'd found and zipped the bag hastily before evacuating the area. Now very scared, confused, and unsure of who he could really trust, he thought, if Sandy's visit weren't a dream, why was she carrying a gun?

When Bill re-entered the main chamber he headed directly for the chair opposite Marvin and sat upon it, prior to being quizzed by a very concerned Marvin. "You were gone a while, is everything OK because you look like you've just seen a ghost?" Bill slightly shook whilst retorting. "I'm fine. I'm just a little bit tense about later that's all, do you fancy our game now?" Marvin did and whilst Bill dealt each man their two cards Marvin inquired, "What's up Bill?" When Bill didn't react Marvin spoke again. "I know something's on your mind and it's not just tonight. You know you can trust me with whatever's bothering you, I'm your wingman remember, and I've told you I'll make sure we pull through together. Now what is it?" Bill ogled his opponent; his head totally mashed and unsure what normality really was any more, and he feared today was going to be his last, so if anyone were going to kill him, he'd rather decide who yanked the trigger. Eventually he gave Marvin his response, "there's a gun in that room tucked behind a bench, it's in a bag halfway down on the left. Why don't you go and get it and pull the trigger to put me out of my misery once and for all. Then you'll get to walk free and I'll elect how I die." Marvin shook his head in disbelief, he was curious as to what had happened to make Bill have such a negative attitude, so he reassured him how well he was going to perform, by completing all of the tasks and strolling away a very rich man. Bill wished he could have faith in what Marvin had declared, however after Sandy's visit, Bill knew tonight would bring a very different finale. Bill stood up and began to pace around the room prior to warning Marvin, "I can't tell you why I'm afraid, I've been sworn to secrecy and all I know is, I don't know who to believe anymore and I genuinely can't handle it. I want to be dead!" Marvin responded sternly, "Stop being so negative and come and sit down, a problem shared is a problem halved so they say. You can trust me I'm your wingman. Now, if I'm going to do my job properly and we're to survive, then I need to know everything that's going on in your brain, good or bad." Bill suitably did as he was told and whilst taking a seat, he opened his mouth.

Once he'd started, he couldn't contain himself any longer and let it all out. "Last night I had a visitor in my sleep, it was Sandy, and she lay beside me on the bed whilst whispering several things in my ear. First came a warning that I couldn't trust you, as you're not the person that you portray." Marvin tried to interrupt but he didn't get chance seeing as Bill wasn't stopping. "Then she told how my wife's a slag who's been shagging two men behind my back, although with one a lot more than the other. Next, she told me that I've been set up by someone, I don't know who or why, but obviously the boss is some sort of sick pervert who gets his kicks making innocent people play a part in his deceitful game. Sandy then told me how she wants me to take her back home to Ringgold, where she'll become my mistress and we'll have hours of fun frolicking in the hay. Finally she said she hated the sleazy life she's found herself trapped in and apologised for playing her part yesterday before confirming that she wanted to make amends, which she did in the most marvellous and delicious way which I could ever have imagined, when she finally let me love her." Marvin chuckled whilst commenting on how vivid a dream Bill must have had, since he was sat on the couch the whole time and no one had entered the area until breakfast. Bill then began again. "OK smart arse, if you don't believe me go and have a look in the bag that contains the gun. Inside it you'll also find an empty aerosol of whipped cream. Sandy and I emptied it last night whilst squirting it over our nipples prior to us licking it off each other. You won't remember Sandy coming in because she slipped a little something into your drink to make sure we weren't disturbed. Please go and check the bag, and when you return, you can explain who the real Marvin is." Bill was frustrated and annoyed, he wanted answers and he wanted them now. Marvin acknowledged the irritation in his face and chose to appease him by taking a look for the bag alone. Thus enabling him to use the excuse of wanting a pee if someone happened to wonder in. Bill consented and observed Marvin's body disappear when he walked through the door.

Bill sat patiently whilst awaiting Marvin's return, hopeful that when he did, it would bring back a bit of sense to his shambolic life, when Marvin fathoms out that he too was drugged. His mind pondered regarding Sandy, at first, about how much he'd appreciated her physique, before switching firmly towards figuring out a way of making her wishes come true. But he knew the only way it could work would be to see Shelly securely out of the way, thus permitting them to spend the rest of their lives together. Bill secretly wished Shelly had been frolicking with Conner and he knew that if he could prove it, then he could file for a divorce and she'd be chased out of the county as a tarnished slut; followed swiftly by Conner frantically struggling to escape the end of his barrel. Bill's thoughts shifted towards Marvin's extended absence and judging by the quantity of occasions he'd replayed seeing Sandy's large breasts bouncing uncontrollably, it seemed at least an hour must have passed. Bill's feelings were brought to an abrupt end when he heard Marvin ambling through the door stating. "Sorry I was gone so long partner, I've had a really good luck and I couldn't find any bag, so I took the opportunity to have a pee while there. Now you need to understand what's going through your mind is just the aftermath of the cocktail, the bartender did say it would create life like dreams." Bill disagreed; the bag was definitely present earlier when he'd stared at it. Determined to prove Marvin wrong, Bill stormed back into the area and travelled straight in the direction of the bag. Only Marvin was right, and it wasn't there. So Bill marched towards the exit, and whilst being extremely confused with the bag incident, he questioned himself whether it had all been in his mind, or had Marvin repositioned it. With this idea racing through his head he turned around and once again started to search. Bill didn't get very far when, within what seemed like seconds, a voice screamed from the doorway. "Hey what the fuck are you doing in here. It's time to go and you better not have touched anything, otherwise the boss will find out and he'll be incredibly annoyed." Bill took one final glance towards the back of the room, before withdrawing to re-join Marvin back in the orgy room.

Bill returned to find Marvin accompanied by half a dozen men, all stocky and heavily armed. Feeling uneasy he questioned himself as to what sort of trouble these men were anticipating whilst evaluating the amount of firepower on display? One of the men sarcastically apologised for retrieving them so soon, prior to clarifying how the boss had demanded them in Vegas earlier than was originally intended, since someone was waiting there who he'd like them to meet. Bill peered towards Marvin, who gazed back, then both men shrugged their shoulders with perplexed heads from what the man had just reported. Marvin queried his colleagues whether the limo was out the front. No one replied, so he addressed it differently. "Like that then is it. I'll remember this when things are back to normal tomorrow and one of you needs an errand." The six men stared in Marvin's direction and whilst giggling, the biggest replied. "With a bit of luck you're not going to be here tomorrow after the boss has finished with you." Marvin's heart plummeted to the ground, while wondering what he had done which was so bad it's potentially ended his life prematurely. "Time to go," the big man commanded towards one and all in a military fashion, and when they were led from the room, Bill paused next to a table, before taking his time while he picked up the cards. He was more determined than ever to finish his simple game with Marvin. Only now he knew it would have to be on the plane.

Chapter 8

Wow! Look at all those bright lights

The eight departed the orgy room but instead of descending the two flights they'd climbed the previous night; they went through another door hidden in a small recess, and whilst watching Marvin, the big man spoke. "There's reports hovering from the local snouts that something massive is going down, so we're going to the roof where the bosses chopper awaits, and we've been ordered to get you on that bloody jet before you could potentially fall into the enemy's hands. Then if we're successful, we can finish our duty and relax. Why the hell are you two so important the boss has laid on such generous protection?" The big man awaited a response from either detainee, unsure of the answer themselves, neither reacted. Deciding instead that until they were sitting in the safety of the aircraft, the shrewdest and securest thing to do would be to say as little as possible. The door pinged and opened sideways whilst disappearing into the wall. This wasn't an ordinary door; it was an elevator door and all eight men somehow managed to squeeze in. It was a tight fit with most of the accessible area preoccupied with the vast amount of weaponry which each man carried. Once securely in, it started to rise, along with the temperature generated by the mass of bodies crammed firmly in like a tin of sardines. After a short assent, the lift came to a halt and the door pinged. The leader ordered three of his battalion to go and confirm the coast was clear while the rest stayed with the captives, and he emphasised how they were only to come back for them when they're sure nobody was nearby, before he concluded by enlightening them how the FBI scanner is distressing the boss since it's been buzzing with action all day. A couple of minutes later one of the men returned and publicised that the coast was clear. The big man led followed by Marvin, who in turn was shadowed by another man, Bill was placed behind him, and the lingering two took up the rear. After a brief stroll, the eight were all sat securely inside the chopper when it became airborne prior to making its way towards the airport.

Bill couldn't comprehend what all the fuss was about when people became thrilled from experiencing a helicopter ride. He assumed it would be a gratifying experience, not the ear-splitting one he was enduring. Bill was powerless to hear himself think over the constant noise of the engine powering the spinning blades, and whilst gawking around, he spotted all of the others were wearing matching TRAS branded headphones with a microphone attached to the right-hand side. He then noticed Marvin pointing to the ceiling directly above him, signalling for him to look up, and when he did, his face illuminated when he discovered his own branded set. That's better, he thought once he'd shielded his ears before he peered out of the window with bewilderment at how diverse the city looked from the sky. It was littered with skyscrapers which seemed to stretch for miles into the clouds, and the earth beneath was covered with various sized structures and arteries. However, he couldn't help but notice the absence of green open spaces and sensed how horrible it must be to live in a jammed place like Dallas. His interest was pulled to a huge clock on top of one of the buildings, it was square and black with red digits exhibiting the current time, **14.07**. Uncertain with what bother to expect, he hoped that for some reason, any reason at all, Shelly had refused to board the plane and was out of harm's way on the ranch. After around ten minutes in the air, Bill noticed the built-up areas were now fading away whilst gradually inspecting more open space in the distance. A voice then surfaced in his ears; it was the pilot. "OK chaps we'll be landing in a few minutes and I'll be setting her down, right next to the jet. Then the two commuters are to depart alone and join their formal wear on board immediately! You six will provide covering fire if they're met by any hostiles and Bill, just to let you know, Shelly's boarded her Jet and is safely on her way." That wasn't the news Bill wanted to hear, he'd prefer to take a bullet now for the plan failing rather than for it to succeed and place his attractive wife in danger. The Chopper started its decent, and Bill searched for the big target of Dallas airport, but it was nowhere to be seen. Instead they attempted to land in a dingy little place, were the only plane in sight was waiting for them on the tarmac, without a solitary airport worker in sight. When the pilot touched down within fifty feet of the other aircraft the big man released the door next to Bill prior to whispering with a smile on his face, "Make sure you run fast. I've orders to shoot you, at my discretion of course, if I think you're moving too slow." Once he'd finished, he heaved Bill out and he felt a crunch and a sharp pain in his side when he landed on the tarmac. This was the type of noise and pain that Bill associated with every time that he'd previously fractured a rib. Whilst Bill lay on the tarmac, Marvin got shoved out, and somehow managed to remain on his feet just inches from Bill's bonce. With an outstretched right arm he gestured for Bill to grab hold, and when he did, Marvin pulled him up from the ground and they both ran as fast as they could towards the open door. They were both nearly there when from behind, they could hear the unmistakable sound of a semi-automatic rifle firing, trailed by a couple of loud bangs. Both Marvin and Bill didn't bother to look back and see what all the commotion was, they were too busy using all of their energy whilst seeking to board the plane. Bill arrived first, shadowed almost instantly by Marvin and as soon as he had both feet firmly aboard, the door shut, and a voice chatted from above. "Welcome aboard gentlemen. Please do have a seat as we'll be airborne in less than sixty seconds and I'd hate for you to hurt yourself during take-off. If you don't, I could always leave the jet here and let you find out what all of the commotion is about." They didn't need a second warning, both men scrambled for a seat and fastened their safety belts as snugly as they could, and when the jet took off it flung them firmly in their seats, prior to the voice from above congratulating them on making the right selection.

Bill commented how this was much better now he could hear himself think without a bloody stupid set of headphones on, before questioning Marvin what all of the commotion back there was about. Marvin shrugged his shoulders whilst stating "dun no! But whatever it was, it didn't half scare me." Bill agreed before unfastening his strap, then whilst rising, he justified that after what they'd just been through, he was desperately in need of the loo, and he strode towards the rear to find it. Whilst admiring the quality of the jets finishing's on his travels, he pondered how anybody could make so much money, legally, to be able to afford one of these, let alone two. Bill opened the door in the centre of the bulkhead and was greeted with a lovely fresh scent, curious where the aroma was coming from, he entered the room and found an entertainment area, with a piano in one corner, a couch in the other and a small bar stretching along one side. Spotting all of the optics hung behind the bar made him thirsty, and after what he'd been through, he opted to reward himself with a sizeable bourbon and slammed it back in one. Following a loud belch he continued on his quest to find the bathroom and stumbled across another partition door further towards the rear. Upon opening it he became thrilled with what he'd found; a bathroom complete with a rolled top metal bath; a double shower, bidet, foot massager along with a heavily decorated loo. Bill sat down to do his much-needed business and began to sense some dizziness prior to thinking how stupid he'd been for having such a large beverage. Now regretting his actions and within a few minutes of sitting, Bill had managed to fall sound asleep.

Bill was startled by Marvin's voice coming from the other side of the door. "Are you OK Bill? You've been gone ages? Do you need any help?" Bill opened his eyes and became confused as to why he was sitting on such a posh lavvy at twenty thousand feet. When reality struck, he answered. "I'm fine. I'm just finishing off. I'll be with you in a minute." After standing he used lots of luxurious paper before washing his hands and exiting the bathroom. Only to be greeted by Marvin updating him on how they were now halfway to Vegas and it would soon be time to freshen up and change. Bill peered at Marvin with intrigue in his eyes and reminded him about their little game of truth or dare. "We haven't got time Bill, maybe some other day once this mess is over and we're relaxing on a beach." Marvin commented, and whilst he did, he noticed Bill staring back with a determined look in eyes before he reiterated how he had some very important questions that he needed some answers to, and how he wasn't going anywhere until he'd got them. Marvin didn't like what he'd heard. Aware of the consequences if either of them were not suitably dressed the moment the jet arrived and accepting how serious Bill was about his threat, he decided that he had no choice but to play his stupid game. "OK I'll play. But due to time restraints we'll limit it to only three hands. Agreed?" Marvin held his right hand out towards Bill and waited for him to shake, he did, so the two of them walked back towards their seats at the front. "I'll be dealer!" Bill remarked whilst he grasped the cards and started to shuffle; however, he struggled due to their unusual size. Marvin received his first card, then Bill, followed by another one each. Bill didn't peek at his while waiting to discover his opponents next move. Marvin glanced over his and smiled whilst informing Bill of his intention to stick. Not phased in the slightest by Marvin's poker face Bill turned over his cards, to reveal a seven of hearts and an eight of clubs. "Fifteen's too low a number to stick on, I'll have to twist," were his thoughts, so he turned over another card to unveil the king of spades. "Bust, what have you got?" He cried out in gloom before Marvin showed him his pair of nines'. "I won, what would you like a 'truth or dare?" He requested with a smirk on his face. Bill was frustrated he'd lost but he knew there was no backing out now, "Truth" he replied. Marvin chuckled while asking Bill whether he promised to tell nothing but the truth. "I do as long as so do you," Bill retorted with a sneer on his face as he did. Marvin agreed; therefore he raised his question with Bill.

"What exactly did Sandy say about me last night and I'd like it word for word if possible, Please?" Bill paused for a short while, his brain was struggling to remember exactly what she'd said, still muddled with whether it really happened or not he gave his response. "I can't remember phrase for phrase what she told, but it was along the lines that you're not the person you make out to be and can't be trusted. What did she mean by that?" Marvin sniggered whilst declaring. "Nice try partner, trying to change your response to a query. You'll have to wait your turn and win the next game before you get to quiz me." Without hesitation Bill dealt the next hand, and once Marvin had squinted at his, he gleamed again prior to informing Bill of his intention to stick. Bill didn't enjoy the sound of sureness in Marvin's tone; however, he revealed his cards; a ten of spades and a two of diamonds. Confidently, he shouted "Twist" and received the eight of diamonds. "Stick, beat that." Bill invited. Marvin satisfied Bill's request; he had twenty-one and joyfully yelled "I win again. What's it to be this time truth or dare?" Bill didn't like losing again, he had one important question that he needed answering and if his luck carried on this way, he'd never get the opportunity to ask. "Truth again please?" he reacted, enabling Marvin to pitch his next topic. "Do you think Shelly has been sleeping around behind your back?" This was a question that he didn't really want to answer; distraught at the thought of his wife's naked body being kissed and caressed by another man or two, he informed Marvin how he hoped not, but after Sandy's visit, he now feared the worst. The two men stared at each other and Marvin was feeling confident of winning three in a row; he had a really personal question that he wanted to raise regarding tonight. Bill dealt for the last time and grabbed a quick peek whilst Marvin requested another, and it was a six of spades which made him broke. Bill turned his over, and already knowing his hand, he grinned when he revealed his twenty-one, a king and an ace. Bill queried Marvin whether he was ready for his question. He looked a bit nervous with the prospect of facing Bill's upcoming interrogation, sensitive that he'd promised to tell the truth, he instructed Bill to go for it.

Bill's question had been playing on his mind since Sandy's visit, so without further delay he asked Marvin straight out. "What's the real Marvin up to?" The cabin fell silent once he'd finished and remained so for a good two minutes before Marvin gave his account. "I'm not a happily married man like I portray I am, in fact I'm lonely within my marriage, with no friends only work colleagues, so I suppose that I'm one of those people who are married to their job; maybe that's what Sandy meant. But I can assure you that I'm trustworthy, especially tonight, because we're going to need trust to see this thing through together and come out the other side alive. You do trust me don't you Bill?" Unsatisfied with his answer Bill didn't. He suspected Marvin was holding back something significant, unwilling to tell him this and possibly put his own life in danger, he countered. "Of course I do but not quite as much as I'd hoped." Bill's words were then interrupted by the voice from above. "Arrgh, isn't that nice. You two love birds having a little heart to heart over a game of cards. We heard everything and Marvin, the boss won't be happy with you. He'll be very suspicious about you from now on and will probably sift through your life with a fine-tooth comb to see what anomalies he can discover. We'll be landing in Vegas in an hour so both of you go and get yourselves changed." The two men stared at each other, now worried with the knowledge that every word they'd spoken since boarding had been eavesdropped and probably recorded. Between them they decided that Bill would get a shower first while Marvin took a drink at the bar. When the two men entered, they noticed their formal attire hanging on a rail next to the piano. Bill picked his up then headed for the shower, and after hanging them on the wall, he changed to his birthday suit before showering. It was delightfully hot, and the shower gel revitalised his body as he scrubbed away. Bill remained in the same position with his face towards the wall for the remainder of his shower. Then before exiting, he span around, rubbed the soap from his eyes, and his heart skipped a beat when he saw Marvin standing naked with one finger covering his lips, gesturing for him to remain silent. Marvin opened the cubicle door to share and Bill strained to squeeze out past him, but he couldn't find a way around Marvin's bulk. He was terrified, tentative as to why Marvin felt it necessary to gate-crash his shower. He didn't have to wait long to find out the motive when Marvin approached and whispered in his ear. "I'm really sorry but I didn't tell you the whole truth back there. I suspected that somebody might have been listening; that's why I've had to join you in the shower, hopefully the noise of the flowing water will conceal what I'm about to tell you. Now please don't ask any questions, Sandy was right and if I told you the truth, then it will probably put your natural life in peril. I'm not the person I appear to be. I'm better than that, and all I'm prepared to say about the matter is, that if you trust me one hundred percent, I promise we'll still be alive tomorrow when it will become apparent exactly who I am." Bill was thankful upon receiving Marvin's speech. Now knowing that his fears of being asked to bend down for the soap had evaporated, so he escaped and left Marvin to freshen up whilst he dried himself off with a big fluffy towel prior to getting changed from one suit to another.

Once Bill was ready, he left Marvin in the bathroom to finish off and prepare for tonight. However, whilst en-route to re-take his seat at the front, he was unable to resist and paused at the bar for another large bourbon first. Fifteen minutes later Marvin joined him and re-took his seat opposite Bill, then for the rest of the flight the pair remained silent. Bill used this time wisely to gather his thoughts about his upcoming contest, and after paying particular attention to what Sandy had voiced about facing the queen, he was displeased with the prospect of needing to exterminate her to survive. After Marvin's little confession, Bill was confident Sandy's visit was real and smiled with the thought of last night's exploits. His smile turned to a frown when it dawned upon him that his wife had been unfaithful. It changed back to a smile with the thought of being able to turn it to his advantage and divorce Shelly, thus leaving the way open for Sandy to become his wife instead of his mistress. Bill's thoughts were distracted when he gazed out of the window and observed the enormous towers in the distance; each one covered in bright flashing lights and lasers shining into the sky. He noticed how a lot of other planes where all converging on the same spot and thought how that must be the airport. His thoughts were unconfirmed when he heard the voice from above. "We'll be landing at a lovely secluded spot in five minutes so please remain seated, with your safety belts fastened, then prepare to depart the moment we land. The boss has very kindly organised another chopper for your onward travel, so I'd like to take this opportunity to thank you for flying with TRAS airlines and we'd love to welcome you aboard again soon." Once the voice had disappeared, both Marvin and Bill could hear laughter, lots of laughter; the pilot had forgotten to switch off his microphone and it sounded like there were quite a few different voices, all laughing loudly together at them.

Chapter 9

What the hell is he doing here?

The jet landed, not at a big airport like Vegas, but a smaller half derelict one which had no sign of any movement. As the aircraft taxied towards a huge hanger, it was unable to continue its journey due to another one being parked outside, along with two waiting limousines and a helicopter nearby. As the jet ground to a halt the voice reappeared from above. "I'm ever so sorry about the delay in you joining your new flight crew, for what I'm sure will be an exciting ride. However, until the passengers on the other airplane have vacated, I'm afraid you'll have to sit tight." Curiosity got the better of Bill and he gazed out of the plane window and observed no movement through it. The stillness ended when a body appeared on the stairs of the other aircraft and once he'd glanced towards it, he had to stare even harder to distinguish that his eyes weren't deceitful. It was Shelly withdrawing from the plane, followed by no fewer than six burly blokes who were each carrying a fantastically large pink suitcase. Bill chuckled to himself, knowing that Shelly had made the most of the in-flight freebies, his mood soon changed to anger when he pictured her lying on the kitchen table undressed, having just been ravaged by Conner. Bill needed to be sure what Sandy had stated was true, and he knew the only way he could find out, would be to hear it from the horse's mouth. However he realised that this would have to wait, seeing as he had more important matters to deal with first. Eventually Shelly and her army of helpers managed to stow all of her new possessions inside the limousines and they departed for the venue. Then the jet door opened and the voice from above encouraged them to exit quickly; some reports had just come over the airways of hostiles approaching from the north. Not again, Bill thought whilst swiftly making his way down the stairs with Marvin following a very short distance behind. They sprinted as fast as possible in the direction of the waiting chopper and as they approached the door opened, and two men dragged them on board. The pilot was in that much of a hurry he took off with the door still open, thus allowing Bill's legs to dangle helplessly in the air until two of the new security team managed to repatriate him. One of the men asked whether their flight had been pleasant. Both Marvin and Bill looked at each other and were sceptical with how to answer, so they bowed their heads then avoided making eye contact with anyone by peeking out the window. They didn't have much time to take in the sights whilst gazing, because within a couple of minutes they'd landed. Only this time not at an airport or in a field, but high up in the sky right on top of tonight's location. One of the security team then warned them. "The boss wants to see you right away and he's not in a very good mood today, hence he's searching for someone to take it out on." He laughed then escorted the detainees down two flights of stairs, through a set of double doors and into a large conference hall.

The room was big and plain, it had no tables or windows, only four chairs spaced somewhat apart, and lots of stocky looking heavily equipped men guarding the occupants of the two reserved chairs. The talking man from the helicopter ordered Marvin and Bill to have a seat and warned them not to look around or say a word to anybody else. Otherwise if they did, he'd carry out his orders and stop them with his weapon. The two men approached the empty chairs, and careful not to make eye contact with anybody else, they sat down with their eyes firmly stuck glaring at the floor. Bill's mind was totally confused, and he quizzed himself as to his whereabouts? the identity's of the others? and more importantly the reason for their presence? Marvin and Bill sat in silence, as did the other two strangers, until after about thirty minutes it was broken by a voice bellowing out from one of the guards walkie talkies. "Send Sandy in now. I'm ready for her." Bill believed his ears where deceiving him how Sandy was in the room. Instantly he was alarmed for her safety as she'd specifically asked him not to tell another sole about her visit and he'd broken her confidence by informing Marvin.

When Sandy entered the room she was instructed by the boss to "Come in. Take a seat and make yourself at home," whilst he sat directly in front of her behind a very large desk. Once she'd taken a seat, he started to clarify the reason for her attendance. "You've been a naughty girl. Haven't you my dear? You went somewhere off-limits last night didn't you!" Sandy was afraid and hesitant how to reply: she didn't get chance when the boss shouted. "So you're giving me the silent treatment, are you? Well I'll teach you a lesson for that! I recorded the whole thing from start to finish, and I saw you give Marvin a drink to help him rest, followed by you lying next to Bill and murmur something in his ear. I enjoyed watching what you did with a whip and loved the strawberries and cream. Sandy, I saw and heard everything apart from what you whispered in Bill's ear. NOW what did you say to him? and if I believe you. I'll let you live." Sandy didn't know how to respond, she didn't intend to get Bill in trouble and there was no denying what they got up to; the cameras had been rolling the whole time, so she reluctantly started to tell her tale. "I'm really sorry boss for going off limits last night. It's just I'm really attracted to Bill and I got wind that he'd volunteered to be the contestant for tonight's game. Knowing no one had ever lasted all seven challenges, I was desperate to have at least one pleasurable night in his company and hopefully send him to his grave with a smile and that's what I told him." The boss sniggered when he delivered his reaction. "Do you think I was born yesterday you stupid little slut! I've just given you the opportunity to come clean and I don't think you have, so for that I'm going to have to punish you. I just haven't chosen how. You can leave the room now via the door behind me and someone will be waiting to chaperone you to your room, where you will remain until I summon you once I've decided on your punishment." Now extremely worried, Sandy did exactly as she'd been instructed, and once she had vacated, the boss spoke through his walkie talkie, advising his staff that it was now Marvin's turn.

Whilst he entered, the bully told him to take a seat and listen carefully to something very important that he had to say, and how he expected his full attention. Marvin sat and no sooner had his backside lowered his boss began. "Marvin my friend, firstly I'd like to thank you for being the impeccable employee which you've been over the past four years. You've never been late or phoned in sick, all the customers love you; a lot of my staff respect you and until now you've never given me a reason to doubt you. However, I found your story about a dying friend knowing all about our special game very strange, so I started to do a bit of digging and I'd like to know how you came to befriend Fred Jones before he died?" Marvin hesitated with his response, doubting whether the boss knew anything about his relationship with his late friend and hoping he was calling his bluff, in due course Marvin answered. "Fred was a lovely man who lived in the apartment opposite us for years. He was always away on business, so we kept an eye on his place; water his plants, take in the mail you know things like that. Then whenever he got back from his various company trips, he'd return bearing a wonderful gift for my wife. His death was very sad and sudden after he was mugged one night whilst out jogging. The attackers stabbed him several times and the doctors tried their best to save him, but sadly he only lasted a couple of days before his body surrendered." Marvin wiped a tear from his eye once he'd finished whilst his mind reminisced regarding what an inspiration and role model Fred had been, and how he missed him dearly. The boss laughed prior to replying in a sarcastic voice. "How very sad that your friend came to such a horrible end. You see I've done some digging on Fred Jones and you've told me the truth about your relationship with him and how he died. Although, I'm a bit intrigued as to why you felt it necessary to tell Bill on the Jet that you were a lonely old man, when you're married and have a very understanding wife. You've got your reasons and I have to respect you for that; however I can't ignore the fact that I had to get your friend murdered not once but twice. The fools I sent to knife him to death were incompetent and paid for it with their lives. When I got reports he was making a full recovery in hospital, I had no choice but to bribe the doctor to give him a lethal untraceable jab and prevent him from talking. I don't know if you already know what I'm about to tell you. However as I see it, whether you do or not is irrelevant, because in my eyes anybody who befriends an undercover FBI agent who was trying to bring down my cult, requires eliminating. It's nothing personal towards you Marvin it's simply a precautionary measure to protect my interests. I'm sure you'd do the same thing if you were in my shoes." Marvin knew what was coming next, just not when or where, and whilst sitting silently he was scared with the thought that he probably didn't have very long to live. Marvin pleaded with his boss to be quick and get it over and done. He agreed before inviting him to exit the door behind him to meet some friends of his, then he concluded by clarifying that when it was time, he would personally instigate the bang. Whilst Marvin exited, the boss consulted his walkie talkie again, this time requesting Conner.

"Come in have a seat, I'd like to say it's a pleasure to meet you, but I'm always suspicious about a man who snubs my money. Now, I've got a very important question that's been spinning around in my head. What's the real reason you sent Bill to me?" Conner sat once the boss had stopped, feeling wary of his surroundings and terrified by the way he'd been kidnapped so forcefully, he decided to give an honest reaction. "Shelly, Bill and I go back a long way, twenty-nine years to be precise. We met at her 21st birthday bash which was held on her father's ranch. I attended along with Bill, my brother and ten other local lads. We had a few too many drinks and everyone, apart from Bill, messed about in the barn having a game of spin the bottle. Things got a little bit out of hand when Shelly started to undress, and after we saw her unclothed, the atmosphere changed when everyone started to fight for her attention. She wasn't shy and knew how to satisfy a man, sorry several men. However, things were brought to an abrupt end when her father came in and battered the living daylights out of us for abusing his angel of a daughter. He warned us with death if he ever found us within a mile of her. My brother and I were the only two who remained in the county and we keep our distance from Shelly and her family at all times. The other ten felt that ashamed they moved far away and the last I'd heard of them; they had all gone into partnership together and are now quite successful. With hardly any other men left in the area, and those who remained totally terrified of Shelly's father, this left her all for Bill. Who took full advantage of the situation when she became his bride. I didn't bump into her again until a couple of years ago. It was just after her father had died and my brother and I had bought his ranch. The moment our eyes crossed again after nearly thirty years apart brought back the pleasure of the barn, and we had rampant sex over the kitchen table. Once we'd finished, we had a little chat about that night, and Shelly recalled how she really enjoyed being penetrated by so many in such a short space of time. But she remembered how the most pleasure she got was when it was with me. Then, while feeling relaxed, she confessed to a secret that her father had stated shortly before his death. He didn't stumble across them by chance that night. They'd been set up by Bill, who used his initiative and seized the opportunity to have Shelly all to himself by running as fast as he could straight to him, before grassing about the predicament that his angelic daughter was in. Upon hearing this I knew I had to get my revenge and make him pay for the years of suffering that all twelve men present that night have endured since his actions, and that's why I don't want payment from you. With Bill out of the way it'll pave the way for Shelly and me to live happily ever after." The boss roared prior to revealing how he liked his way of getting revenge; he saw it as a little bit devious but a clever way. The boss ended by enlightening him how he didn't really trust him, and as a precaution, he would have him closely examined. Next the boss ordered Conner to leave the room via the door at the back, so that he could get accompanied to his room. Where he's to remain until he's determined his fate.

Bill was sat nervously in the conference hall while waiting for his name to be called when the security man's walkie talkie bellowed with the tyrant's voice. "Bring me the last one now and be quick about it. I've still got to get suitably changed for this evening." Whilst uncertain with what awaited him on the other side, Bill stood up and proceeded towards the same door that the other three had walked through, and all he knew was, three people had previously taken the plunge and not one had re-emerged. Slightly concerned he pushed hard and found the boss grinning in his direction whilst sitting alone behind his large desk. Once inside, Bill began asking his very important questions, "What's going on? What have you done with Sandy and Marvin? Did my ears hear right? and if so, what the fuck is Conner doing here?" The boss was laughing uncontrollably by the time Bill had finished and beckoned for him to take a seat. When he did the boss responded. "Don't worry about Sandy, she's tucked up safely away inside her accommodation while I conjure up an appropriate sentence for her violating my orders, when she spent an evening with you. Did you enjoy the cream by the way? I can't wait to see the look in Shelly's eyes when she witnesses you wince from the whip." Shelly viewing the recording didn't bother Bill, he was happy the boss had put some clarity on Sandy's visit. Now all that he had to do was to come up with some credible evidence regarding her infidelity to be able to file for divorce. Bill didn't get an option to answer before the boss broke some bad news. "That's the least of your worries though. I've got to dispose of your wingman." Bill didn't like the sound with what the boss had said. Then reality kicked in and he realised that before he could even think about gathering evidence, a much more pressing engagement required his immediate attention, and one which had just been made a whole lot harder after hearing of Marvin's plight. Bill pleaded with the boss and hoped what he was about to say would save Marvin's life. "Why have you got to dispose of Marvin he's done nothing wrong. I need him to keep up his part of the plan and entertain Shelly while I'm busy and it won't work without him." While chuckling the boss gave his reaction. "Don't worry about Marvin and his plan, I've taken care to put alternative arrangements in place. When you leave here, you'll go for a drink at the bar alone and don't get any funny idea's though as you'll be watched like a hawk. Then you'll be joined by an attractive lady and a man; this will be your cue to call Shelly from her room to join you for the evenings fun. You will not say a word to this other couple, then when Shelly arrives, they'll introduce themselves to you and that's when the man will disgrace Shelly, forcing a reaction from you. Do you understand?" Bill nodded in agreement, he was scared from the prospect of what the night had in store, especially a possible deadly encounter with the queen. The boss further enhanced Bills curiosity with what he said next. "Before you walk through the door behind me and get ushered to the bar, I've got something very important to tell you which will result in me raising a very important question which you should think long and hard about before replying. Your response will potentially be the difference between your life or death." Bill was utterly confused with what he'd just learned but keen to find out more, hence he piped up. "Come on then put me out of my misery. Tell me what you've got to say and ask me your important question because I've got a busy night ahead of me." The room fell silent, the boss was unsure what action, if any, he should take over Bill's sheer attitude and cheek with his statement. Eventually he saw the funny side and started to speak.

"On your way in you queried why Conner was here. Well he's present because I invited him to come and explain why he wouldn't accept my payment for setting you up. Yes you did just hear me right, you've been set up by Conner and he wants you eliminated from Ringgold forever so he and Shelly can live a happy life together. They've been shagging each other for the past two years right in front of your nose." Bill's heart sank upon hearing confirmation that Shelly had been adulterous, prior to the boss resuming. "He also told me why he wanted revenge after you sneakily blew him and his friends up to Shelly's father so you could have her all to yourself. Is that true Bill? Did you go running to him or did you stay and watch like you told Marvin? Now think carefully about your answer as your life depends on it." Bill sat motionless with his mind working overtime

117

and was struggling to cope with the mixed thoughts which it contained. After considering his response for a brief spell he gave it to the boss. "I did stay and watch for a while. I won't deny it and I enjoyed watching. However, I managed to sneak out unseen after I'd sufficiently satisfied myself, and as I started the long walk home, I was spotted by Shelly's father who asked if I knew of her whereabouts. I couldn't help myself and it just popped out, "she's in the barn." No sooner had the words left my mouth I regretted saying them and feared for my safety after telling tales on the others. I did a deal with him and told him everything that I'd seen in return for his protection and daughters hand in marriage. Then he made me watch the beatings he inflicted as a warning what to expect if I ever disrespected his angel." Hearing this the boss stood up in anger and slammed his hands on the desk whilst yelling. "You weasel, you ruined a dozen young men's lives by your actions that night. However, I've got to admire you for showing intuition in manufacturing a situation to suit yourself, so I'll let you know your fate once I've decided. Now you won't see me again tonight but I'm warning you. I'll be watching very closely and if you want to get out of this situation alive, you better do everything exactly as instructed. Stroll through the door behind me and you'll be escorted to the bar, where you'll wait until it's time to make the call. Now go!" Bill didn't waste any time in doing so and within minutes he found himself standing at a large bar, which was situated in a gigantic banqueting room, surrounded by lots of people laughing and giggling amongst themselves while they plied themselves with alcohol.

Chapter 10

Bill grows big balls

"Can I have a large Bourbon please?" Bill asked politely and then patiently waited for the bartenders reply, none came so he inquired again, only this time a little bit louder. "CAN I HAVE A LARGE BOURBON PLEASE?" This worked, but only for him to be advised the boss had given strict instructions not to serve him any alcohol, only soft drinks were permitted. Bill didn't fancy anything else; he wanted a bourbon to help soothe his nerves. Whilst rotating his body the thought of trying to make a break scurried through his mind and while eyeing up any possible escape route, he studied his surroundings, bemused with the size of the chamber and the sheer amount of people it held; around ten thousand he believed. Situated at the very far end was a raised stage area, it was a good two-hundred-foot-wide with matching dining tables strategically positioned either side. In the centre stood Bill's main competitor for the night, the very large wheel of fortune and he knew if he triumphed then he'd walk away an exceptionally happy and rich man. Abruptly the room fell mute as hundreds of screens illuminated the walls, Bill glanced at one and instantly recognised the logo it presented. The silence was broken by the bosses voice rumbling from it, "Good evening ladies and gentlemen. I'd like to thank you all for coming and I hope you're looking forward to tonight as much as me. This evening we have a special treat for you; a non-member volunteer and we all know how the queen loves sinking her teeth into an outsider don't we!" He paused and commenced laughing, as did everyone else in the room whilst their eyes were hooked on the screens waiting to learn some more, so he continued. "Now tonight is a very historic one as for the first time we introduce a new way for you to have a flutter, with our brand-new APP. It's available on both Apple and Android so you'll never have to leave your seat for a chance to win big. Before I go and get changed for the evening here's some of our latest odds; bleed heavily after first whipping 3-1; fail to pleasure a large ugly lady 7-2 and to face the queen will get you even money. Sorry folks, I know the odds aren't terrific for this one, but we all know how often this contest occurs with a volunteer, and we all know how it normally ends. Now, here's some of tonight's big money bets; face the twelve life like statues and come out smiling 75-1; enjoy a flogging that much he begs for more 150-1 and tonight's outside bet by a long shot is for him to survive an encounter with the queen, which will pay you a whopping 10000 -1. Place your bets now ladies and gentlemen the main event will be opening soon." When his speech fell mute the room erupted with applause and roars, and Bill's immediate thought was how his mind hadn't deceived him yesterday when he was in the gimp suit room, and one of the statues did move. He wasn't looking forward to the prospect of having to face them again tonight, seeing as they were creepy enough yesterday when they remained motionless.

While Bill was stood at the bar and after having just put two and two together, he came up with the conclusion that if he refused to take part it would cost the boss big. Presuming this put him in a very good bargaining position, he asked the bartender his question again whilst expecting the same reply. He didn't get it. Instead he was approached by a couple of thugs, who recommended that he halted demanding a drink as there was no chance of him getting one, and if he inquired again, they would take him out the back to put him out of his misery. Totally out of character Bill laughed with what had been stated, right now he'd prefer a bullet in the back of his head rather than have to face the statues, consequently he mouthed in one of their ears. "Now look here big boy, you don't scare me anymore. I know by this time tomorrow my wife will be a widow. How she becomes one is irrelevant to me and if you execute me your boss will lose a lot of dollar, then it will be all your fault. So be a good boy and tell him I want a word with him NOW, otherwise I won't be playing his stupid contest." The man was startled and unsure what to do, knowing Bill was right with the contents of his speech he radioed for guidance. "Sorry to disturb you whilst you're getting changed boss, but he's refusing to compete until he's had a conversation with you, and he's more than willing to die at my hands, but he's indicated how much money you'll lose if he does. Should I take him somewhere quiet?" Whilst glaring at each other and wondering what instructions he would provide, the three men waited patiently for his reply. "I don't want everyone hearing what I'm about to say so give him your radio and make sure he's got an earpiece in, then switch to channel 7 now!" The man did exactly that and Bill found himself listening to an incredibly furious tone in his ear. "Now you listen to me fuckface. You will play the game or else Shelly will have a very nasty surprise for her birthday and probably won't survive. Don't think I'm making idle threats since I warn you this will happen if you don't play my game. Do you understand!" Bill sniggered then gave his stern response. "Oh I understand all right, but I don't think you fully comprehend me, because I don't give a shit about that slut anymore and you'll be doing me a favour by getting rid of her for me. It will save me a lot of time and money by not having to file for a divorce. Now, I know how much cash you stand to lose if I fail to play, so I propose a deal, you let me have a stiff drink or two and give me your word that if I complete all seven challenges, I'll walk out of here alive with my winnings in cash, accompanied by a very special lady called Sandy. Do you agree?" Bill fell motionless and whilst standing there as cool as a cucumber he showed off his best poker face to the bosses men and waited for his reaction, he didn't have to wait long when he heard it. "OK if you agree to give it your best shot and go the distance whilst making it brutal for the gang, then you walk out of here with thirty million in cash and your life. But it's Sandy's decision if she wants to accompany you. As for Shelly, you have to be extra nice to her, otherwise if she suspects in the slightest that something might be up, I'll assassinate you personally. Do we have a deal?" Now with a huge grin on his face Bill agreed prior to demanding that the boss ordered him a large bourbon, and before he'd had time to give back the equipment, the bartender had placed Bill's drink on the bar. The goons then backed away and left Bill sat sipping his favourite drink, whilst feeling extraordinarily content with what he'd just achieved.

The chamber soon came alive with a hype of activity from citizens scrambling to grab the best seats in the house, the ones with an unobstructed view of the screens. There was also lots of shouting between tables whilst friends and colleagues compared their bets on tonight's strange events. Bill had finished his drink and was eager for another, so he summoned the bartender politely and was rewarded with an even bigger glass. A loud tone then echoed around the room, encouraging everyone to take a seat because the action would be starting very soon. Bill turned around to see the MC stood on the stage with a microphone in his hands, it was his voice that he'd heard. The voice then updated everyone on the latest odds whilst encouraging them to download the APP to wager. Bill knew he'd be getting called upon very soon so he sank his drink in one, prior to receiving a refill and a warning that this would be his last. This news didn't bother him, he was feeling relaxed and calm enough to win anything. While sat calmly at the bar his eyes observed all of the pretty woman nearby, trying to figure out which one, if any, were his cue to call. Sandy's man approached from the back entrance accompanied by a classy looking dazzling blond lady; hair past her backside, with lovely long legs and a set of red stilettos which stood out due to their immense size. Her breasts where well-proportioned and her outfit left just enough on show for one's imagination. Bill was questioning himself how Sandy's man could end up with a delightful lady like her, when he spotted a bulge in her neck and whilst chuckling, he thought, it's a man, before his eyes deflected to the other beautiful women present, searching for his cue. Sandy's man approached and stood next to him, along with his lady friend, Bill couldn't resist and uttered in his ear. "So that's how you get your kicks then, dating transvestites, does the boss know? I'm sure he would like to. What's her name, Jeremy?" Sandy's man wasn't impressed, his face turned bright red with rage after receiving Bill's insult and he went to swing but was stopped in his tracks by his lady friend's arm interceding; thus preventing any contact. The lady subsequently muttered in Bill's lobe. "Have you forgotten something very important that you've got to do?" before handing him his phone. Bill took a moment to gather his thoughts after hearing the lady's voice and he was trying hard not to break into laughter when he realised that Sandy's lady friend was actually the boss in drag.

Trembling when reality finally sank in with what his was about to do, he dialled Shelly's number. After a few rings she answered, and immediately asked if she could join him to demonstrate how sexy she looked in her new outfit. Bill didn't give Shelly any time to add anything else. "You certainly can my love, I'm in the main bar waiting for you and I've finished all my competition business for the night so I'm all yours. I've missed you honey, and I can't wait to give you your surprise." Delighted that she could now come out of her room, Shelly opened the door to be greeted by the sight of two butch men waiting, who made clear how they'd been sent to chaperone her safely to the bar. Ecstatic that she'd be reunited with her husband within minutes she let the men lead, whilst her thoughts made her excited with what treats her husband had in store. As Shelly walked through the main entrance, she immediately caught site of her husband and ran straight towards him with her arms stretched out wide, as were his. Then they embraced in their smart attire, but before they had a chance to say a word, Sandy's man approached Shelly and asked what she saw in a loser like Bill, prior to trying to encourage her to spend the night with him; so she could experience what sleeping with a real man was like. Bill was ready to take a swipe; however he was stopped in his tracks by Shelly countering the man's request. "My man's not a loser, he's won me this lovely weekend away for my birthday and he's a real man unlike you city types. You'd run a mile if you had to do some of the things that I've witnessed my husband do over the years. He's the bravest man I know, especially when he has to calm down a rampant bull." Bill didn't know what to do, laugh or cry, that was his cue to club him and Shelly had just interfered. There was then a short silence which was broken by Sandy's Man. "I bet you've got a lovely trimmed pussy that tastes delicious, and I'd love nothing more than to feel it quivering around my cock while I fuck you." Sandy's man didn't have time to finish, he

126

was now lying on the floor after being on the receiving end of Bill's finest right hook. Bill then whispered in Shelly's ear. "That'll teach him for disrespecting you sweetie; you look gorgeous tonight and you know I'll always be here to protect you." The classy lady then introduced herself as Tallulah, tonight's host and after apologising for her partners remarks, she insisted they join her at the core of the action on the main stage. Bill and Shelly gazed at each other, before Shelly rotated towards Tallulah and expressed her delight while she accepted.

The three of them found themselves on the long walk to the stage accompanied with a standing ovation and lots of clapping and cheering, when the MC announced that Tallulah was in the house accompanied by a couple of very special friends. Shelly loved the attention, she waved at the crowd and even stopped to sign a couple of autographs before eventually arriving at their destination. Once there, they were shown to their seats and Tallulah grabbed the mic to commence her welcome speech. "Good evening ladies and gentlemen, I do hope you're enjoying yourself but times running out to place your opening bets, so come on you know the drill. Now as of this moment we're opening the betting on one of our favourite little punts. 'What happens next', are you ready, 3-2-1, gamble. Whilst you're making some lucky bookmaker fatter, I'm going to take a short break while I get to know my special guests a little better, and I'll be back for the main event in thirty minutes." Tallulah joined Shelly and Bill at the table and immediately asked Shelly to spill the beans regarding herself and what had brought her to Vegas. Shelly, still really excited, then began. "My names Shelly. I'm a country girl from Ringgold and today is my 50th birthday." Tallulah interrupted and gave her congratulations prior to advising how a magnum of champagne would be making its way over as a gift from the management. Shelly embraced this news and gave Tallulah a great big chesty hug before progressing. "I'm here tonight because my gorgeous husband Bill has been truly lucky and won a competition, with lots of posh clothes and a weekend away in Vegas for the prizes; I can't believe I'm so lucky. I was picked up by a jet earlier today, it had the most amazing choice of garments inside for me to pick from and keep. Next, I got carried here in a limousine and I've spent a couple of hours trying them on. I do hope we get the same jet back; I'm not happy with a couple of things which I've picked and was hoping they'd let me do an exchange."

Tallulah sniggered upon hearing this, but her amusement was cut short when a couple of deputies' approached and demanded a word with Bill. "What's the problem officers, can I do anything to help?" Tallulah inquired in a concerned manner before one of the deputy's replied. "It's OK madame nothing to worry about, but we've had a complaint from a member of the public who says this man has just assaulted someone at the bar. We do have several witnesses who watched the incident and have verified what happened, so we just need this gentleman to accompany us down to the station for interrogation." After arresting Bill he removed some handcuffs from his belt and introduced Bill's wrists inside. Shelly was distraught and pleaded for Bill's freedom; citing the other man deserved what he got after communicating with her in the manner which he did. The deputy assured Shelly how they wouldn't be long seeing as it wasn't a serious matter, and if he pleaded guilty, then he'd almost certainly be back within a couple of hours upon receiving a small punishment. Tallulah butted in. "OK officers, please be quick because this lovely couple are here to celebrate a big birthday and I'd hate for this magnificent lady to have to spend it alone." While the deputy's departed with Bill, Shelly dreaded the thought of being alone while Bill was trapped in his prison cell and frantically attempted to accompany them. Tallulah managed to calm her down when she clarified how one of her friends was a high-ranking police official and promised to put in a good word. Then whilst finishing off, she enlightened that how to cheer her up she was prepared to break all of the rules, just this once, and let Shelly have the important job in tonight's main event, By having the pleasure of being one of the shows stars, and the one with the important responsibility of spinning the circle for the chance to win big money. This worked and Shelly stood up and waved at the crowd while she basked in the glory of her extended fame.

Chapter 11

Let's get this party started!

Tallulah's voice echoed whilst she welcomed everyone to the main event. "Good evening ladies and gentlemen may I take this opportunity to thank you for attending our annual gathering which is brought to you in association with our main sponsor. The Real Adult Superstore, were just one visit really can change your life." The crowd retorted enthusiastically with heaps of applause and several guests banged on tables whilst hollering "bring out the queen" and "let's get the party started" amongst other things. Embracing the mobs enthusiasm she wasted no time in continuing. "Tonight my friends, we have a very special treat for you, as we're privileged to be joined by a delightful lady called Shelly, who's specifically travelled over one thousand miles today to let us join in her 50th birthday celebrations. So please stand and give her a big ovation after we've sang Shelly the birthday song." Every person in the room did as they were asked and waited patiently for Tallulah's lead. "Happy birthday to you, squashed tomatoes and stew, happy birthday dear Shelly, happy birthday to you. Hip-Hip hooray, Hip-Hip hooray, Hip-Hip hooray." The sound of applause deafened, and once it had ceased, Shelly jumped up and waved frantically at her brand-new friends. The host then toasted her with a huge grin on her face and once the applause had climaxed, she begin chatting again. "Congratulations Shelly, we do hope that you have a lovely evening with us, and I'm sure that if you ask nicely, some of our male guests will willingly give you the Vegas bumps." The room fell silent as she handed the microphone to Shelly whilst encouraging the birthday girl to say a few words. "Thanks ever so much everybody for making me feel so welcome. You don't know how much it means to me and I'd like to say a big thank you to my long-standing husband Bill for finally fetching a birthday present which I'll truly remember, but sadly he's at the police station and won't be back till later. Thank you everyone." The mass clapped vigorously whilst Tallulah retook to the mic.

"Now Shelly, apart from being here to celebrate your big day is there any other purpose why you and your husband are with us?" The audience silenced when Tallulah thrust the microphone in her face, then they patiently awaited her response. "Yes, we're here because my husband entered a competition were the main prize was a weekend away in Vegas and he won! I'm so excited, and on the way here, on a private jet I may add, I got to choose a whole new wardrobe. I even chose a sexy new nightdress, but please keep that to yourself. I want to surprise him with it later." After extra cheering and whistling from the gathering one voice shouted, "you can show it to me any time you like sexy lady." This statement filled the room with delight as one by one several other people pitched-in with, "and me." Once the room had fallen silent again Tallulah renewed her quizzing. "Shelly are you happy with your present so far and what would Bill normally of given you if he hadn't been our lucky winner?" Eager to answer her questions, she smirked and wrestled the mic from tonight's host. "I'm over the moon with it. The jet was luxurious with a well-stocked bar and it had a dance floor with a pole in the corner as well as the walls and ceiling being completely covered in mirrors. I loved them; I could get a really good view from every angle of how big my bum looked in my gorgeous new outfits. The room here is lovely with the softest mattress I've ever felt on a bed and I'm really enjoying the warm welcome which everyone has extended to me. It's such a wonderful surprise and Bill's certainly made up for some of his 'disaster presents' which I've received over the years. One year he bought me pans for Christmas and a cold weather survival kit for my birthday. I mean let's face it when does it ever get cold in Ringgold. To be honest with you though, he's caught me completely by surprise this year and I was only joking with Conner the other day regarding how much I was looking forward to receiving 'over 50's life insurance' now I qualify." Tallulah giggled and inquired, "would he really do that?" Shelly relished being the centre of attention and when the free champagne arrived, she took a big swig prior to sounding out her reply. "Yes he would!" Tallulah had a sip of her favourite cocktail, a Porn Star Martini, before continuing to help everybody get to know tonight's special guest a little bit better. "So who's Conner then? That's a strange name for a girl?" You sensed the horde appreciated Tallulah's witticism when the wolf whistles started, only stopping when Shelly's voice echoed. "Conner's a man, who's a very good friend of ours and he'll do anything for me when he's round and about on our ranch helping in any way that he can. Conner's one in a million and I don't know what Bill and I would do without him. Bill's going to take him on a night out when we get home in appreciation of his kind actions towards me." Tallulah enlightened everyone regarding the upcoming little break in which they'd hear the latest odds from their sponsor, whilst allowing them to stock up on beverages and guarantee they didn't miss what was coming next. Following a big round of applause, she sat next to Shelly and poured her another glass, prior to excusing herself while she went to powder her nose.

Whilst sat alone with her eyes gazing at the various faces of the crowd Shelly's mind wondered towards Bill's plight, hoping he was safe and well, while in custody. Her thoughts disappeared when her sight became drawn to the illuminating TV screens as each one displayed a different flutter, such as 'Bleed heavily after whipping NOW 2-1 favourite'; 'kill the queen NOW 50000 -1'. She didn't appreciate what to think after seeing these messages and questioned herself as to what type of 'hotel' Bill had booked. When Tallulah returned Shelly didn't hold back in her probing. "What type of place is this? It's not one of those hotels where you all put your room keys in a bowel is it?" Tallulah couldn't contain herself from laughing and giggling prior to reacting. "No Shelly dear, it's much more exciting than that." But before Shelly could reply Tallulah had already picked up the microphone and commenced. "Ladies and gentlemen. I know you're all dying for the action to begin, but before it can, I've got three more very important questions to ask our special guest." The troop fell silent and you could sense their anticipation whilst waiting for the host to resume. "Shelly do you trust your husband?" The room remained mute as one and all eagerly anticipated her response while Tallulah held the mic in front of Shelly so she could. "Of course I do, I trust him more than anyone else in the world, dead or alive." The congregation retorted to her answer with laughter, therefore Tallulah waited for the venue to fall quiet prior to raising her second question. "Would he lie to you?" Shelly squinted right in her the eyes whilst educating everyone how he wouldn't. The room filled with more laughter then fell subdued when Tallulah asked her third and final question. "Did Bill come up with the idea for this years present all by himself, or did he get a helping hand?" Shelly thought how strange a question to be asked, however the bubbly was beginning to relax her when she gave her final answer. "I had to help him a little as there was no way I wanted a present which I'd hate forever, so when he asked me for a clue I told him to surprise me and use his imagination because I want it to be a birthday where I'll try new things and experiences that awaken my body and mind, things that I'll never forget and if I like them, I'll do them again." Tallulah moved the mic towards her mouth while inviting the group to put their hands together for tonight's special guest who'll be the lucky one with the privilege of determining the contestant's destiny." She concluded by alerting the crowd how she'd be right back after a short break.

Urgently requiring another trip to the bathroom, Tallulah left the stage; enabling her to powder her snout, which left Shelly and the champagne alone. Tallulah had been gone quite a while and when she returned, she was greeted with a delightfully happy Shelly asking if she could be cheeky and have another delicious bottle of fizz, while she tipped the empty bottle upside down to prove it was. "No problem," Tallulah sang out in a beautiful voice and ordered not one, but another three from the bar. Then the mass started to chant Shelly's name and whilst jubilant and tipsy, she became overwhelmed when the host encouraged her to stand on the table and give her audience a bow. Which she did before getting off as quickly as she possibly could since the champagne had now started to take effect. Tallulah helped Shelly back to her seat and encouraged her to enjoy herself by getting into the swing of things, seeing as tonight she was in for a really big treat. Shelly grinned like a Horny devil before letting out a great big belch and the room erupted when she did.

Tonight's host asked the assembly nicely, "Ladies and gentlemen, can I have your attention please?" The area then silenced when she started to state. "Now before we get down to tonight's game let's have a recap of what we have learned so far. Our gorgeous special guest is the delightful Shelly from Ringgold who's here to celebrate her 50th with her husband Bill; who's an honest man and would never lie. However sadly, he won't be present until later once the police have probed him." Tallulah stopped for a sip of her cocktail and made sure Shelly was OK before enduring. "They're here because Bill entered a competition for a weekend away in Vegas and won; coming up trumps with this years present in the process. Which due to his past performance has surprised Shelly who was expecting 'over 50's life cover'. While travelling over one thousand miles by jet to be with us tonight, she got to choose lots of new outfits for her wardrobe, including a sexy nightdress for tonight; but remember to keep that one to yourselves. The jet had a pole in the corner of the dance floor with mirrors everywhere and her mattress is very soft. They have a good friend Conner who's a real big benefit to them, often inseparable at times, and Bill's going to take him for a pint once they get back home as a way of saying thanks. Finally, when Bill was unsure what to get Shelly for such a special birthday he asked for a clue, so she told him to surprise her and use his imagination." Tallulah then fell soundless and encouraged the bunch to make some noise. They did by chanting her name, then once the chanting had ceased, she resumed. "Shelly, I promise you that tonight your husband Bill is going to do exactly as you've asked him to do by surprising you with lots of presents that will awaken your body and mind, and hopefully you'll want to try them again. Now until he returns let's keep your brain occupied by playing the TRAS wheel of fortune."

The mob couldn't contain their excitement, now knowing that the beginning of the show was imminent. Everyone was cheering, clapping, and chanting Shelly's name before they sang, 'let's get this party started' over and over again, until Tallulah asked for calm so that the game could commence. The chamber fell soundless and she thanked them prior to enquiring whether Shelly knew about the prize money that was up for grabs? She looked back at the host with a squint in the eye and her voice happened to be a little slurred when she gave her reply. "Bill did mention something but I've absolutely no idea what he meant." The host topped up Shelly's glass and poured herself one at the same time; having consumed all of her cocktail, before she excitedly, and in a very loud voice, educated everyone how Shelly will now be given the chance to win a possible sixty-four million dollars, and all she has to do for it, is spin the wheel of fortune seven times, then for each challenge that the competitor successfully completes, the prize fund will double. Starting at one million dollars for finishing the first. After the end of the game, and if the challenger had managed to do what nobody else had ever done beforc and complete all seven, she'll be asked one multiple choice question with only three possible answers, and If she guesses correctly, she'll walk away with a cool sixty-four million dollars, as will the competitor. Shelly couldn't believe what she'd heard and sought reassurance from Tallulah that becoming rich was genuinely so simple. "It's simple for you but not so for our competitor," she responded, then inquired, "do you want to play?" Without hesitation Shelly shouted out at the top of her voice, "YES I DO." That was Tallulah's cue to ask for the lights in the room to be cut, thus leaving a solitary spotlight shining down from the ceiling illuminating the two ladies and the huge wheel.

Romantic music began playing gently in the background before Tallulah started to tell. "Shelly, I've a confession to make and I'm ever so sorry to have to break you this very sad news, but BILL'S A LIAR!" Shelly chuckled whilst totally denying the accusation that had just been made so Tallulah retorted. "OK let me prove it. Now what I'm about to tell you may seem a little bit farfetched, but I promise you it's real, and all that I ask is for you to remain silent from now on with an open mind, apart from if I ask you a question of course. Then at the end I'll ask you the important sixty-four-million-dollar question and if you get it right, you'll instantly be a multi-millionaire. Do you agree to my requests?" Shelly was pretty muddled with all of the weird events and accusations which she'd heard so far, however feeling a bit tipsier than earlier, she agreed hence Tallulah started to explain. "Shelly your husband Bill who's an honest and trustworthy man DIDN'T win a competition for a weekend away in Vegas. He's here tonight because he volunteered to compete against the big wheel. Otherwise, he'd be spending the next twenty-five years in prison for statutory rape after sexually assaulting a woman in my sex shop in Dallas." Shelly smiled, while accusing Tallulah of lying and trying to play with her mind. So the host reminded Shelly how she wasn't allowed to utter a word. She apologised before Tallulah restarted. "What Bill didn't realise is that he'd been set up by Conner who wanted him out of the way so that he can have you all to himself. Do you believe me Shelly?" After a brief pause and still laughing at the nonsense she was hearing, her answer was a very firm "NO!" Some guests in the gathering shouted, "it's true," before Tallulah asked the congregation for complete silence from now on, thus enabling Shelly to be able to give her full attention and concentration to what she was absorbing for the first time. When the silence was restored, she continued. "I found it hard to believe, at first, that he'd been set up by Conner, so let me take you back to the beginning, yesterday morning and I'll tell you what Bill's told us so far." Tallulah paused to take a drink before telling. "When you gave him the hint about what you wanted for your 50th it was taken by him that you wanted to experiment with some sex toys and that's why he made the trip Dallas in the first place; to visit The Real Adult Superstore. Upon arrival he was asked to complete a questionnaire which contained some bizarre questions that the store allegedly required in order to process his membership. While completing it he spilled the beans about how the two of you met for the first time and what happened that night. Do you remember that night twenty-nine years ago?" A little bit apprehensive at answering the question, and unsure were Tallulah was going with it, Shelly confirmed that she did, prior to taking a stiff drink. "That's good, would you like to confirm to us what we already know?" Tallulah invited. Shelly's response was a long time coming. "What do you mean when you say, 'confirm what we already know', you know nothing about me and my husband, but I'll play along with your stupid game because I want to win big."

Tallulah couldn't resist and explained to the troop about Shelly's 21st and her father inviting the residents of their neighbouring ranches over to help her celebrate, including 13 local men. Tallulah stopped and queried Shelly whether for one million dollars, she would finish telling the tale to the crowd. It didn't take long for her answer. "If I tell you, do you promise you'll give it to me?" Tallulah duly promised before elaborating. "Now that I've made a pledge to you, and I expect you to vow to tell me the truth otherwise you don't get the money. Promise?" Shelly's face smiled to the point of cracking with the thought of becoming rich so easily and she knew that she could make up a load of old 'cods wallop'; seeing as she was in the company of no one who was present that night, they couldn't disprove what she said. Feeling smug with herself and thinking of all the nice things she could buy with the loot; her reaction was a simple one. "I Promise."

Shelly held her glass in front of her lips for a long time, before replacing it with the mic and letting everyone have her account of how she met Bill. "My father had arranged for several competitions and events that day allowing the men to show off their strengths and skills.

He was determined to find me a nice strong man who could take care of me. After we'd eaten the hog the parents were talking and drinking moonshine whilst waiting for the second one to spit. My father then approached and bribed us to get out of the way with moonshine, so the parents could get to know one another better." Tallulah interrupted by asking "in what way did they want to get to know each other 'better'." A voice bellowed from the horde, "they're swingers." The rest of the crowd laughed loudly at this remark and once soundless, Shelly resumed. "They wanted to chat shit about monotonous things relating to the ranch and country life, the men and I just wanted to get sozzled and have a good time. When we found out that all we had to do for a crate of moonshine was re-stack some hay bales, we agreed. I think we'd already drank a couple of bottles by the time we got to the field and Bill volunteered to re-stack them all by himself. I thought this was the kindest gesture any of the men had performed all day. The other men were just trying to get in my knickers, but I really admired Bill for being different, so I gave him a little kiss on his cheek to show him how interested I was. The men and I then ended up in the barn getting drunk and having some fun. When it was bedtime my father came and ended the party, whilst informing the men how they could stay in the barn for the night. He asked where Bill was, but no one knew; the last time we'd seen him was in the field. I was sad not seeing Bill again that night since I knew he was the man for me. Can I have the money now please?"

The group were clapping once Shelly was done, then the area was filled with "You're a LIAR so no money for you!" when Tallulah shouted through the microphone. The gathering hushed instantly in anticipation of an explanation and with Shelly staring directly at her, Tallulah spoke once more. "Shelly my dear, we do not tolerate liars in our clan, in fact we despise them and take great pleasure from punishing fibbers heavily. However, seeing as you're a new member to our family then I can excuse you just this once. But be warned! You've just used up your one and only life, and if you fib again then I'm sorry, but you'll forfeit any prize money, and instead of you getting to spin the wheel for the contestant, they get to spin it for you. Now I'll ask you again, but before you answer, I want you to pinkie promise that you'll tell the truth and I'll know if you're lying because I was there. I've also got Conner and Bill's version to compare with mine." Shelly became bedazzled with what she'd just learnt, her brain was now completely jumbled whilst thinking how Tallulah was really trying to play with her mind, as there wasn't another woman present that night. Knowing that Conner and Bill where, but uncertain with what they had said, she opted to tell the truth but only after getting Tallulah to agree to giving her two million dollars instead.

"I was feeling merry by the time we got to the barn and a few of the men were trying anything to get into my panties. I was enjoying the attention when one of the men suggested that we play a game of 'spin the bottle', I'd never played before and was eager to try, but I wish I hadn't as I'm ashamed of what I did next. Now Bill doesn't know about this and if he did, we'd be history, so you've got to Promise not to tell?" Shelly used the time it took for everyone to swear wisely by having a stiff drink and gestured for a refill once she had. After everyone agreed she continued. "The top of the bottle pointed towards me after the first spin and one of the men informed me that I'd won so I had to take something off. I was a little bit drunk and decided it was my bra from under my blouse; letting my assets hang free. I could tell the men approved by the look in their eyes and seeing as I won, I got to go again, and it pointed at me. This time it was my skimpy's from under my skirt and before long I was bare. I'd won every time! One by one the other men began to win and soon Simon accompanied me. I'd never seen a man's dagger before and when it transformed into a sword, I felt a tingling run through my entire body. I couldn't help myself and had to ask if I could touch. He agreed as long as he got one in return. I didn't mind and before long his weapon had popped my cherry." While Shelly paused to have another drink the mob took to their feet whilst clapping and cheering her name, Tallulah asked for silence and encouraged her to continue. "After Simon had satisfied himself, I used his shirt to wipe myself down and Brian was paying particular attention to what I was doing prior to inquiring if he could help. I agreed, and he did a very good job before making me messy again, if you know what I mean."

Shelly was really starting to enjoy reliving the events of that night and murmured in Tallulah's ear how she wished Bill were present right now because she was feeling extremely naughty. Tallulah laughed, prior to repeating to the audience what she'd just learnt, and several voices yelled out querying whether Shelly wanted the 'Vegas bumps', eager to resume she didn't respond. "After Brian had made a mess it was Vincent's turn, he was ugly and shy, but asked ever so sweetly so I agreed, as long as I didn't have to look at his face. He suggested we could do it like his dogs, I'm awfully glad we did because what that boy lacked in the beauty department he certainly made up for elsewhere, and that's all I'll say about that. One by one the rest of the men asked nicely, so I obliged. I was thoroughly enjoying myself and continued to drink heavily when I thought it would be fun to line the men side by side. Watching them standing proud made me really horny therefore I walked towards Tony and knelt to give him oral sex. Bobbing up and down so quickly made me dizzy and I lost my balance, so I used his body to steady myself, but I pushed too hard and he fell over backwards. The sight of his penis pointing skywards excited me, and I couldn't help myself." Shelly stopped suddenly, before she stood up and approached Tallulah, then whispered in her ear, "I need a wee, where are the toilets please? I'll tell you the rest once I've been." "OK" she responded prior to announcing it was time for a quick comfort break. Tallulah warned the mob not to go anywhere, guaranteeing they didn't miss a piece of the action. Tallulah then expressed how she had a weak bladder and never passed on an opportunity to powder her nose, so she instructed Shelly to follow.

The two ladies struggled while making their way through the mass towards the VIP toilets whilst Shelly frequently stopped to chatter with fellow members of her warm following. They all sought to shake her hand and query what happened next, however she managed to keep tight lipped and refused to spill the beans until she'd had a pee. Tallulah was conscious with the length of time that they'd been struggling to make their way through the gathering and how little progress they'd made. Luckily, she still had the microphone in her hand, and used it courteously when ordering the troop to make some space. They did what they'd been requested and very soon after the two ladies made it to the toilet just in time for Shelly to prevent a disaster. Sadly, there was only one cubicle, so Shelly invited Tallulah to join her while they made use of the time intelligently by having a private chat. Tonight's host educated Shelly on her suggestion not being a good notion by expressing how she probably wouldn't like what she'd find, consequently she gestured for Shelly to go first. Shelly thanked her and within seconds found herself sitting listening to the sound of cascading water while she felt relief in her bladder. "Tallulah can I ask you a question please?" She hollered from inside the cubicle, then paused for a breath before resuming. "What did you mean when you said you where there that night?" The silence which ensued eventually turned to noise with her direct reply. "Darling I'm ever so sorry but the regulations state that only I get to ask the questions, and how you have to make up your own mind at the end of the night whether I'm telling the truth, by what you're told alone. Guess right and your rich." Shelly's mind was actively working with trying to work out the truth while feeling lightheaded. Once Shelly's waters had stopped flowing it was Tallulah's turn to powder her nose, and before she had finished her business, she recommended that Shelly should wait for her assistance with helping her back through the group. However, Shelly couldn't reply because she was nearly halfway back by now, revelling in the warm welcome she was receiving from the mob. On returning to her seat, she emptied her glass and whilst pouring another, tonight's host re-joined her and asked for hush therefore enabling Shelly to wrap up.

"Are you ready to earn yourself some money?" Tallulah queried. Shelly was and started to talk. "After I'd left Tony satisfied, I saw William standing proud, so I attempted to give him oral and again lost my balance; accidentally pushing him over. Keen-sighted with his weapon I couldn't help myself and made good use of it. However, he took ages to make a mess, but when he did, it was massive. Once the others had lined up next to each other I approached in the same way which I had previously. Only this time while I knelt, I deliberately pushed in a domineering manner. Hours later and after losing count of how many times the men had made a mess, I was asked if I'd like two at once. Nervous with what they suggested, I reluctantly agreed. Conner lay on the floor while I straddled and blinded him with my beasts, then Keith approached from behind and just as I felt a little prick my father walked in." She rested to have a drink and someone in the audience shouted, "he's behind you," everyone laughed, then another yelled, "oh no, what did he do?" After she'd finished drinking, they found out. "He grabbed Keith around the throat and only let go when his face turned blue. Once Keith had been dropped, he set about teaching the others a lesson in what happens when someone disrespects his angel. When their experience was over, they apologised to me and my father, then he whisked me away to my room whilst informing me that I had to join the local church to make me change my ways." She paused for a moment, regained her breath then asked for her money. A couple of voices from the back of the horde shouted, "liar demonstrate it to us then we'll believe you." Tallulah sniggered while asking whether the crowd thought she was telling the truth and the outstanding response was a definite yes. Tallulah began writing out a cheque whilst encouraging the audience to give Shelly a round of applause in celebration of her earning two million dollars. They went wild, as did Shelly who jumped with joy from the idea of suddenly becoming rich. Tallulah congratulated her as she passed over the cheque before enlightening the crowd that it was time for another a quick break.

Chapter 12

Spin the wheel time

The crowd were vibrant during the short time Tallulah had been absent from the stage, when she returned the lights dimmed leaving Shelly and she illuminated in the centre, stood right next to the big wheel. Tallulah placed the microphone between her lips and ordered the gathering to be silent while Shelly became acquainted with it, They obeyed so she read out some of tonight's encounters. '2 AM'; 'You Decide'; 'Twelve'; 'Off Ground Tick' and 'Joy Time'. Once finished she asked for Shelly's thoughts on what any of these might be. Shelly didn't respond, her eyes were hooked on the wheel and quizzed herself whether it was already spinning. Tallulah remarked to the audience that Shelly's silence must have been brought on by the excitement of the barn and they chuckled whilst she read out some more. 'Ouch'; 'Pleasure or Pain'; What's That?'; 'Impossible'; 'Musical Chairs' and 'Survival'. Shelly was still obsessed with the big circle when Tallulah placed the mic in front of her mouth and queried which one, she liked the sound of. "Off ground tick and musical chairs. I used to love playing both in my younger years," she countered. Knowing how shocked she'd be while viewing their interpretations' the crowd giggled at her reply. After the audience had quietened Tallulah read out the rest. 'Yes Please'; 'Head To Toe'; 'Guess who?'; 'Twisted'; 'Double Trouble'; 'It Takes Two';

'Hammerhead'; 'Welcome To The Jungle' and 'Would you'.

Once finished, Tallulah became concerned for Shelly's well-being; she was clearly showing signs that her room was starting to spin. Realizing if she passed out it would spoil everyone's entertainment, she encouraged her to take a seat while she listened to something very important prior to her first spin. Tallulah then requested total quiet before she began to explain. "Shelly, I've promised to tell you the truth, so I'll come clean with you, all of us gathered here are members of a sexual cult." Tonight's special guest interrupted the host. "I'm not putting my keys into one of your bowls to be picked out by some pervert. I knew this was one of those places." Tallulah chortled; summoned silence then continued. "As I said we're members of a cult and we're gathered here tonight for the highlight in our busy calendar, our version of the wheel of fortune. Normally our contestant and his wife are brought to us by one of our many scouts who are dotted all over the country. However, these scouts aren't looking for people with talent, quite the contrary, they're looking for people who wouldn't be missed if any encounter went wrong." She paused for a drink, and observed Shelly as she did, whilst wondering why she hadn't given any response. Deciding to leave her to sober up, she resumed. "Now our scouts get a hefty commission for sending a suitable candidate our way, but to my surprise the scout who sent us Bill didn't want what he was due and told us we'd be doing him a favour by eliminating him from your life, because he's been sleeping with you. Have you Shelly?" The audience gasped as they waited for her account, none came so Tallulah reminded her how she'd promised to tell the truth and that the prize money depended on it, prior to gesturing for the cheque to be returned to sender. Shelly looked at the host before viewing the cheque and shouting, "Yes but it's over." The crowd heckled and hissed, someone even called her a Jesse-bell, so Tallulah asked for calm again and motioned for Shelly to elaborate on what she's just stated.

"Conner and his brother had just moved into my father's ranch and I'd baked a cake for a moving in present. Bill and I were supposed to be taking it around together but one of our cows went into labour, so he had to stay with it. I was a bit nervous about seeing the two brothers after the lengthy period. However when I arrived, they were ever so nice and polite which made me feel very welcome, so I stayed for a drink or two and we got talking about that 'night'. A few rude comments passed between the three of us and somehow, we ended up back in the barn, replicating the scene before my father interrupted. I'm not going to say any more about what happened. I'll leave that to your imagination, but we remained there for a long time." She then took a long gap and filled her lungs with air, before progressing. "I only slept with the two of them that night; Conner wanted me all for himself, and it was actually nice getting some fresh attention. He was different to Bill in so many ways, thus allowing me to really enjoy a regular orgasm again.

Over the last two years we've been making plans about our future together, but I couldn't leave Bill effortlessly after all these years. I do love him it's just you get bored of doing the same routine over and over again. Conner's been pestering me to tell Bill it's over and I agreed that I would, if my 50th present was useless. When I found out yesterday what he'd won I told Conner we were history. I regret hurting him but I'm a married woman who's sticking to her vows. Whilst arguing we were interrupted by a knock on the door, Conner handled it; I was too upset by some of the hurtful things which he'd said. It was some men questioning if they could check the field where the jet was landing, so he offered to show them as we said our goodbyes. I've not seen or spoken to him since I do hope he's all right? I've told you the truth can I have my money now please?" Tallulah denied her request, advising that she'll have to play the game for some more winnings, prior to telling her that she had something else which was very important to say. "Those men who came to yours last night had been sent by me. Not to check for a suitable place to land but to bring me Conner seeing as I was intrigued by his reasons for him refusing my payment and as a result, he's here with us in Vegas. Do you believe me Shelly?" Due to her immense laughter she couldn't answer the nonsense that Tallulah had just waffled. Once she'd stopped, she did. "You're really striving to do a good job at playing with my mind

but I'm not falling for it and I think you're lying to me."
The bunch cheered briefly, while Tallulah reminded
Shelly how it was nearly time for her first spin. However,
before she did, there was another question that needed an
answer. "Conner also told me that just before your father
passed, he confessed how Bill grassed on you about that
'night', after he'd watched you perform with all of those
young men. Is that also true?" Her face filled with anger
as she replied, "No it bloody well isn't."

Tallulah stood next to the big circle and invited Shelly to
join her while she clarified the rules. "Just grab hold of
any of the big black knob's and spin as fast as you can
before letting go. Then when the wheel stops, whatever
task it's pointing to, is what our contestant has to
complete. Shelly grabbed one of the black knobs and
span it as if her life depended on it. The crowd then
egged her on, every one of them thrilled and full of
excitement while willing for it to stop on one of their
favourites. They started chanting 'survival' every time it
came close and when the wheel slowed the tension in the
room rose, until it abruptly ground to a halt on "You
Decide'. Tallulah bawled the wheel's selection through
the microphone while the audience applauded, then they
silenced when she started to explain this debut challenge.
"This one's easy Shelly all you've got to do is make a
simple decision, but before you do, I've got something
that you need to know. We've had to make this challenge
up especially for you and I'm so glad it's come up; it'll
make the night much more fun. When Conner confessed

152

to your little business earlier, I sent him to his room, uncertain what I should do with him. However, when Bill waited in the bar for you to join him, he started to get cocky and threatened me with his refusal to compete. So I put Conner on standby just in case Bill carried out his warning. After we had a little chat, he withdrew his threats, thus all was good again apart from for poor Conner. Therefore for tonight's first challenge you get to decide who plays Conner or Bill?" Unexpectedly there was movement and noises on the stage as a massive screen replaced the wheel and the gang clapped as soon as the screens came to life with two figures, dressed in identical bright red 'Gimp suits', standing in the arena.

Following a good long look at what she was witnessing, and unsure what she was, Shelly asked "Who the hell are they and what are they wearing?" Shelly burst into laughter once she'd spoke and the gathering joined her, finding amusement from her question. Tallulah invited hush before reacting. "I've told you Shelly it's Conner and Bill, and you've got to decipher which ones which, then decide who plays for prizes after seeing them compete in three easy challenges. Now seeing as you've been on the receiving end of both of their affections, you should be able to work out who's who by studying their actions while they perform. You've also seen both of their sex organs up close, haven't you?" The room fell voiceless whilst anticipating her reaction. "Yes, but you can't trick me. I've sobered up a bit and I've worked out your game. They're two complete strangers! Conner's back home and Bill's in the police station; you witnessed him getting taken away. What the hell have they got in their mouths? I need a drink!" As she walked towards the table, she stumbled and recovered just before the point of no return, prior to reaching for her glass and sinking the contents back in one. Tallulah responded. "Muzzles, that's what they've got in their mouths and the two deputies were fake. It was two of my employees in fancy dress. The man he assaulted also works for me and it was a simple diversion tactic merely to explain Bill's absence for the night. Now quiet please everyone, Shelly needs to focus because the contest is about to begin, but remember Shelly DON'T tell us who's who, you MUST keep that all to yourself." There was movement on the screens when the contestants were joined by two glamorous ladies who approached from the left and stood behind them. They grabbed their arms and positioned them to their rear before restraining their wrists in matching red handcuffs. The ladies then moved to the front and momentarily obstructed everyone's view of the contestants and when it was restored the swarm cheered upon noticing the men's meat and two veg poking out from the paltry hole in their suits. Shelly was gawking at the screen in disbelief with what she saw. However she decided on playing along as her thoughts had already made plans for spending the majority of the money.

Tallulah instructed her to get up close and take a good look before falling silent. Shelly did and scrutinised every ounce of meat that was on show. After a couple of minutes the screens went clear and the host queried whether Shelly had chosen a contestant yet, before inquiring whether she'd like to see some more? Shelly sat down and poured herself a fresh drink whilst shaking her head in disbelief with what she was undertaking for money. Once the glass had emptied, she gave her reaction. "I'll see some more please?" After she'd answered the screens lit up to reveal the two men stood sideways back to back, each with a lady kneeling in front of him. Tallulah enlightened Shelly how for this part of the challenge she had to imagine it was her performing what the ladies were about to do, while she observed the men's body movement for anything that appeared familiar. As Soon as the host stopped talking the action began.

It was the man on the left of the screen who twitched first when the lady took hold of his little tinker and gave it a gentle rub. Slow to respond, the gentle rub soon turned into a hard yank or three. They did the trick and soon it was pointing upwards, so she introduced it to her mouth. While her head bobbed repeatedly the man's body began to shake, the more it shook the quicker the lady nodded, until when it seemed like he was about to have some sort of a fit, she ceased nodding, before standing up and leaving the man unsatisfied for the congregation to see. Next it was the other man's turn, he didn't need much encouragement, so the lady replicated the motion of licking a lolly whilst paying special interest to its shiny red end. Once she'd had enough tongue action she began to bite. Small one's on the edge at first before putting her mouth around and sinking her teeth deep in. The man winced when she did and she decided that it must have been sore, so she opted to rub it better; that worked and soon his body trembled like the other man's had earlier. Then she stopped. The audience came to life with cheers and whistles when the screens went blank whilst Tallulah questioned Shelly whether she'd made her mind up while there was more to see. Shelly didn't respond, her mind was on Bill, hoping he'd be back soon to rescue her from what she was viewing. Her thoughts quickly focused on the money when she heard Tallulah voice's stating she'd go home with nothing unless she gave an answer.

The throng started to chant Shelly's name, whilst willing her to answer seeing as their fun hadn't really commenced yet. "See some more," was her reply and with it the screens brightened once again. Shelly was horrified with what she witnessed, the two ladies were lying down next to each other, both naked apart from a headband which had something small and square sticking out of the front and their legs were wide apart. The men were stood proudly by them, so the ladies wrapped their legs around the men, who in return, launched a thrusting action. The screens filled with the lady's on the lefts view. It was of a man muzzled in his gimp suit thrusting as hard as he could, but he was useless, failing to even make the lady quiver, let alone scream. The picture switched to the other lady's view, she was clearly enjoying herself, while her body twitched, and her legs

156

quivered before she let out an enormous scream. The more she screamed the faster he thrust, the faster he thrust the more she squealed, the more she cried the harder his thrusting became until finally the lady let out a massive yell, and the man became released from her grip. The picture switched to the other view and nothing had changed. This man was making a feeble attempt of taking his lady to heaven and back. Frustrated, she released him from her control and the screens went plain while everyone remained silent whilst waiting for Tallulah to speak. "Well Shelly, what did you think of that? Have you made your mind up? Which lucky man are you picking to perform? Now please don't say anything apart from left or right." The venue fell soundless after Tallulah had requested her decision, the silence remained for what seemed like a perpetuity before she revealed that she'd seen enough and didn't want the money anymore. The horde booed along with the host, so she declared that prior to Shelly stating her final answer, they'd take a short break.

The big displays exhibited the latest odds. 'Left man' 150-1', 'Right man' 2-1, while Tallulah sat down beside Shelly and murmured in her ear, quizzing her whether she didn't approve of Bill's present seeing as it did exactly as she'd requested. After all it was a body and mind awakening experience. Shelly went to pour herself another drink, but the bottle was dry, as were the other two, therefore Tallulah responded by taking to the mic and ordering some additional supplies. Shelly gazed her in the eyes and explicated that it was quite the opposite and how delighted with it she was, ecstatic in fact. The problem being that after she'd done what she'd been instructed and imagined herself with the men, she was missing Bill and wished him back. Thus enabling the showing of her new negligee while sinking into her lovely mattress together. Tallulah smiled, before inspiring her to imagine how special a night she'll have after winning big money, and to understand how pleased Bill will be with the thought that his magnificent wife had changed their lives forever with her actions tonight. Something Tallulah had just said must have tugged on her conscience, because like a mad woman Shelly bounced from her chair and jumped for joy while she shouted, "I've made up my mind." Eager to prevent a potential fall the host signalled for her to sit back down, which she did, and no sooner had she, the replenishments arrived. Tallulah dispensed a glass each then raised hers and proposed a toast to Shelly's life changing decision. As their glasses chinked the ladies toasted 'cheers', and after they'd taken a long drink, they strolled towards the centre of the stage, ready to announce Shelly's decision.

"Ladies and gentlemen, can I have your attention please, Shelly's got something to say." The host requested, before telling Shelly to make the crowd happy by not only telling them which one's going to be the lucky contestant, but how she came to her decision. Tallulah then passed her the mic and in it she spoke. "When you told me to imagine myself with the men, I did. Now, if you had to pick between screams and frustration, I think I know which one you'd choose. I know neither of them are Conner nor Bill, so if I've got to watch people having sex to win, I'd much rather watch someone who I could learn a thing or two from, and for that reason I'm picking the man on the left." The group gasped in disbelief with her choice, they wanted vigorous action with lots of noise. Although those who'd placed money on the outsider were shouting and applauding whilst celebrating their win. They didn't rejoice for long when Shelly announced how sorry she was, but she meant to say right. The rest of the group sprang into voice, their cheers drowned out the boos, while Tallulah inquired whether Shelly was sure, seeing as she would have to take her next answer as the final one. After the room fell silent Tallulah queried Shelly. "Could you please confirm once and for all, which contestant is playing tonight's game." The room erupted once her voice clearly stated RIGHT and the crowds jubilant celebrations began when the cheque exchanged hands while the screens exhibited her prize fund aggregate.

Chapter 13

Bernard's first challenge

After a short comfort break Tallulah re-took to the mic and asked the audience for peace and quiet while she revealed something important to her special guest. Shelly's ears pricked with the mention of her name and when she gazed towards the host, Tallulah started to tell. "Congratulations on successfully completing our first challenge, sorry I meant to say congratulations to our contender 'right' man on being lucky tonight. Now we don't know whether it's Conner or Bill, so I'm going to refer to him as Bernard." Amusement filled the space once Tallulah had performed her renaming ceremony, but the fun diminished when she chatted again. "Shelly, I've told you all about us and our cult and how you've ended up here tonight, whether you believe me or not is entirely up to you; I don't give a damn. Now for the next part of 'Bill's story' I'm going to introduce you to someone who was actually there and let you hear it directly from them what happened next. I wasn't you see, and I'd hate for you to decide based on some second-hand knowledge incorporating some of my own extravagant spin. Ladies and gentlemen, can you please put your hands together as we welcome Marvin to the stage." The applause deafened, and upon him reaching his destination, he made a bee line straight towards Shelly and murmured in her ear. "I promised Bill I'd take care of him, which I will, because I'm a man of my word. However, you can't

160

trust anybody except for me, and your life depends on it. Now slap me across my face as hard as you can." The crowd cheered after hearing loud and clear, the whack when her right hand contacted with his left cheek. Tallulah then instructed Marvin to pop over and stand beside her while they had a little chat. He obeyed and she asked him with what he had said to provoke such a reaction. Composed, despite the fact he was a condemned man, he grabbed the mic and enlightened everyone present with what he'd just stated. "I told her she was a SLAG not worthy of a decent man like my friend Bill, and how I hope she's chosen Conner to play tonight seeing as it's going to be horrific for him." The horde erupted, they were starting to take pleasure from the twists and turns that were unfolding right before their eyes. Tallulah re-took to the microphone and clarified how Marvin's a dead man walking since, after tonight's entertainment had finished, she was personally going to pull the trigger. The crowd gasped at this news, before the host continued. "It wasn't an easy decision for me, seeing as Marvin's been a model employee whilst being popular amongst staff and customers alike. He's reliable, honest, trustworthy and he'll be hard to replace; however, Marvin is probably the only member of my staff who didn't have a clue about our antics, yet somehow, he knew all about our little game. When I checked out his story it stacked, so you're probably wondering what he's done to deserve a bullet when he's been such a model employee. Well he's done nothing more than live next door to an undercover FBI agent who was trying to infiltrate us, who happened to tell him about our game whilst he lay dying from the injuries that were inflicted by us. Now it may merely be a coincidence, but I couldn't take the chance and chose to terminate his life. However, after hearing what he's just stated I'm starting to have second thoughts. She then paused and rotated to watch him in the eye before progressing. "I'm starting to like you Marvin and I'm going to give you one chance to save your skin. So if you promise to tell Shelly the truth about Bill's antics this weekend, and you join our close family, then I'm prepared to let you live. Do you promise?" Marvin squinted towards the gathering once he'd pinched the mic and confirmed how he did and was looking forward to getting to know every person personally.

The troop chanted his name, so he took a bow while Tallulah grabbed the mic and requested quiet again, prior to giving some further instructions. "Go and sit beside 'the slut'; your words not mine, and examine her eyes whilst you explain, truthfully, how we know so much. I don't require it word for word, just a synopsis will do as I'm led to believe that Bernard is eager to complete his next conquest." Marvin did as instructed, but Shelly was uncomfortable with his close presence and he sensed this, so he grabbed her hands and gently rubbed her palms. This did the trick, now relaxed she encouraged him to commence. "I'd just been for a pee and I noticed a nervous man waving at the end of the alleyway enquiring whether he was in the right place. I confirmed that he was and then clarified the registration process; that's when he told me all about the 'pan present' and how your sex life has dwindled ever since. Bill asked me not to tell anybody the secret that he was about to spill. The one which he'd kept for twenty-nine years. That 'night' after he'd regained consciousness from his little accident, he sought to find you, and when he approached the barn complex, he was alerted to your whereabouts by your screams. Tentative with what to expect, upon entering he armed himself with a pitchfork. Then when he spotted you naked amongst the other men, he disappeared behind some hay and scrutinized everything. When your father ended everyone's fun, he was petrified, but somehow managed to remain hidden throughout and heard everything that was stated. Shortly afterwards Bill joined the church, safe with the knowledge there'd be no competition in winning your hand. Once he'd told me, I promised to take good care of him during his spending spree by being his wingman for the day. Sadly, I've let him down and that's why you're with me tonight. Please trust me and if I can do anything to assist my new 'partner' in the future, I will." Marvin subsequently rotated towards Tallulah and reassured her how he'd told the truth, apart from omitting the bit about the presents; unwilling to spoil Shelly's other surprises. Upon hearing this she nodded and gestured for the congregation to make some noise in appreciation for honest Marvin.

Once the silence was golden, Tallulah instructed him to take a seat on the opposite table to Shelly; he wasn't out of the woods yet and might be called upon again later, and while he was executing his orders the wheel re-emerged while the main lights extinguished. Tallulah then inquired how Shelly was feeling. "I'm enjoying it so far, the booze is lovely, I've already spent over a million of my winnings on lots of designer handbags and shoes; whoever came up with the story you're telling must be on drugs to have come up with such a devious plot. I'm missing Bill though; how long will he be?" The crowd laughed from her latest remark as did the host, prior to questioning Shelly whether she was starting to become a believer? Shelly remained silent whilst sat at the table gently shaking her head. "Speak up we need an answer now" Tallulah shouted into the mic. This startled Shelly from her thoughts, so she retorted her answer "NO."

The screens illuminated once again, filled with the figure of Bernard standing alone with his body covered in red from head to toe, apart from his manhood, which was in plain sight and a bright green ball strapped between his lips while his arms were restrained to his front. The arena was bare apart from a metal cage in the far-left corner which had a weapon hanging nearby. Tallulah invited some clatter from the crowd whilst Shelly joined her for another spin and when she did, Tallulah quizzed her which game she fancied next. By now Shelly was starting to get into the swing of things and stated she'd quite fancy 'Twelve'. The host picked up on this straight away and couldn't resist, when she laughingly reminded her how she already had. Shelly didn't respond to Tallulah's remark, however the mob did and reacted with a thunderous ovation. Then they fell silent when Shelly grabbed hold of another big black knob and gave it a ferocious spin. The convention cheered once more at the sight of 'Survival' whenever it neared the top. However it wasn't to be, although they still gave out a loud roar when the wheel eventually stopped whilst pointing towards 'What's That!' Tallulah requested hush, seeing as this was one of her favourites and a guaranteed gathering pleaser. Then, while the mob were still jubilant in their celebrations, she announced a short break while Bernard prepares.

Tallulah made the most of the intermission by checking on her guest. Judging by the shaking in her legs it wasn't good; she was clearly more advanced following her latest binge than her earlier spinning room, so she queried whether everything was OK? "I need the toilet NOW!" She retorted before hastily quitting the safety of stage. Tallulah thought quickly and wisely and utilized the microphone to summon a parting of the waves, before insisting how Shelly mustn't come to any harm. Tallulah used the gap and tracked her guest just to play safe, and upon entering the latrines she was greeted with the commotion of Shelly's voice repeat-ably stating "I'm going to be sick." Tallulah turned to her right and caught site of Shelly kneeling by the pan. But her head was nowhere to be seen, therefore Tallulah queried whether she was OK? Shelly's reply was slurred and slow. "I think I must of drank too quick on an empty stomach, but I'm sure I'll be fine once I've been sick and had a bite to eat." It must have been the mention of food that tipped Shelly over the edge, because as soon as she'd finished talking, the lavatory started to fill. While bumbling away, she remained in this position for a few minutes although a perplexed Tallulah couldn't understand a word. Once Shelly had produced a few more funny noises, she stood up and wiped her mouth, before begging for a munch. Tallulah stated how she'd organise for something after the challenge, prior to confirming that her order would need to be placed soon to qualify for rapid delivery. Shelly thought for a while as to what tickled her fancy, undecided whether it was to be gammon or steak she eventually confirmed it was the latter; a well done 30 ounce one with peppercorn sauce and triple thick chips. Tallulah directed Shelly to stroll ahead while she placed her order, and when the host repeated it into her wedding ring, a voice appeared inside her right ear confirming it had been received.

Once everybody returned to the stage the lights were dimmed and the wheel became replaced by the massive display, before Tallulah placed the microphone between her lips and invited the group to remain noiseless for the next challenge. The room fell silent before the blank screens lit. However, it filled with cheers and laughter once they did, after Shelly had took one look and shouted, "What's that!" In a calming voice Tallulah answered her query. "That my darling is either Conner or Bill dressed in his gimp suit whilst exhibiting some of our most popular toys." Upon hearing this Shelly scrutinised the screen and studied hard for the popular toys that were mentioned, but she couldn't distinguish any, all she could see was a man stood side on, and apart from his exposed tackle, he was completely covered from the neck down in red. His arms were shackled by his sides and his head covered in a black mask, with a phallic symbol poking up from the top along with another from his mouth. Tallulah inquired whether Shelly adored what she observed, "interesting" was her reaction, hence the host started to describe the test. "This is a two pronged one, pardon the pun!" The audience did and gave her a quick applause before allowing her to continue, "I'll tell you about the second part if Bernard fulfils the first and all he's got to do to win is very simple. If his manhood points towards the sky he's failed. However, nobody's allowed to touch it and if they do Bernard wins. Did you get that contestant?" He nodded, and Tallulah ordered that from now on he would only respond when he was addressed as Bernard.

The venue fell silent and dark as the camera rocketed out to reveal two woman present in the room with Bernard, one approached and stood in front, then the other behind. The one in front was a petite red head with perfectly formed beasts, and whilst standing completely naked, her hands explored her skin. The one behind was entirely covered in shiny black PVC with spikes sticking out from her head and breasts. The naked lady accosted Bernard and rubbed her hands on his chest, then she gave him an all-mighty backwards shove. Luckily, the covered

lady caught him and lay him gently to the floor.
However, Bernard was powerless to prevent what
happened next, when he peered upwards then witnessed
the naked lady's vagina heading straight towards his
mouth, before he felt something push against his teeth as
she connected with his toy. Bernard was endeavouring
not to look at her beautiful body whilst it pushed
skywards before returning, and as her breasts bounced in
perfect harmony with each other, her clitoris repeatedly
came in and out of focus whilst it made some noise. Her
body movement began to increase and when it did the
pain in his teeth intensified. However, and thankfully for
him, she replaced her up and down rhythm with a side to
side circular one which was much gentler on Bernard's
eye's and teeth. He could sense a little twinge in his
Harry as he paid attention to the woman's constant
moans and to his delight his little spasm faded when she
forcefully thrust up and down again, only this time a lot
more vigorously than earlier; thus the pain killing off his
pleasure. After continually grumbling for some time they
increased in volume until she let out an enormous
screech and Bernard felt a tear in his eye. Then abruptly
she stopped and removed herself from his toy, when she
stood up before rotating 180 degrees, and rested back
down. Whilst bent, she replicated her previous actions,
only now she blew gently on his limp love gland
whenever it was close by. Bernard wished she weren't, it
was truly starting to work, and he could feel he was
about to fail when he spotted a lonely hair sticking out of
her peachy backside. Then whilst managing to focus all
of his attention towards it, he prevented an imminent

disaster. It didn't work for long; he soon felt another ache, only this time a considerably bigger one. But, fortunately for him, it disappeared when the woman sat up and he found his eyes now focused on the split between her cheeks. The pain in his teeth intensified when, for a short while, her thrusts became faster and harder until the area filled with another almighty scream. Then once silent, she stood up and the two women departed.

The mob cheered when the screen went blank, so Shelly took the opportunity to have a much-needed drink, shocked after what she'd just witnessed. They calmed when Tallulah's tone filled the room commending Bernard's bravery in part one, before explaining part two. "For his next role he must move to the beat, it's really that simple." No sooner had she finished the screens brightened yet again and Bernard had been joined by two different women, both of whom were dressed in matching yellow PVC with killer heels. The only way you could tell them apart was by the black whip which one of them held in her left hand. The woman without the whip released Bernard's hands from his side-cuffs then repositioned his arms in front of his belly, prior to replacing his restraints with a smaller pair; thus enabling his arms to be suitably restricted for the next event. Once Bernard was suitably shackled, she carefully unzipped the piece of her suit that was protecting her Amazon jungle, while the whip woman grabbed hold of Bernard by the cuffs and led him to what resembled a small

169

operating table with a stand positioned either side. The jungle woman lay on it and spread her legs wide apart, then the whip woman left Bernard standing alone, when she moved towards the jungle woman and restrained her extremities tightly to restrict any unnecessary movement. After double checking the straps for tension, she lowered the make-shift bed and once it was of suitable height, she forced Bernard onto all fours, whilst taking her time to ensure his head was positioned exactly where it was required.

Some disco music began playing and the whip woman's body danced to the beat, as the music got louder her prancing got faster until it suddenly fell quiet when the music was replaced by an almighty crack from her whip. Bernard's body jolted, and the toy disappeared before the woman gave out a loud jungle roar, and once Bernard's toy had returned into view, the music commenced once again. After a few seconds it stopped before restarting and stopping three times in quick succession. However, once it stopped for the fourth time, Bernard's body jolted an equal number of times. When the music resumed the whip woman set about Bernard and removed the part of his suit that concealed his rear, but it wasn't the same disco music as before, this time it was a lot louder with a heavy metal kind of sound. Then when it stopped the whip woman took great pleasure in leaving a nice red smudge on Bernard's rear, and whilst his pain intensified, the woman's jungle roars developed louder and more frequent, until eventually culminating in dramatic fashion after Bernard had received 15 hard strikes in quick succession and the woman screamed out "no more I'm done." The whip woman man- handled Bernard to his feet while the camera zoomed in on his jewels, verifying his resounding victory.

The screens turned bare when the stage became well-lit once again, and the bunch cheered then screeched whilst pleading for more. Tallulah took to the mic to congratulate Bernard on his success before inviting the crowd to make some noise for Shelly; who's now got another million dollars added to her cheque. They went wild, with lots of banging on tables and chants of Bernard's name. When order was restored the host queried Shelly for her thoughts on what she'd just viewed and queried whether she would like a go. Slightly confused with what to say, while knowing that she's got to tell the truth to win big, she countered. "Painful, did you see those marks on that poor man's backside. I feel so sorry for him. He won't be able to sit down for a week. The hairy woman sounded like she enjoyed herself though so it's not a definite no." Tallulah requested for some din and for everyone to get betting; hopefully, there was still lots more to come after they've taken another brief pause. Once the chamber illuminated a waiter approached the stage with a tray, he placed it down in front of Shelly and removed the cover to reveal a huge 30-ounce peppered steak with all the trimmings just like she'd ordered.

Chapter 14

A very royal occasion

After fifteen minutes had passed, Shelly's plate was still half full and the bunch were getting agitated whilst readily waiting for the main event to resume, when the latest odds displayed simultaneously on the screens; 'Who's Bernard? Conner, 10 -1; Bill, Even money'. Tallulah approached Shelly inquiring whether she was going to be long, in between mouthfuls she replied. "Don't mind me you carry on, just shout when I'm needed." "I need you now!" The host sternly yelled, then she gave her some time to clear her palette, prior to resuming. "Shelly, I hope you're appreciating your present so far, but can I query how much more of Bernard's earnings have you spent?" She glanced at the host prior to grabbing the microphone from her and educating everybody as to how she fancied a world cruise aboard a luxury ship with immaculately dressed sailors in smart, sexy uniforms. Tallulah sniggered before regaining control of the mic, and enlightened Shelly how she was now going to meet the lady who handled Bill's next part of his voyage to Vegas, before gesturing everybody to give a big hand to a member of their very own royalty, the enchanting Sandy. The males in the crowd turned berserk with excitement after recognizing how they were now in the company of such an important figure, and the females curtsied as she made her way to the stage, then once there, she found herself summonsed to stand next to Tallulah whilst she was formerly introduced.

"Ladies and gentlemen, we all know who this stunning lady is, and we've watched her antics here many times before. However, Shelly doesn't have a clue about her and how important a role she's played so far and has still to. Now, I think it's only fair that we kill her suspense as I hand you over for Sandy to take over from here." The crowd shouted her name, while she sat next to Shelly and opened with how she's not sorry for any of her actions, seeing as Bill's a pervert who deserved everything that he got. An enraged Shelly stood up and shouted her reply. "Don't you ever speak about my husband like that again or I'll knock your block off. Do you understand!" Sensing trouble aloft, Tallulah managed to calm the situation down by reminding Shelly about the money and how she needed to hear what Sandy had to say to get it. After she'd regained her composure and sat back down, she picked up her knife and fork, prior to instructing Sandy to continue with her lies while Shelly finishes her steak. "The first part I had to play to make the plan work was to process Bill's registration and advise him about the store's strict no touch rule, even though for the scheme to work, Bill had to break it. From that moment on with every move I made, I did it with the sole intent of making him horny so he couldn't resist but choose me. When he saw me for the first time, I was naked from the waist down, and once I'd started striding towards him, he didn't know where to look at first, until his eyes eventually became glued to my vagina. Then I teased him by undressing fully after I'd told him how I wanted him to explode in my mouth. All was going well, and I'd finished with him for now, when Marvin, who knew nothing about what was going on, gave him the option of a personal shop, accompanied by his own personal model to demonstrate any product of his choice. The plot worked. I was chosen and from that point on I had Bill firmly in my grasp." Shelly had finished her steak by now and wobbled her head in doubt with what she'd just been informed. Feeling much better through a full stomach she poured herself a drink and summoned Sandy to continue.

"For our first stop I needed to lead him into our 'Appetisers and Stimulants' room. This was easy, and it was here he told me about his one and only experience with a little blue pill; do you remember that night Shelly?" She glared with amazement in her eyes after listening to what she'd just heard, and for the first time of the night, she had the faintest thought that what they were saying might be true, before she quickly dismissed it with her answer. "Bill's really gone to a lot of trouble to arrange all of this; I really do get the money at the end if I go along with it?" Tallulah nodded so Sandy continued. "After I'd changed from my fluffy gown into my birthday suit, I convinced Bill to take a 'Dallas Pill' to give him a little help with ensuring that he didn't break the golden rule, by declaring how it would keep his sexual urges at bay, so to speak. However, I lied and actually got him to take one of our best-selling slow acting stimulants. The next stage of the strategy was for me to get him alone in the gimp suit room thus enabling him to choose a fitting costume for tonight. I didn't have to do much persuading as Marvin inadvertently did it for me. Bill was a bit uncomfortable with what he observed in this room. The twelve life like statues modelling our newest range. Following a little persuasion with my bodily movements, I managed to get him to pick one and try it on. It was at this point that the 'Dallas Pill' began to take effect and he nearly broke the no-touch rule. I alerted Marvin by way of a loud scream, he entered and upon hearing what had happened, decided to shackle Bill for his own safety. I decided to choose the rest of your presents alone while Marvin took him to the special room to await me." Shelly interrupted by inquiring what presents she had in store, "nice ones" Sandy retorted before concluding. "I won't tell you much about what happened in this room, seeing as I don't want to spoil what Bill's bought for you. All I will say is everything went to plan, and Bill broke the golden rule."

The horde cheered the moment Sandy ended, and once Tallulah had instructed her to sit next to Marvin, she invited Shelly to join her centre stage while the wheel re-emerged. The audience quietened when she grabbed another knob and gave it an enormous spin, then they continuously chanted 'survival', followed by 'joy time' as the wheel rotated a few times before finally halting on 'Hammerhead'. The flock cringed with the thought of what was coming next; they'd seen this one before. Then the big circle got substituted by the screen and on it appeared Bernard standing alone, covered in red from head to toe with only one part on show: his tackle. "You're in for a treat Bernard" Tallulah sniggered while she spoke. "What you're about to get is going to improve your sex life no end and enable you to take Shelly higher than heaven, when she experience's the thrill of an 'Albert'. The mob exploded in noise upon hearing these words, and Bernard's image transformed into one showing several different types of 'Prince'. The troop silenced while Tallulah educated Shelly how, for the next step to her becoming a multi-millionaire, she must choose which crown Bernard shall receive. Shelly laughed as she shifted towards the screen for a close up and after having clearly been taking comfort from the bottle, she found herself mesmerised with what she was studying, consequently she scrutinised each one at length. The first one was a simple ring with a bulge halfway around. The second looked more like something the dentist would use, it was cylindrical in shape with hollow sides which could only be described as a few clasps forming the outer cylinder, and it had a thick metal bar running through its centre. The third was a 2-inch-long metal shaft with balls on either end and little spikes running all around. Lastly there was a ring with a chain attached to another lying side by side. Shelly was fed up with their silly game by now, and with having no interest whatsoever in what she was viewing, she pointed at the last one and yelled, "Bernard can have that." Tallulah commended her choice before declaring another short recess.

During the break, the screens flickered with the latest odds; Succeed - 50-1; Fail 2-1. Shelly paid particular attention to these; she knew her dreams of having overwhelming wealth rested with Bernard's success. Tallulah re-took her place then asked for quiet while the challenge began, before the screens illustrated Bernard lying on the same table which the jungle woman had occupied earlier, with his legs bound the same, as was his body, along with a couple of scantily clad ladies stood either side whilst gently stroking his chest. The lady on the left opened Bernard's inner thigh zip, thus exposing this part ready for surgery. Then they were joined by two others, a lady dressed as a nurse and a man masquerading as a doctor, complete with stethoscope. When he strolled towards Bernard and used it to listen on his chest, the room echoed with the sound of his heartbeat, pounding hard and racing away. Then the nurse paid particular attention to his penis and she took ample time in cleaning it to prevent infection. Another lady then entered carrying the silver tray which contained Bernard's prince and all of the necessary implements. The doctor picked up all of the prince's parts and positioned them in place while he made his mark, and after he'd placed them all back, he picked up a large hook shaped needle, which appeared extremely sharp, prior to moving it towards Bernard's inner left thigh. Once he'd stabbed the needle and checked his heartbeat once again, the group cheered with the sound of its galloping speed. The doctor then returned to his needle and gave it an invincible push before it disappeared into Bernard's flesh. Then he paused from pushing to observe his heartbeat once more, thus allowing the gathering to hear how rapid it had now become. The two ladies standing either side ceased stoking when the doctor did what he did next, causing Bernard's body to jolt when the end of the needle reappeared from hiding. The nurse handed him a slim ring from the tray, and he tried to do what came next as 'carefully' as he could, then after quite a lot of movement from Bernard's body, he'd successfully completed the first part of his prince, hence the camera whizzed in on its new home embedded in Bernard's thigh. The screen turned off as Tallulah took to the Mic, requesting Shelly's opinion on what she'd witnessed. "Delightful" was her reply prior to requesting another bottle or three. The host obliged and announced a quick comfort break, whilst instructing the crowd not to be long seeing as the best was still to come.

After the short adjournment and as soon as Tallulah had re-took her place, the room dimmed as the screens lit with the sight of Bernard on the table surrounded by everyone who was present earlier. Only this time the ladies were securely restraining him for the procedure that he was about to endure by holding his chest rather than stroking it. The doctor took to his chest once again and it was a lot swifter than earlier, so he returned to his position in between Bernard's open legs. After exploring his penis in great detail he requested for the nurse to give it a quick clean, before he approached Bernard and muttered in his ear. "I hope you like pain" whilst checking his heartbeat yet again. It was off the scale at this point and the troop praised when he took the needle from the tray and returned to 'Bernard's bits'. By now the nurse had finished her cleaning, so with his left hand he grabbed it around the end, and with the needle in his right, he pushed making the end disappear into his urethral. Bernard's body grimaced on the table when the doctor left the needle jabbed in Bernard's organ whilst he checked his beating drum once again; it sounded like it was going into overload with its near constant thumping. Without further ado the doctor grabbed hold of his needle and Bernard's flinching became frequent and violent whilst the eye returned into view. The crowd clapped energetically at the patients success so far and as they were willing him to succeed, the doctor gave Bernard a short break from becoming the newest member of the 'royal family', before he grabbed the other shiny ring from the tray and forcefully prodded it through the small incision which he'd just created. His body lurched harshly while the doctor finished off and he made sure he did this as un-carefully as he could. Bernard's body constantly jolted; the doctor was clearly struggling to make it fit, and after numerous attempts and oodles of wrestling with Bernard's bit's, he surrendered, therefore the ring was replaced with a much fatter needle than earlier. Unable to proceed due to Bernard's constant movement from the agony, he summonsed another six nurses to help, and as they reported for duty, he directed each one to where he wanted them to pin the contestant down. They obeyed and he took hold of his new needle once again, prior to pushing as harsh as he could. However, at first, he struggled, until he pushed with all his superpower and ultimately the job was complete. One of the nurses then handed him the ring and again Bernard's body joggled until finally his prince was crowned. The doctor then attached the small chain to either ring before all the screens went out.

The room filled with the sound of voices while the bunch were chatting away, busy comparing notes from each other's post-mortem on what they'd just witnessed. The victorious ones were smug whilst bragging to their friends about how much they'd just gained, when Tallulah took to the Mic once more, educating everyone with how much she cringed at the thought of how considerable pain Bernard was in. Then while rotating towards Shelly, she requested her opinion on 'Bernard's Royalty'. "I can't see the point of it myself." However, Tallulah grabbed her attention fully with what she said next. "Darling the purpose of having a prince is to give you both a little bit of help in completing your journey to heaven and back more pleasurable and believe me it does. Congratulations your cheques just grown by another two million dollars." Shelly turned wild, as did the audience upon hearing this news and once calm had been restored, Tallulah took to the Mic enlightening everyone about the hour they now had to kill while Bernard took time to recover. She asked for peace and quiet while she took up some of this time, to tell Shelly what happened to the ten men, who were that afraid of her father, they upped sticks and ventured out into the nasty big wide world.

"The following morning they woke early in the barn, battered and bruised after the previous night's encounter with your father, and not only were they hell bent on getting revenge for the injuries that he inflicted, but also on you for acting so innocent and sweet by pretending that we'd taken advantage of you. A few days later ten of them held a meeting at Brian's family ranch and concocted a devious scheme. Fortunately for you on the night that they were executing it; whilst on their way to yours, heavily armed and expecting trouble, a suspicious passing deputy blocked them and while he approached the overcrowded truck, he sensed something afoot with the amount of hardware they carried, so he grabbed his radio to call for back-up. One of them panicked whilst trying to hide his weapon and it went off, then the deputy fell to the ground. Convinced they were all destined to spend the rest of their living days behind bars, they agreed their revenge would have to wait until another day and decided to flee the county together. They made a pact to collectively stick and watch out for one another as they ventured into the hustle and bustle of Dallas. The pact between them still stands to this day and they are now very wealthy, powerful, respectable citizens." Tallulah paused when she heard a voice in her ear, informing how Bernard's made a good recovery and is eager to get on with the rest of the show. Receiving the good news she announced it to the mob, who all cheered before the host queried Shelly for her thoughts on what she'd just discovered. Shelly started clapping, and applauding the plot so far, while she enlightened Tallulah on how much she was beginning to love it, and despite it being so unbelievable, it made perfect sense to someone who was a raving NUTTER like her. The congregation couldn't believe someone would dare insult Tallulah in such a way and they remained unspoken whilst unsure what response to give. When Tallulah laughed it off, they erupted, and she announced another quick breather.

Chapter 15

Your throne awaits your highness

Shelly remained seated when Tallulah exited the stage; taking full advantage of one more opportunity to powder her snout, and the audience were in good spirits, smiling and giggling while discussing the show thus far. She gazed towards the other two detainees and took great interest with their awkward posture and silence, so she stood to approach them and inquire what was the matter. But before she could get anywhere near, she was apprehended by a pair of burly blokes, who insisted she re-took to her seat, and no sooner had she, Tallulah unexpectedly appeared prior to her requesting for silence to allow for the next piece of the puzzle to fall into place. The crowd gave her a big cheer, then they fell silent when she announced that the next part of Bill's day would be told, as seen through the eyes of Marvin. The venue erupted with clapping for their newest recruit as he walked towards Shelly before he sat down beside her, and like before, he gently rubbed the palms of her hands, prior to recalling his memories of what happened just after Bill had perpetrated his cardinal sin. "I heard Sandy's screams from inside the room. As I entered, I was shocked and immediately told Bill to Freeze and put his hands in the air. Several of my colleagues also responded and came bounding in, but I knew that I had a promise to keep so I took control of the situation and rapidly handcuffed him more securely than earlier. Now whenever someone breaks the no touch rule, the stores procedure requires them to be marched to the boss immediately for interrogation. So I led him through a series of corridors until we reached the bosses quarters, and we were greeted by another two of my colleagues standing either side of his door. They offered to take over, but I feared for Bill's safety; the act he'd committed was upon one of their girlfriends, therefore I declined their kind offer to ensure the boss heard the truth. After a short delay in his recreation area we were eventually invited into his office for Bill to learn his destiny and I was ordered to leave them alone while they had a little natter. Whilst I was sat in the room to where I'd been dispatched, I started to mull over Bill's options, prison or death." Shelly intervened, and smiled, before communicating. "I've worked it out; what my presents are and If what everyone's telling me is true, then Bill's been to a sex shop to buy me some toys. I'll tell you this now, if he bloody well has then I'll kill him, the dirty perverted bastard! What do you mean prison or death?"

The spectators detonated upon hearing her interruption, they soothed when Marvin continued. "The act which Bill committed was a very severe one which in Texas is punishable by a long prison stretch. However, the bosses preferred way of dealing with problems like Bill is to make them disappear; this way avoided any unnecessary attention from the authorities. I was feeling guilty about allowing Bill to find himself in his current predicament and remembered what I'd been told by my dying friend

Fred, about the police chief and his cult. That's when I told them all about my plan to give Bill a fighting chance of survival. Ultimately after Bill and I had managed to work out the small print, the boss was given the green light by the cult and the plan was put into action, with his call to you. Thankfully, he was convincing with his explanation of his day's experiences and you've wound up in Vegas. After the call finished Bill was a given a big cocktail. When he asked what was in it, the bartender expressed how it was a wonderful blend of the world's finest ingredients, each one specifically chosen to help calm and relax the body and mind, allowing him to slowly drift into the best night's sleep he'll ever have. Along with the most life-like dreams that anyone could ever wish for, dreams that felt so real you'll question whether they were." Shelly interrupted and insisted she had one of those concoctions seeing as it sounded so lovely and refreshing, before inquiring what narcotics Marvin had been using to come up with such a ridiculous idea. He rebuffed her comment by reassuring her he was telling the truth and reminded her how his life depended on it. Marvin closed by telling her how after a quick bite to eat, the beverage took effect, and Bill drifted off into a wonderful deep sleep.

Tallulah grabbed the mic and thanked Marvin for his honesty whilst acknowledging his ability to keep a secret, then she demanded the mob made some din for the looming challenge which was about to begin. The venue's enthusiasm overflowed with the prospect of something gruesome about to happen, and as the host invited Shelly to take centre stage, the wheel started to materialize. Once she was in position Tallulah queried her thoughts so far. "I'm enjoying myself, free booze, good food, half decent entertainment, but I tell you now if it's sex toys that Bill's got me, then I hope to god I've picked him as judging by what I've seen so far, he's certainly getting his just rewards." The gang adored this remark and banged uncontrollably on the tables while hailing Shelly's name. The host restored order by directing Shelly to grab hold of another knob, she obliged and span the wheel like in the past. As it span the usual chants reverberated from the crowd, 'survival and twelve', and the big circle appeared to speed up just before it ground to a halt when it reached 'Off ground tick'. Shelly jumped for joy with her choice whilst yelling out informing everyone how much she enjoys playing this game. Tallulah revealed how she would ask Shelly if she'd still like to play after she'd viewed their version. The laughing of the gathering was ear-splitting, even though they were absolutely unaware of what they were about to witness, so they urged Tallulah to get on with it and not take a break. She agreed as long as one million dollars was placed in bets within the next sixty seconds. Following on from this, she encouraged the horde to reveal their phones and commence betting once the countdown had ceased. 10-9-8-7-6-5-4-3-2-1, BET! Twenty seconds had elapsed, when the screens filled with the amount raised so far, $80721 then the group became extremely active from everyone frantically striving to reach their goal. However, the screen refreshed after forty seconds to reveal a disappointing $238542, so Tallulah took to the mic and enthusiastically encouraged everyone to bet some more seeing as time was against them. It worked and after another twenty seconds the screen flashed $1287632. Mission accomplished and the host encouraged everyone to give themselves a big pat on the back for making some lucky bookmakers night.

The wheel had been replaced by the screen during their little flutter, and while Tallulah took to the microphone to explain the new rules, the screen lit with the site of Bernard bound and gagged alone. Again he was covered from head to toe in red, apart from his weapon, which was erect and pointing towards space. As the camera whizzed in and the horde sighed with disbelief when they caught site of Bernard's bright red unchained swollen prince. Then Tallulah educated everyone how Bernard had been given a little assistance via the form of a 'Dallas Pill', in order to prevent his warhead from aiming for the floor, because if it did, he'd fail. She concluded how he must also remain seated with his feet off the floor at all times. The camera rocketed out providing a clear view of the entire arena and to Bernard's right, sat a solitary black chair. It was quite a big one with a high back and slender base which were both covered with lots of shiny pointy things protruding out. Then a very large naked lady holding a whip in her left hand appeared and whacked him on his rear, thus instigating his body to tremble from the sudden pain, so she ushered him to have a seat, which he did, and his body winced with pain after it had been simultaneously stabbed by thousands of tiny little pricks. The whip lady made sure he was resting comfortably, by taking a seat and having a little bounce. Bernard's body cramped from the prickling pain throughout, then to his relief she stood up. However, his relief didn't last for long as the pain in his penis intensified when he heard the crack of the whip and the group springing into life with a synchronised "Ouch." Fiercely the lady hit it yet again, and again and again, so the camera zoomed in and paid specific attention to the swelling around his prince, before moving to decipher it's angle. Bernard was doing well it hadn't drooped at all. However, with her last whip she made direct contact with the prince's crown and Bernard's body rocketed while his feet narrowly avoided contacting the ground.

The screens turned blank and Tallulah quizzed Shelly's opinion on 'Bernard's Prince'. "Sore and painful, which is just what he deserves if he's got me sex toys." Tallulah chuckled from her response; she was feeling proud with her efforts of orchestrating the drama so far. Her chuckling crashed to an abrupt end when the screen revealed the sight of Bernard on his throne surrounded by a dozen stands, each one varied in height and bore a different sized burning candle upon it. An even larger naked lady entered and made a bee line for Bernard's knee, upon arrival she bobbled hard and Bernard's body was lifeless; unable to move a muscle whilst being pinned so firmly, but luckily for Bernard the lady gave up after completing a few firm bounces. She stood and grabbed the biggest candle before placing it directly above the base of Bernard's love tool. Then she wobbled her assets directly in his face, prior to tilting the wax light sideways. Bernard's body solidified; the crowd could sense his pain when they witnessed his teeth sink deep into his muzzle, and to his credit, Bernard was doing incredibly well considering his discomfort whilst having somehow managed to remain gratified. Unsatisfied with her feeble attempt the lady tried again, only this time with two approximately halfway up his shaft. When his body congealed and hands clenched, the lady smiled, while she observed his rocket dip slightly towards the floor, but before replacing her candles on their stands, she decided to rest her legs and take her vast weight from her feet with a well-earned leap. Rest over and it was her final attempt to succeed, and for it she chose both big and little. After impressing the crowd with her wobbly twirl, she went straight for the jugular by repeatedly alternating between huge and modest as she poured the wax directly on Albert. The gathering applauded after Bernard came his closest yet to failure, when his feet missed the floor with just a few millimetres to spare, but somehow, he'd managed to still stay proud. After one final close up of Bernard's battered bits all of the screens turned blank.

Tallulah queried her distinguished guest for her thoughts. "Not painful enough for that dirty little bastard," she retorted, whilst instantaneously the screens brightened

189

again revealing Bernard's swollen prince. The camera
sped out and focussed on a giant of a lady pounding her
way. Her huge mass appeared completely naked;
however it wasn't, it was covered by a thick carpet of
hair. In her right hand she grasped a purple super soaker
size dildo, then as she pointed it towards Bernard and
offered it a big squeeze, a lightning bolt raced from one
bell end to another. Bernard's body shuddered after it
made contact, and the conference roared with approval
after witnessing such a barbaric act. As the lady
inspected it closely the camera whizzed in on his now
enormously bloated plum prince, before she took the
weight off her feet by standing on his thighs, thus forcing
Bernard's base to experience thousands of tiny pricks.
You could tell how much pain he was suffering by the
way his cheeks bulged from his mask and after another
brief bounce the lady inspected his organ again; seeing
how sore it looked she decided to kiss it better. Whilst
she bent over and introduced it to her mouth, her head
remained motionless while her cheeks repeatedly puffed
in and then out. Satisfied that her embrace had worked,
and Bernard was well on his way to defeat, she stepped
back and gave her penis an extensive squeeze. Bernard's
body shook violently and resembled somebody fitting,
and when his body had reverted to its normal posture the
lady re-examined his bits. Excitedly she jumped into the
air to celebrate her victory when his weapon momentarily
pointed down. However, her celebrations were premature
when she looked again and saw Bernard had recovered
and remained impatient for more. She obliged by
bending over and sinking her teeth deep into the end of

his proud sword, and the audience cried out a synchronized "Ouch," when she pulled away to reveal her perfect pattern. Conscious her time was running out, and determined to succeed in bringing Bernard down, she placed his penis inside her sweaty cleavage and bounced up and down like her life depended on it. Bernard did well to retain his stamina, even though he must have been in some considerable pain after what he'd withstood so far in this horrendous test. But little did he know that the worst was yet to come, when the lady turned towards the camera and gave the audience a bobbly twirl, then she aimed her penis directly at Bernard's shiny ring and pressed her button for what seemed like infinity. His body stiffened, then shook dynamically, before collapsing limp; he'd passed out from the pain, but somehow had still managed to win. The screens became obscure and the crowd applauded while Tallulah congratulated Bernard on his resounding success, she then notified Shelly that in doing so he'd added another four million dollars to her clothes fund. Shelly became ecstatic with the thought of winning such an enormous amount and she displayed her excitement by waving towards the group, before interrogating Tallulah whether Bill had really bought her sex toys. Tallulah smirked as she countered. "You're not allowed to ask questions, remember Shelly, so I can't answer that I'm afraid and you'll have to figure it out for yourself." Someone in the group shouted out, "he has," then the host demanded silence again because she still had her tale to tell.

"Now Shelly, let me tell you what happened to those poor ten men who'd been driven out of their homes by your father and you, well that's how they see it anyway. What happened in your barn that night had awoken them sexually, so to speak, and they wanted to explore their horizons some more when they arrived in the big bad city, but they had to adapt very quickly to survive. Between them they managed to scramble enough dollar together and acquire a video camera. However being the eighties, it was extremely heavy and large. Vincent then came up with the idea of advertising in the adult magazines offering a free of charge satisfaction service for lonely housewives; so long as the men got to keep any revenue from potential sales. It was an instant success and they soon found themselves very popular with all of the ladies throughout Dallas. Vincent never performed though; he'd always do the filming and continuously remained anonymous by being unrecognisable in his director's costume. None of the other men really knew why Vincent would never been seen out in public without wearing some sort of disguise. I wonder if you have idea Shelly?" The horde sighed as they waited for her reply, however, Shelly's mind was still full of thoughts about being married to a pervert when she muttered, "was it because he was an ugly bastard?" The mob adored this remark, however Tallulah didn't, and she showed her disapproval by yelling at Shelly for being so cruel all those years ago. Tallulah then educated her how the remarks she made to Vincent, about only letting him if she didn't have to look at his face, have stuck with him right throughout his life, and that's why to this day, he's never seen in public without being dressed in some sort of costume. The audience screamed "bitch" and became quite intimidating towards her. Thankfully, Tallulah calmed things down by announcing a well-earned break, before declaring that as a reward for being such a friendly swarm, all of the champagne for the rest of the night would be on the house. The gatherings hostility's soon turned to joy when waiters emerged from nowhere and distributed a magnum or two for every table.

Chapter 16

You're lying

Shelly seized on the opportunity to pay another visit to the toilet, as did the glamorous host, and after an uneventful journey Shelly quizzed Tallulah regarding the sex toys once more, she gave in and muttered in her lobe. "Darling you know I'm telling the truth when I tell you he's got a big purple one, and I hope you enjoy as much as Sandy did." Shelly's body froze while she digested what she'd just learnt before she sounded her reply. "The cheeky bastard, he's got me a used dildo for a present! I'm getting a divorce; I do hope Conner's OK." Shelly was eager to get the next contest out of the way; her thoughts had turned to Conner and the life that she now had planned for them, therefore the ladies powdered their noses prior to returning to the stage. When the lights dimmed Tallulah took to the Mic. "Ladies and gentlemen, can I have your attention please, since I've a declaration to make. Shelly knows what her presents are; I've just snitched, and she now wants a divorce." The gathering hailed this news, and several invited her to worship the cult. Sadly, she declined before the host introduced Sandy once again to carry on telling Bill's tale. The crowd booed Shelly's refusal while Sandy swapped her seat on the stage, finding herself sat comfortably beside Shelly once again, she began to educate everyone regarding Bill's Friday night in Dallas. "I discovered Bill had been sent to the orgy room for the night, and I was desperate to see him and make up for the part I'd played in his earlier entrapment. I don't know what had come over me, but for some reason I was unequivocally falling for him. Understanding he'd be facing certain death the following day; I charmed the sentries into letting me in by stating that I was attempting to figure out who the real Marvin was. After I'd entered with a couple of drinks and used my trinkets on him, it didn't take long for the little something I'd put in his drink to take effect and soon he was having a snore. Then I turned my attentions to Bill who was lay fast asleep on the bed, so I mouthed in his ear how sorry I was for snaring him, and not to trust Marvin as he isn't who he appears to be prior to insisting for him only to trust me. I concluded by telling him about your deception, along with the danger that he was in, and that the only way to triumph was to kill the queen. I couldn't help myself with what happened next, and without going into too much detail, Bill and I had amazing sex." The audience praised her upon hearing this, cries of "your majesty" resonated around the room whilst Shelly took to the mic notifying Sandy, that in order to believe her confession over Bill's adultery, then she'd require a bit more detail. The crowd appreciated this statement and they cheered and chanted Shelly's name. Sandy then asked if she was sure. Shelly concurred, so Sandy did what she'd been invited to.

"I unzipped his pants and became awakened with what I found, then once I'd stood and stripped naked, I straddled him; this startled him, and he awoke to the sight of my sizeable beasts inches from his face, so I inserted my pierced nipple into his mouth, where it stayed for a while, and to my delight, he nibbled and sucked away adequately. After I'd removed my bullet and substituted it with my vagina against his moist lips, I started to moan when his tongue penetrated, and the deeper it went the more I groaned. Soon afterwards I rotated my body and wiggled Bill's trousers over his hips, and I Instantly realised how excited he was with the sight that welcomed me. At this point I was gushing and grabbed hold of his weapon and gave it a gentle rub before inserting into my mouth; it didn't take long for it to go off. Bill was lying motionless whereas I wanted more, so I got to work on his wobbly weapon with my breasts and before long, it was rigid. By now I was desperate to sense him inside me; hence I squatted down upon him, then I let out a great big scream when his mighty sword inflicted it's punishment for the first time. Whenever I reached the lowest point of my squat, Bill thrust his hips towards the sky and this rhythm continued until I could feel it was nearly time for Bill's second twinkling of the night. Thankfully, I managed to catch it all to ensure no evidence of my visit was left behind. I then turned around to help Bill have a bird's eye view of my monsters bouncing uncontrollably whilst I continued to squat, the more of Bill's excitement I could feel, the hornier I got, until without warning he exploded right inside me. At that moment I uttered in his ear with concern seeing how I wasn't taking precautions."

"By now I was rampant, so I stripped him naked before toddling off to get some accessories and I returned not long after holding a bag and a whip. Then I placed the bag on the floor and whacked his tackle with the whip. However, disappointedly it shrank! In anger with the prospect of my nights pleasure being brought to an abrupt end I repeatedly struck fiercely, he must have liked this and before long, it was proud again. When I placed the whip down on the bed and picked out some strawberries and cream from the bag, his face was a picture. Next, I covered his nipple with cream and placed a big strawberry on the top, before I licked away the cream. Finally I picked up the strawberry with my mouth and squashed it prior to releasing all of my created juices over his erect tower. After I'd received great pleasure from doing a very good job of cleaning him up it was my turn, therefore I lay beside him while he repaid the compliment. Bill was enthusiastically dining when his fingers began to wonder while he tackled the strawberry, and in no time, it was gone. Thus resulting in my almighty scream. After dessert, his fingers continued exploring, until he replaced them with his tongue. What a treat that was, your husband certainly knows how to use his, then I couldn't help myself when I grabbed the back of his head and pushed it down with all of my might. Ultimately, he broke free of my grip, and with the sight of my legs wide open he couldn't resist, and he propelled himself inside me for the final time."

The bunch offered Sandy a standing ovation, they were extremely appreciative with the quantity of detail. Tallulah then inquired how Shelly was feeling towards Bill after Sandy's graphic confession, as a result she stood up and grabbed the mic to give her reply. "Now I know that you're lying to me, there's no way on this earth that Bill could perform like that, and if you're telling the truth then I feel hard done to seeing as he's never played like that with me." Everyone chuckled at her response while the wheel moved into position and when Shelly joined it the crowd became lively as she clutched hold of another big knob. Round and round the wheel went, and it seemed like it was accelerating faster with each spin while everyone repeatedly shouted 'Twisted' whenever it climbed high. The big circle came to an abrupt halt and the crowd cheered with what they saw; the pointer clearly pointing towards one of their favourites, 'Head to Toe'. While the screen substituted the wheel, Tallulah queried Shelly for her thoughts as to what this challenge may entail, the crowd laughed loudly at her reply. "I've absolutely no idea what you sick bastards have in store, but I bet you it involves poor Bernard in his red gimp suit." No sooner had she finished, up popped poor Bernard dressed exactly like Shelly had described. However this time, completely covered in red from head to toe, with his arms confined to his sides. The camera whizzed in on his hidden prince and the crowd sighed when they caught sight of his gigantic jewels hidden underneath his protective layer.

The camera zipped out to reveal a bed of nails on the floor to his left while Tallulah took to the mic and provided Bernard with an account of what he needed to do. "This one's easy my dear, you only have to do one thing, and that's not bleed." The camera switched focus to the petite oriental lady who entered the room, she was stripped apart from a pair of purple shin length lilac boots. When she stood next to Bernard, she greeted him by giving his bulge a firm squeeze, prior to laying him down in his starting position. Getting prepared herself, she positioned her body at the foot of the bed before raising her right boot in the air. Where it hovered for a short while before it came crashing down on his right leg. Bernard's body didn't move, and the crowd remained hushed until she repeated her actions with her left. Then when his upper body momentarily jerked skywards prior to returning to earth, the troop roared with delight when she took her next stride and her right boot landed right on top of his prince. Bernard's head shuddered from side to side; it was the only part of his body that was able to move freely, while the lady relocated her right foot by rotating it a little before she moved her left and stamped it down upon his chest. Poor Bernard's legs rose from his bed and his head shook forcefully when her right one met her left. After remaining stationary for a while, the oriental lady checked to see if victory was hers by dismounting Bernard and assisting him up from his bed. Then she made him perform a little pirouette for the cameras whilst encouraging them to zip in on the hundreds of little holes to verify the result. The victory was Bernard's, so the lucky bugger got to fight another round.

The camera zoomed out and focussed on the tall lady who had just arrived, she was also bare apart from a pair of purple wedges. After giving Bernard another grab for a greet, she violently dragged him to his nails and forcefully hurled him upon them. Using her wedges she checked to make sure he was lying comfortably, which he was, therefore her battle could commence. While stood behind him, as viewed from the screen, she lifted her left leg high, then stamped it down as powerful as possible bang on top of 'Bernard's bits' and his body arched from the pain she'd just inflicted. However, not content with her punishment, the tall lady pushed down hard on her left foot while she drifted her right directly above his chest, where she balanced one footed for a short while. Poor Bernard's body remained unresponsive whilst she did, as it did when she went for the jugular and stamped down hard, before rocking her hips from side to side. Detecting victory she terminated her hostility's and hauled Bernard to his feet, thus allowing the cameras to decide which one was victorious. The gang let out an enormous sigh at the sight of poor Bernard's backside, it was riddled in holes, as was his limbs and back. Though, the sighs turned to cheers with the sight of no blood, thus confirming that poor Bernard could potentially go the distance. The camera whizzed out for the final time and focused on the extremely large lady who was now present alongside him. Then it rocketed in again to reveal the size of the heels on her very high and pointy plum stilettos. The large lady greeted Bernard with a punch to his prince, prior to picking him up and tossing him on his bed with all of the muscle she could muster. There was a loud thud when his body connected, and he lay limp until the large lady repositioned herself into the same starting position as the previous one, then she raised her left heel before digging it right into Bernard's left groin. He didn't move a muscle, so someone in the crowd shouted, "She's killed him!" Luckily for them she hadn't, and his body flinched back to life with her next move, when she repositioned it into his left shin. With his upper torso raised, the throng could sympathise with his pain by observing the clenching of his teeth. Once his body lowered the large lady snatched her opportunity for success and jumped for joy whilst aiming to land near Bernard's crown and neck. The group roared while they observed Bill's lifeless body being dragged from his bed. Barely conscious and unable to stand, the large lady propped him up for the judges to announce their decision, she swiftly let go with the sight of no blood. The screen darkened and the crowd applauded while Tallulah took to the Mic, expressing how concerned she was feeling towards Bernard and hoped he'd be OK to carry on before she swivelled her body towards Shelly and congratulated her on the prize fund increasing by another eight million dollars. The mob turned wild, along with Shelly who was leaping in the air, revelling with the thought of her new lifestyle. Tallulah then requested for some order to be restored while she continued to tell the outcasts story.

"Vincent turned into the money man and came up with lots more cunning programs, all to do with sex. Their next venture came in the form of chatlines and they make an absolute fortune from these to this day. Quite early on in the phone sex industry they realised the world was populated with sick bastards who got their weird fantasies satisfied whilst clasping a phone. Then somehow, they discovered the creepier the fantasy the more they could charge, consequently that's what they did, and it wasn't long before they found themselves running the entire porn industry in Texas. From this they founded the cult for other like-minded disturbed individuals and our numbers swiftly swelled. Nevertheless, despite Vincent being positioned at the top, he never personally attends any of our gatherings, and opts to send a representative instead. So in one-way Vincent's got a lot to thank you for, by giving him the inspiration to make his fortune. Though, I'm sure he'll never be able to forgive you for having to live his whole life behind a mask, following the complex that your remark gave him nearly thirty years ago." The horde roared with applause when Tallulah closed prior to quizzing Shelly whether she believed them yet. Fifty-fifty was her response, before reiterating how Bill better not have bought her any toys. The chamber then crammed with cheers when the host announced yet another short intermission.

Chapter 17

We need a plan now!

The recess was a short one, less than five minutes in fact, when a tone in Tallulah's ear urged her to hurry because poor Bernard was in an horrific state, and if she didn't get a move on, then there was a good chance that poor Bernard may be no more. Sprinting back to the stage she urged the audience for silence whilst the next challenge got under way. After a flurry of activity while the mob re-took to their seats, the room fell still when Tallulah took to the Mic. "Shelly my darling, poor Bernard is a bit worse for wear and we're going to have to speed things up in order for you to win, so for the next part of Bill's journey I'm going to invite back someone who was there. Now ladies and gentlemen can I please have a big round of applause for Marvin who's going to tell you briefly, what happened next." The crowd recited his name while he sat down beside Shelly. However upon grabbing her hands, he sensed the hostility which she now bore towards him, when she swiftly pulled away. Un-fazed, he took to the mic and started to rationalize.

"Bill woke around 11 AM after what I thought had been an uneventful night for him, and whilst he was having breakfast one of my colleagues interrupted when he came running in with a phone, instructing Bill to answer. He failed and had to call you back before the pair of you had a brief conversation. After you eventually picked-up that is. While my colleague was leaving the room with Bill's phone someone recommended playing a game of cards to kill some time by having a game of truth or dare, and luckily for us, my colleague agreed to return with some nice ones from the store. Before he left, Bill asked for the toilet and was informed where he could find it. However, he was gone for a while and returned a very frightened man. Upon retaking his seat he confessed about Sandy's visit, and how he thought it was a dream at first; until he'd just discovered the bag which she'd used on his way to the toilet, and it contained a gun. Then he broke down and asked me to retrieve it, so I could put a bullet in him right away. Thankfully, I managed to calm him down by going to have a look for it myself once I'd advised him that it was only in his dream; I believed I'd been watching guard over him all night at this point. I searched high and low for the bag, but I couldn't find it. However, Bill thought I was fibbing and insisted on having another peek for himself. He didn't get far when six of my heavily armed colleagues burst through the door updating us that due to a change of strategy, we were leaving for Vegas immediately. I can remember Bill picking up the pack of cards from the table, though I can't remember at what point my colleague had returned with them."

"Then they led us into an elevator to meet a waiting chopper on the roof, and when one of my colleagues inquired regarding our importance to the boss, they gave us the impression that something big was happening due to their snouts chatter. The helicopter ride was uneventful until we were forcibly evicted at the other end, and after sighting the waiting aircraft not far away we were told to run; my colleagues had been given orders to shoot any stragglers, so to speak. Then as we approached nearby, I heard gunfire, but I didn't dare look to see from which direction it was coming whilst I ran as swiftly as I could. I desperately sought the safety of the jet and luckily within sixty seconds of succeeding, we were airborne. While Bill vanished to the toilet, I took the opportunity to get a quick forty winks. Then about an hour later I awoke and became startled to find Bill still hadn't returned, so I hunted for him and found him in the bathroom; I think he was asleep, and I surprised him. He was determined to play his game of cards, consequently I agreed but only if it was limited to just three hands of twenty one's. I won the first two and questioned what Sandy had said to him and whether he believed you'd been playing around. Bill won the final hand and asked me who I really was, so I told him that I'm not a happily married man like I portray, that in fact I'm lonely within my marriage, with no friends only work colleagues, therefore I suppose I'm one of those people who are married to their job, and perhaps that's what Sandy meant. But I assured him that he could trust me, and when I asked him whether he did, he smiled before going for a shower. I took this as a come on and thought he might be Bi like me, so when I joined him, I whispered sweet nothings in his ear about my feelings for him. Sadly, he didn't feel the same and departed. We haven't spoken since, we remained in silence for the rest of the journey and upon our arrival here, a big room awaited were we joined two others and sat in silence while waiting for our audience with the boss."

Tallulah commended Marvin on recalling such a fine tale and acknowledged his honesty, especially for having the audacity to 'come out'. The horde responded to Tallulah's pun by providing a great big growl, before she span towards Shelly and queried her nerves. "When will Bill be back?" she retorted, and quick as a flash, Tallulah countered. "If you believe what we're saying then he's already here darling, only none of us know if he's poor Bernard or the lucky Gimp who's currently residing in my luxurious office. Only you can possibly know" The gathering celebrated her remark and chanted loudly, "he's Bernard." The stage then filled with noise while the wheel appeared, and the lights extinguished. The room silenced with what Shelly had to do, only this time she stretched for the big one at the top, then wrestled it with both her hands, prior to giving it a big yank. Then an embarrassed Shelly nearly fell flat on her face when she let go and it rotated for a perpetuity before it came to a gradual halt on 'Twelve'. The crowd turned silly, bar the queen, this was their favourite, therefore Tallulah quizzed Shelly for her thoughts. "I haven't got a clue, but I bet it's painful for poor old Bernard" she replied. The big circle developed into a screen and when it brightened Bernard was nowhere to be seen. A shocked Tallulah urged the group to create heaps of noise, seeing how

Bernard was scared and needed encouragement to re-appear. The mob did as requested and went nuts whilst jumping, clapping, chanting, and whistling away, so Tallulah seized the opportunity to talk into her ring and inquire as to Bernard's whereabouts. She didn't like the response. "He's finished, doctor's just given him something to liven him up, but it'll probably take about an hour to kick in, possibly longer seeing as he's that far gone." Tallulah instructed them to get the other Gimp from her office and substitute Bernard, although she was rightfully informed by the voice in her ear, how this wouldn't work whilst reserve Bernard was missing one vital thing, hence she ordered his immediate crowning. However, the voice delivered more bad news by alerting her that the piercer was now pissed and wouldn't be able to perform. Realising the other Bernard was of no use anymore, she warned her ring that she would send someone up soon to take care of the alternative Gimp once and for all.

Tallulah insisted on calm, while she sadly broke some dreadful news, the masses spirits were dampened when she announced the end of the contest since poor Bernard had thrown in the towel. Shifting towards Shelly, she passed on her condolences regarding the sad news of her loss and recommended that she go and party with her new pals like it was her last night alive. Shelly then stood up and boldly screamed. "What do you mean I've won nothing. You go and tell Bernard from me that he'd better get his bloody arse into gear and win me my money." The gathering booed at Shelly for showing her temper so freely, while the host clarified that Bernard was too badly injured to go on so therefore, as he was unable to continue, her cheque would be ripped into pieces because he hadn't overcome the wheel. Shelly stunned everyone with what she suggested next. "If Bernard can't fucking well compete then I will. I'll do anything for my bloody money!" Tallulah didn't know how to react; such a decision had never needed to of been taken before. Thinking on her feet, she responded by alerting her ring regarding an emergency meeting of the board in her office in five minutes. Cool as a cucumber, she addressed her gathering and told them about her requirement for some temporary unauthorised absence while she took care of some very important business which had just materialised. The crowd booed as she vacated the stage, and after Marvin had been ordered to follow, they hastily made their way in the elevator to the bosses office which was located within the very top floor. Upon opening the door they were greeted with the sight of the bosses nine business partners, all sat around a large blue oval table waiting for Tallulah to lead. She advised Marvin to take a seat and listen hard; now he could be trusted, she was considering enlisting him for an awfully important part to play later.

Tallulah took her seat as the head and began to chat. "Gentlemen what should we do? We all know it's highly irregular to let the challenge continue while the original contestant is still alive. However like you, I've been waiting years to get my revenge on that bitch and now we have our opportunity. Shelly's providing the congregation with lots of amusement and the betting profits are through the roof, so I personally think we should let her; I wouldn't mind nudging her again. Now I've never told you this before, but she's the only woman I've ever had sex with." The others gasped with disbelief upon hearing her news, Brian added how he wouldn't mind another go, then one by one the other eight all gave their opinions concerning Tallulah's suggestion. Everyone was in favour apart from Dick, who expressed severe doubts as to whether continuing the challenge was really necessary, because from where he was sitting, he saw no need; the cult members had lost lots and along with the TV rights, they should easily clear in excess of fifty million. He suggested the wiser thing to do would be to dispose of all three in the usual way, thus allowing the real partying to begin. An enraged Tallulah stood up before banging her hands hard on the table. The other's took note of her disapproval and pleaded for her to calm down, which she did, before revealing something that hopefully would make Dick change his opinion.

"Brothers, all of our lives we've looked out for each other and that's why we've got such a unique bond. You are all like real brothers to me. However, may I remind you who's the brains behind this operation and please, for once, look at things from my prospective. Only you have ever seen the real Vincent's face, for years I've had to cover up daily, whether it be as Tallulah, the boss or even old Mrs Brown, and none of you know what it's like having to hide your looks on top of the complex feelings it brings. That night in the barn you all got to have considerably more fun than me. I never got to see her breasts bouncing while she squatted on my missile, nor the orgasmic look in her eye. All I got was a quick BJ followed by a birds eye view of her arse, and that's what made me gay! Yes, you heard me I'm gay, and it's all down to her. I'm not fully gay, I give but never receive and I just want to be able to have the confidence to attract members of the opposite sex. Now I'm prepared to do a deal with you, Dick, my brother. If you agree to Shelly being allowed to take part, then I promise you, I will come out from hiding and reveal myself as Vincent to the whole cult forever. Please my comrade, back me and release me from the horrible life which I find myself trapped in."

Tallulah sat down and clutched her head between her hands, totally exhausted from the emotions that she'd just expressed. The other men sat silent and stared at Dick whilst they waited patiently for his answer, and after a short while it came. "OK I'm in, but on one condition, we're going to have to rethink the challenge as there's no way I'm standing getting touched up by another man dressed in a gimp suit while waiting to see if my knob gets hard, before letting him suck me off, any suggestions anyone?" The room fell silent for a good five minutes while everyone racked their brains trying to conjure up a suitable alternative, then Michael broke the silence with his suggestion. "Why don't we torture the bitch, beat her black and blue like her father did to us, then let the queen finish her." You could see Tallulah's dissatisfaction with his proposal by the look in her eyes, luckily, she managed to control her anger and calmly offered her thoughts. "I'm not looking to hurt Shelly. I just want to be able to look a woman in the eyes while I take her to heaven. That woman's remark has prevented me from having that privilege all of my life, so we need to think of a challenge that will enable this. Please gents help me find a way. I'm tired of hiding and I just want to be able to lead a normal life." The room hushed again prior to Marvin querying whether he could suggest something. The partners all looked towards their chairman of the board and left the decision to her. She agreed and for the second time that weekend Marvin explained his plan.

"I think I know a way how you can take full advantage of the situation and make a lot more dollar from the crowd whilst each one of you remains anonymous. You'll all get to pleasure Shelly one more time and it will also freak the fuck out of her if she succeeds. However, more importantly, it will hopefully help Tallulah bury her complex." She interrupted, by telling him how she now liked him and the way that his mind functioned, before promising a big promotion if it was decent and worked. He resumed. "OK, please hear me out fully and then you can comment. You change the challenge to ten, blindfold and handcuff her naked to a frame then, instruct her to do it like the dogs do, one by one, with each of the ten life like statues that have just entered the room. That's you nine plus Tallulah. Tell her the truth about Vincent being present in the room and to win she has to guess which cock is his. A waving of her right hand will indicate when she believes it's Vincent's, or her left one if she believes it isn't. Whoever is chosen then gets the privilege of watching her squat on their knee prior to Shelly uncovering her eyes. The look on her face will be priceless if she guesses right. Hopefully if she does boss, this will help you find the closure that you seek for her horrible comments from the barn." The room instantaneously filled with applause once Marvin had finished, whilst everyone present showed their approval for his proposal and Tallulah expressed how glad she was that she'd not disposed of him earlier, seeing he was now proving to be an invaluable asset. Brian saw a slight flaw in Marvin's plan and queried Tallulah who would host in her absence. "Marvin" she said, whilst spinning towards him, "You can host the show, it's easy, all you have to do is entertain the pack for half an hour while my brothers get improved. Only joking boys. I'll give you my ring and earpiece so we can communicate when we're ready for Shelly to be brought to the arena. Then I'll take good care of her from there. Are we all agreed? All those in favour raise your right hand in the air?" It was a unanimous vote, hence Tallulah handed Marvin her equipment and ordered him to entertain the crowd. "Just one slight problem" Marvin warned, "I don't know where the arena is." Tallulah approached him and whispered. "It's behind the cash office, seeing as that's the most secure place in the building, but you'll need the code 682034 to get in. However make sure you get it right as you only get three attempts before a 50000-volt electric shock will fry you on the spot. When you enter, you'll observe a door on the very far wall, go through it, turn left and it's the fourth door on the right. Oh one last thing, when you get back to the stage tell Sandy it's time for her to go and get changed into something a bit more appropriate, and whatever she does, make sure she kills him; she'll know what I mean. Now what's the code?" Fortunately, Marvin had a very good memory and correctly repeated it before navigating his way back to the stage.

The atmosphere in the venue electrified with the sight of Marvin returning alone, and upon his arrival back on the stage, he did exactly as instructed and repeated Tallulah's orders to Sandy. When he picked up the microphone, he was a bit nervous about being the host, consequently he started to speak in a soft calming voice. "Ladies and gentlemen, can I have your attention please, I've got a very important declaration to make." The silence was golden, the audience desperately wanted to know if the show would go on, so Marvin resumed. "Shelly, I have some good news for you, an adapted version of 'Twelve', which will now be called 'Ten', has been approved by our hierarchy. For the show to continue I need your agreement to participate, hence everyone, including you Shelly, please remain quiet while I explain." The audience respected Marvin's request and remained mute. "Shelly if you agree and keep your odds of winning big alive, you will be stripped naked, blindfolded, then bent

213

over and handcuffed to a frame. You will then be joined
in the room by ten life like statues who, one by one, and
in your owns words may I add, 'will do it to you like the
dogs do'. One of these ten will be Vincent and all that
you've got to do is wave your right hand when you think
it's him behind you, or your left one if it isn't. Whoever
you choose will take a seat while you get freed from your
frame, then you'll be invited to squat on his knee. Once
you've had enough pleasure, you'll remove your
blindfold and if you've guessed right, you'll have
doubled the size of your cheque. What do you say about
that Shelly?" The audience erupted with the prospect of
seeing this new version of 'Twelve' by chanting Shelly's
name, they were eager for her response and it didn't take
long before it came. "So, I've got to go and have sex
with ten men and one of them is definitely Vincent, then
if I guess right, I get another sixteen million dollars?"
The audience screamed "yes" before Marvin gave his
confirmation. To the troops delight and with a smile on
her face Shelly stated, that as long as Bill or Conner
would never find out, she'll gladly do it seeing as she'd
know Vincent's cock anywhere, and how for years, she's
always dreamt about the day when she could experience
such an intense orgasm again, just like she did that night
with him.

The bunch transformed into the wildest they'd been all
night, now they finally knew the show would go on.
Marvin again requested silence while he explained about
the time which they now had to kill whilst the challenge

was getting prepared. He asked the audience for any suggestions as to what they could do and someone shouted, 'Off ground tick', then another 'Musical Chairs'. The recommendations came thick and fast until Marvin heard one that he liked the sound of, 'spin the bottle'. After retaking to the mic, he rotated towards Shelly and asked if she fancied playing? She didn't need much persuading and grabbed one of the empty champagne bottles from the table prior to placing it right in the middle of the floor. Excited at the prospect of getting naked, Shelly started to undress in order for her to obtain a slight advantage. Luckily, Marvin intervened before she had managed to get very far when he told her how it was a game of truth and whoever the bottle top pointed to, would have to answer a question from the audience. Truthfully! The throng exploded once they'd learnt this while the screens illuminated with the latest odds for this improvised game. Shelly then Marvin took to centre stage and knelt opposite each other with only the bottle between them. Marvin was a true gentleman and offered Shelly the first spin, so she clutched the bottle around its sides and rotated it hard in a clockwise direction. It span for three full circles before it halted pointing towards Marvin, and Shelly jumped for joy, clearly excited with the prospect of what question the audience had in mind.

Marvin stood up and broadcast for everybody to open their TRAS APP and enter their question in its big box, then he informed them how one of these will be picked at random by the computer for Shelly to ask. He concluded by placing a fifteen seconds time limit starting from now! Every individual in the room typed hectically while the screens counted down, and when it reached zero, the clock switched to Marvin's question. "Are you a giver or a taker?" The mob applauded the computers selection, then they fell silent when Shelly reminded Marvin, how he must tell the truth, before asking the question. "Neither, I've never had sex with a man, or even touched someone else's knob. I'm what they call bi-curious. I've thought about exploring this side of me, but until now, have never found the right opportunity." The audience celebrated Marvin's response while several shouted "come and see me later big boy." Marvin re-took his place opposite Shelly and executed his go. The bottle span for a good five or six times, before it stopped pointing directly towards Shelly. The audience took to their devices once more while the screen calculated down. Shelly became enthusiastic with the rooms activity, however, her enthusiasm turned to fear when her question replaced the clock. "How many times, apart from Conner, have you been unfaithful to Bill?"

Aware she had to tell the truth in order to win, she didn't know where to start. "You need to understand that I've got an extremely high sex drive and whenever I get the urge, I need it there and then. I think it was brought on by that night, because ever since I've longed to experience the length and girth of someone as enormous as Vincent. Bill was always busy doing odd jobs about the ranch and

216

was never there when I needed him most. I couldn't resist and every time a travelling salesman or a repair worker called, I had to see if they possessed what I'd been looking for. So in answer to the question, I would probably say about a hundred. Sorry make that a hundred and six, I forgot about the baggage carriers on the jet." The crowd hissed at her honesty, but they turned to laughter when someone screamed, "you'll do that many here tonight." Before the audience had chance to silence Shelly had her hand firmly around the bottle, eager to have another go. Then Marvin became startled and stood up when he heard a voice in his ear ordering him to fetch Shelly, and after requesting for her to stand, he announced to the gathering the imminent commencement of 'Ten'. Marvin then encouraged them to put their hands together as a way of showing some appreciation for Shelly while she made her way from the empty stage. Marvin didn't express anything to her on the way, she disgusted him since hearing her confession. Now knowing that he's risking his life for a slut, Marvin felt sympathy for his 'partner' Bill. Upon arriving at the cash office he warily entered the code and he knew it was right when he heard the big clunk before the fortress opened. They then entered the bosses money box only to be greeted by Sandy's man sandwiched between two others, and he was now sporting a black eye. Marvin was relieved of his escort duty when Sandy's man stated how they'd take over from here, since you needed privileged access to be able to witness where she was heading, and his had been rescinded. Reluctantly Marvin agreed, even though he was desperate to try and catch a glimpse of

Bernard so that he could see for himself, what sorry state he was really in. Disappointed, he made his way back to the stage and awaited further instructions.

After Marvin had regained his position on the stage it wasn't long before he heard a voice in his ear. "OK Marvin, push the bottom button on the Microphone and be careful not to get hit by the screen, then leave the rest to us. Marvin followed the voices guidance and the screen promptly filled the stage. When he stepped to the side, it illustrated the image of a naked Shelly sporting a blindfold with her hands restrained by a fluffy pair of red handcuffs, and she stood just as Bernard had before he'd commenced the evenings events. The males in the crowd shouted out several obscene comments about her melons while the camera whizzed out, and they witnessed Shelly being led by Tallulah towards a frame which was situated to her right. Once they'd arrived, she bent Shelly's body over it and firmly secured her wrists. The congregation then observed a side on view of the action, her large breasts were dangling down, and her firm backside pointed up. The camera then panned to the left, revealing the nine life like statues who were all dressed in red PVC suits which protected their identity's from head to toe, and each one bore a number on its back. The first statue walked towards Shelly's angled body and removed his dagger from hiding, and as he stabbed her, she moved slightly away. His pelvis repeatedly thrust energetically, but sadly he was unable to make her murmur and Shelly gesticulated with her left hand. Number one signalled to the mass as he departed, and as a result, number two replaced him. Shelly's body moved a bit farther than before when he started his display, and judging by her moans, it sounded like Shelly was enjoying his attention. Number two must have been performing for two minutes or more then Shelly howled out an enormous rumble prior to the flailing of her left hand. Number two waved with both hands while he withdrew, and clearly, he was very proud of his achievement. Number three took his place but didn't occupy it for very long, no sooner had he started he'd finished, and Shelly disappointedly shook with her left. He was replaced by number seven; one can only presume that numbers four, five and six had come over all shy, and when he slapped Shelly's firm backside hard, it's sound repeated thunderously through the loudspeakers. The crowd gave out a growl when he made his mark by sinking his teeth to leave a lasting impression. Shelly gave out a loud scream then demanded some more, so he obliged and gave her a matching one on her other cheek. After another quick slap he started to please and Shelly's body jerked with each new thrust that he made, whilst she moaned and squealed out loudly. The speedier he thrust, the rowdier she grumbled until eventually she let out one final whine followed swiftly by her left-hand waving in submission.

Number seven left and none of the others attempted to replace him, so Tallulah glanced towards the other statues and gestured for them to take their turn but all nine wobbled their heads. Tallulah didn't need any encouragement and as she stood behind Shelly, she gave the horde something to talk about, when she revealed her monstrous cock. She pushed Shelly's backside towards the floor and when he entered, her voice let out a sound like never before while her body banged heavily forward. The group knew Shelly was enjoying her pounding by the way she'd repositioned her hands firmly around the frame, thus helping her push out and allow Tallulah's weapon to further breach. It didn't take long for Shelly to make up her mind and frantically wave her right hand. However, the troop didn't know what to do, they were clearly frightened of retaliation if they made fun of Vincent's formal wear. Tallulah stepped back from Shelly's rear and shifted onto a chair which had been positioned on the opposite side of the room. Then number nine approached Shelly and removed her restraints, prior to guiding her to her prize. Shelly took ages to make the short journey, her lower back and backside twitched with every stride. Eventually number nine positioned her directly over Tallulah's sky-scrapper, and when her legs were either side of the chair a deafening high-pitched squeal filled the arena once he'd given her body a mighty downwards shove. Contact made and Tallulah was gifted with the sight of Shelly's large beasts, bobbing wildly while she took his extensive rod. Following heaps of screaming and crying out Shelly couldn't resist and aspired to know who the owner of such a treasured possession was, therefore, she removed her blindfold to reveal she was getting pleasured by a woman. Shelly's moaning continued and while squatting happily away, she muttered in Tallulah's ear. "I made a

220

mistake all those years ago by putting looks before length, and I vowed never to make that mistake again. I don't care how fucking ugly you are, or that you dress like a woman. All I'm interested in is your cock so give it to me harder NOW!" Encouraged by his newfound confidence since hearing Shelly's words, Tallulah flung off her wig and unfastened her mask, to reveal just how fucking ugly Vincent really was. The two of them carried on kissing and hissing sweet nothings in each other's ears until eventually all of the screens went clear.

Marvin found himself stood unaccompanied on the stage and seeing as he was the centre of attention the mob looked towards him whilst querying what happens next. Uncertain with the strategy, he chatted shit into the bosses ring, "ERRGH Hello, can anybody hear me? What should I do now?" He didn't get an answer, so he inquired again but a bit louder. A voice then appeared in his ear. "The boss is busy finishing off some historic business, just tell them we're going for a short break while we prepare for the final challenge." Marvin did precisely that prior to sitting down and while patiently waiting, his mind worried about poor Bernard, Conner and more importantly Bill.

Chapter 18

Goodbye our stunner

Shelly landed back on the stage first, appearing very happy and smug, she hit the bottle straight away; managing to sink two full glasses prior to Vincent enlisting. The gathering demonstrated their respect for Vincent's bravery by handing him their biggest praise of the night. When he took to the microphone as Vincent for the first time he conversed in a high-pitched squeal. "Ladies and gentlemen. I'm very pleased to personally meet you all for the first time tonight. What that woman sat over there took away from me she has finally given back tonight, and the only comment I've got to say on the matter is. I've got a lot of making up to do!" The crowd burst into jubilation before Vincent addressed the slut. "Now let's get back to business, may I congratulate you on having boosted another sixteen million dollars to your prize fund, so please give her a big cheer." The swarm did, and they made that much noise Shelly stood up to perform a pirouette. Once order had been restored Vincent inquired whether she liked the challenge; he didn't expect her reply. "Like it, I bloody loved it, and if the question at the end is who I am going home with, Conner, Bill, or someone else, then it would definitely be someone else, and that someone would be you! Now I've found what I've been looking for, there's no way I'm ever losing it again." Vincent acknowledged the compliment then commented how it would be best to abandon her decision until after the next trial, which would be getting under way once she's learnt about the final part of Bill's day.

Vincent subsequently commenced, "I was sitting in my study trying to make sense of all of the weird coincidences which the last few days had brought. I had questions that I wanted answering; from four incredibly different people. Conner, whose refusal of my payment aroused my suspicions. Marvin, whose friendship with an undercover FBI agent created stimulation in them. Sandy, who's visit to Bill last night well and truly produced orgasmic doubts, and finally Bill, who I wasn't suspicious of in the slightest; he was oblivious to everything and just transpired to be in the wrong place at the wrong time. As a consequence of this he's now encountering certain death. I'd decided to pop Marvin personally, a decision that I'm happy to have changed my opinion about; he's proving to be invaluable tonight. Bill's fate was set anyway, it was the big circle for him. Conner was to be leant on prior to getting discharged back to his country surroundings; but not until later because I wanted to do it personally. All I required was a suitable punishment for Sandy. I knew this had to be something special and risky, so I came up with something fitting after hearing her confession earlier, and she's currently preparing to fulfil it. Now if you were listening earlier then you'll already know what I'm about to say about your lover, Nevertheless, I'll repeat it again just in case you were too pissed and missed it. After Bill and I had a little chat about tonight he was dispatched to the bar to await his cue. However, he started to get a bit un-cooperative should we say and was declining to compete, so I had to come up with something quick to avoid a disaster, and that's when I then gave the order to put Conner on standby just in case Bill administered his threat. When Bill saw sense, I deviously thought how more fun it would be playing with two. I'm so glad I did; tonight's been so much fun, and the enjoyment is about to get a whole lot better. Now let us see if Bernard's up for the next challenge as we ask the beautiful, sexy Shelly to take her final spin of the night."

The cheering and chanting intensified whilst Shelly made her way across the stage; it erupted after Vincent smacked her on the arse, and in return, she gave him a little peck on the cheek. Shelly grabbed her nearest knob and gave it her biggest yank of the night. Vincent jokingly shouted "Ouch" as she did. The wheel didn't have chance to rotate fully before it landed on tonight's finale, 'Survival'. The atmosphere electrified upon seeing the circle's selection, they'd finally get to see the queen and whether poor Bernard could transmute into the first challenger ever to win. Vincent then invited Shelly to retake her seat while he explained the rules. To her shock when she acted, she was grabbed by four men and each of them stretched a limb and unquestionably secured it to the chair. Vincent approached the screaming Shelly and repaid her peck on the cheek whilst silencing her with a muzzle. Then he reported how sorry he was for what he was about to put her through and warned how her life now depended on poor Bernard murdering the queen. A struggling Shelly was desperate to wiggle free; to no avail, the four men had conducted a professional job in limiting her movement. With Shelly unable to scream out Vincent continued to clarify the rules. "For poor Bernard to survive he's got to assassinate our very own royalty, if not she'll slaughter him; that's why we ask our scouts to send us contestants who wouldn't be missed if they disappeared overnight. Regrettably, you've learnt far too much tonight that you shouldn't really know, so I'm left with no alternative but for you to end up in the same position as our reserve Bernard now finds himself; he's currently making his final journey. We don't appreciate which one of your lovers it is, only you conceivably can. Having seen his last sunrise, his fate is set and the only way you can live to see another, lands in poor Bernard's hands. If he achieves the impossible then you'll be an accessory to murder, and with that hanging over your head, you wouldn't dare have the courage to mention a thing to anybody. Would you!"

The audience ran wild when the screen replaced the wheel while Shelly's body constantly wiggled as she attempted to break free. The commotion intensified when the screens filled with the image of Bernard, unshackled in his starting position, fully covered in red from head to toe. Vincent took to the mic while he explained the regulations as the camera panned towards the red carpet to the left, and on it walked the queen of the cult dressed

225

in full costume, complete with her diamond tiara proudly on display. The screen dimmed momentarily before illuminating brightly with the sight of Bernard detained in a headlock, and his battered body shook whilst he wriggled to free himself from the queens grasp. Punching out, he was trying to connect with any available flesh and force her to relinquish her control. Fortunately for him, he got lucky when he hit the jackpot by landing his fist right in her Mary. A wounded Queen terminated her grip and poor Bernard managed to somehow wiggle free. He didn't get very far crawling across the floor when a loud crack echoed. The Queen had recovered and vaulted onto his torso with the full force of her mass, then she started to assault Bernard's PVC, striving to rip and slice it as best she could. He wasn't defeated yet and whilst she proceeded to stamp down on his head, he managed to grab her leg and twist. This knocked her off balance and Bernard succeeded in wrestling her to the floor. Whilst wiggling on top he tried his best to smother, prior to placing his shovels around her collar and squeezing with every ounce of strength that he could muster. The queen was on the ropes, and her torso twisted sporadically in numerous directions whilst she tried to crack Bernard's grasp. He abruptly let go once the queen had managed to grab hold of his prince and violently shake it from side to side. Bernard was crouched over comforting his crown jewels when the queens right fist connected with his left temple and slammed him to the ground. His body lay unresponsive while she weighed in with a torrent of activity, punching, kicking, biting, and even stamping on it. The mob were joyous in their celebrations while

226

willing their monarch to another resounding victory. However, Bernard wasn't kaput, while the queen took her victory bow, somehow Bernard found the strength to not only stand up but run across the room and remove the weapon from the wall.

Now the queen was worried when she was weapon-less against his mighty sword and he approached while swinging it from side to side, before scoring a direct hit. The monarch winced, then cried out in pain after he'd poked her, but luckily by spiting in his face she avoided being on the receiving end again and managed to liberate herself from his control. This was turning into an entertaining battle for the congregation, and a very lucrative one for Vincent and his 'brothers'. The activity from the hordes betting on their gadgets became immense when the screens displayed the current odds, and for the first time in the cults history, the contender was the favourite. Bernard's energy had dwindled; probably caused by the pain he was suffering from the wounds he'd sustained whilst performing his epic game. The queen stood next to the cage as far away from Bernard's warhead as she possibly could; fearful of the damage that it might inflict. When Bernard somehow summonsed his inner strength and galloped towards her with his weapon standing proudly in front, then just as he was about to shove, the chamber exploded with gunfire and heaps of men shouting "FBI, don't move or we'll shoot." Marvin stood up and accosted Vincent and yelled for him to order the battle to cease. He responded by chucking the mic towards the floor; smashing into several big pieces when it made contact. Marvin's sight became distracted with what he witnessed on the screen; Bernard was lying limp on the floor with his weapon beside him. The queen then wrapped her rods tightly around his collar and using all of her royal superpowers, and unusually for her, she crossed her legs. Marvin raced from the stage, unchallenged by the agents whilst making his way to the arena, and the cameras were still rolling despite several attempts by the Bureau to disrupt the transmission. Everybody in the room's eyes were preoccupied with the image of the queen being only seconds away from gaining another notch on her killing board. They cheered, and her victory was secured, when she picked up Bernard's weapon and returned his earlier poke. The queen had triumphed in doing her duty for the cult and was joyous in her celebration's, utterly unaware of the drama which was unfolding elsewhere. Her festivities were disrupted when Marvin stormed in. As a result she hastily grabbed Bernard's weapon and sought to defend herself from Marvin's advances, but he took one look at her and managed to swerve her incoming poke, prior to knocking her promptly to the ground with his sharpest right hook. Then he made his way over to Bernard to check for a pulse. There wasn't one. Marvin hadn't realised the cameras were still rolling when he began to strip Bernard from his muzzle and mask. He was anxious with not knowing who's face he was about to reveal; hoping it wasn't Bill's and his death had not been gruesome like Bernard's. His face filled with relief when he didn't recognise him. However Shelly, who'd been watching the whole ceremony live, started to cry when she did. Then everyone in the audience caught one final glimpse of Bernard before someone finally managed to terminate the transmission.

Marvin was stationery, and somewhat relieved at the remote prospect of Bill still being alive. He examined Sandy's body for a pulse, there wasn't one, so he hastily tried to remove her mask and administer the magic kiss. He froze when he realised it wasn't her stunning looks staring back. All of a sudden, he remembered what Tallulah had earlier spoke, how it's time for Sandy to go and get changed into something a bit more appropriate, and whatever she does make sure she kills him, she'll know what I mean. Sandy wasn't the queen; he'd put two and two together and couldn't count. Marvin had presumed the boss was telling her to get dressed as the queen and make sure she killed Bernard. The penny dropped when he realised, she was actually getting into something less glamorous, so she could blend in on her journey to the country. Thinking rapidly, he recalled how during one of Tallulah's earlier lessons, she'd reported how the reserve Bernard was enjoying the luxuries of his office. So without further ado, he relinquished his grip, and the arena filled with a loud thud. Hurriedly, he stood up and made for the bosses workplace; attempting to avoid any unwanted attention on the way.

Whilst stood outside the bosses door Marvin had his right ear pinned against it, striving to listen for any clue in educating him with what to expect upon entering. Feeling vulnerable without his weapon, he became somewhat relieved upon hearing a woman's faint voice behind. "Bill just get naked. Don't make it any harder for me. This isn't how I planned for us to end up, you were supposed to kill the queen and rescue me from my horrible life." Marvin seized the opportunity to slip inside quietly and ensured the door didn't bang behind him. Once inside he witnessed Sandy standing in a doorway, dressed like never before and pointing a gun at something; he didn't know what, his view was obstructed by a wall. Her voice wasn't faint anymore and he clearly understood what she said next. "Don't move another muscle Marvin and don't think I won't pull the trigger. I haven't got feelings for you like I have for Bill. However, it's him or me. If I don't destroy him the boss will, and he'll give me a bullet at the same time." Marvin pleaded with her to put the weapon down, before explaining how it was all over now the boss has been detained. She didn't believe a word; how could she when she'd already warned Bill not to trust him, so why should she? Marvin heard the distinct sound of Sandy's pistol cocking, fortunately for him, what he said next stopped her from using it. "I know all about you and Fred, how you were his number one superspy, and all about how you approached him for a way out if you helped him break the cult. Your position was so high risk only Fred new your actual identity, so when he died, they put me in undercover to see if I could contact his inside lady. I had my suspicions that it was you, but I remained under strict instructions that, whoever it was, had to approach me first. Hearing what you've just yakked to Bill has confirmed my doubts that you're the lady I've been seeking." Marvin knew he was right when Sandy lowered her firearm and gently passed it to him.

Marvin's attention switched to Bill, he removed his Muzzle and unzipped his mask prior to administering a huge man hug, while cheerfully telling him how joyous it was to see him alive. "Does someone mind telling me what the fuck is going on. I only came for a dildo and I've been to hell and back. Therefore I think someone owes me an explanation." These were the first words that Bill had been able to say for hours. Sandy stared at Marvin and was quite willing to let him do the talking now she finally understood who he really was. "We've been trying to crack this cult for years, trouble was, we never knew Mr BIG's true identity, and it was imperative that when we smashed it, we took him down to prevent him setting up shop elsewhere. Our troubles were further compounded by the fact that neither Fred nor myself, had ever managed to make it past the bosses door. We'd learnt what had happened to someone who'd previously made the journey, but never witnessed it with our own eyes. When you committed your sin, I seized the opportunity to finally succeed. Thankfully, my explanation to his guards worked and fortunately for us, from that moment on, my training kicked in and I was able to think on my feet, and we're all alive to live another day. Now Bill, I know you're a little confused at the moment, but I told you to place your trust in me and I'd see us through, and we have. In a minute, I'm going to have to ask you a life changing question, but before I do, I think it's very important you have all of the facts."

After taking a big breath Marvin resumed. "You were set up by Conner! He wanted you out of the way so he could have Shelly all to himself and they've been carrying on behind your back for a couple of years now. Shelly's insisted that she finished it last night, but we'll have to take her word for it seeing as he's now dead." Bill disrupted. "What the fuck do you mean he's dead? HOW!" Bill then let Marvin explain. "I'm afraid he succumbed to the queens advances in the final battle. I'd like to say it was quick and painless, but believe you me, it wasn't. I'm just glad Shelly selected him." Bill intruded again. "Me too! Anyway if he set me up then he got what he deserved, the devious little bastard, pretending to be my mate for all of those years when he's been secretly shagging my wife." Marvin agreed before adding some more. "Sorry partner but it gets worse. She's also confessed to entertaining every travelling salesman and repair worker who's visited the ranch over the years. Hence, I think it's safe to say, Shelly's the sort of woman who chases the cock. Now for the next part, I'm going to hand you over to Sandy who'll tell you why, after all of the men she's had, she opted to fall in love with you." Marvin then encouraged her to tell. "I've probably had more men in my life than Shelly, but I did it as a way of surviving instead of living a life in the slums. Once in the life I'd chosen, I realised it wasn't the one for me, and dreamt of the day I found a man who had passion not just punch. I've longed for a man to give me the one thing I've lacked in my life, genuine affection. You did, along with the respect, and that's when I knew I'd found the man of my dreams. After I'd left the orgy room, I knew my life wasn't worth living anymore; that's when I hoped it would be my turn as the queen. I'd sacrifice myself and I'd finally be liberated from my horrible existence forever. My death wouldn't be in vain, I'd die praying that I would rest peacefully in my grave after experiencing you. However instead of my prayers, my fantasies have come true and I'm standing here alive with you."

Bill didn't know how to take Sandy's confession. However, his dagger appeared to like it, judging by the way it transformed into a sword. Marvin took over once Sandy ceased and congratulated their sudden wealth before advising, that between them, they'd be entitled to the estimated fifty million dollars reward for helping to catch the mister massive. He then moved towards Sandy and told her to forget all about her past life now she had a new one under the witness protection programme. Sandy smirked at him and he gave her one back, before he stared Bill in the eyes and asked him his life changing question. "Bill my partner, whatever decision you make I'd just like to tell you it's been my honour and pleasure to serve as your wingman. You have two very different lives awaiting my friend, everybody thinks you're already dead so no one would miss you if you didn't return to your old life with Shelly; who'll probably always be looking for the next humungous knob. What sort of a life would that be? Yes, you'd have money, but would you have happiness? Equally if you were to decide on joining Sandy under the programme, you'd spend the rest of your joyful lives together, knowing she'll never be looking for anyone else's cock seeing as no one will ever love her like you. Her first true love. So, my friend who is it? Shelly or Sandy?

Bill took an extended moment to absorb what he'd just learned; this baffled his already pickled head. As if there hadn't already been enough drama this weekend, he now had to choose which woman to spend the rest of his time with. The room fell deadly silent while the others awaited his reaction. They could hear Bill's cogs clunking in his head while his brain crunched through his thoughts. Eventually he murmured some word's. "OK, I've made my decision, but can I please ask one question before I reveal it?" Both Marvin and Sandy didn't object and encouraged him to proceed. "If you're both telling me the truth, then in order for me to believe you, answer me this. How the fuck did a country boy like Conner know about the activities of 'the cult'?"

Chapter 19

Marvin and his bloody plan's!

Marvin and Sandy both stood with a puzzled look on their face once Bill had finished, neither knew his answer so both remained silent until Marvin shrugged his shoulders and spoke. "I really can't solve that question partner, but I promise to use all of my connections, good or bad, to find out. Now, I don't want to alarm you, but for your own safety, we need to come up with a plan to get you out of here safely." Bill stopped Marvin upon hearing this and interrogated himself as to why his life could be in danger when he was in the hands of the FBI. He didn't enjoy Marvin's reply once he'd asked. "Vincent's a very 'connected' individual, he's wealthy and powerful with a police chief in his pocket. The FBI are corrupt from top to bottom and if I follow standard procedure, then I'm afraid to say, you'll be sitting ducks. Sooner or later one of his business partners will get wind of your whereabouts and you won't hear them knock on your door. For you to be truly safe, I must insist that I'm the only person who knows you're alive. I don't know how we can do it, but if you give me a few moments, I'm sure I'll come up with something.

While Marvin's mind worked overtime trying to figure out his third plan of the weekend, Sandy sat on Bill's knee and wrapped her arms around him as tightly as she could, whilst murmuring "I love you." Their noses touched and the two of them were behaving like teenagers in love, they couldn't stop kissing, touching, giggling, or holding hands. Poor Marvin's face on the other hand was clearly starting to show how much he was feeling the pressure, and while frustrated, he paced up and down from one side of the room to another in anger: occasionally banging his head whilst shouting. "That wouldn't work." Sandy inquired whether she could be of any assistance, after all a problem shared is a problem halved. Marvin didn't acknowledge; his feet were now stomping and his voice getting rowdier. The room fell mute for a few minutes before she asked him again, and this time she got her reply. "It's no good, I've somehow got to come up with a way of smuggling you both out from a heavily guarded building unseen, with Bill dressed like that." Sandy butted in. "Don't worry about the gimp suit, when you entered, I was trying to get him out of it so he could put something a little more casual on and blend in on his way to perish." Marvin acknowledged Sandy for helping to solve part of his puzzle and instructed Bill to change, whilst he revealed the rest. "Once we've successfully vacated, I've got to get you to my safe house, but I can't drive you all of the way because our cars have trackers and following my close association with you, my every movement will be investigated. It's best I keep my distance, the only person I can totally trust to tell me exactly how it is, is my boss, but he's un-contactable on annual leave, mountain climbing up some big hill no doubt, therefore until he's back, we've got to be extraordinarily careful."

Unexpectedly there was a loud thud which came from the direction in which Bill had just walked, so Marvin and Sandy raced to find out what had triggered it and they exploded in laughter when they realised. It was Bill in his red gimp suit wriggling around like a blood worm on the floor whilst trying to free himself. "Are you OK love?" Sandy questioned him in a troubled voice before he bellowed an angry reply. "Just bloody well help me out of this thing will you!" I knew it was trouble the first time I set my eyes upon it, and now it's trying to kill me." Sandy giggled uncontrollably while she assisted him up; then they had some fun getting him undressed. Marvin's pacing was beginning to arouse Sandy's scepticisms; to her it seemed like he was stalling for time, seeing as he's supposed to be a highly trained agent who can work things out quickly while under pressure. She expressed her concerns to a naked Bill, who agreed that his behaviour was a little odd, but persuaded Sandy to put her faith in him; he hadn't failed with a plan yet. Bill asked for his clothes and when Sandy passed them, she burst into fits of laughter with the sight of him trying to wrestle in. Judging by the struggle he was having, they weren't his. Marvin reappeared from the other room with a smug look on his face whilst telling the pair he'd come up with a plan. Sandy and Bill were keen to listen, they wanted out of this place as quickly as possible and demanded to be enlightened, consequently Marvin duly obliged. "We don't get you out, far from it, we hide you somewhere safe and wait until everyone has been evicted for interrogation. Then we'll smuggle you out, but due to the large number of witness's this will probably take some time. The FBI will then do one final sweep of the building ahead of the lock down procedure commencing. Once finished, the power will get turned off, however, the generators will kick in giving power to the emergency exits and it normally takes the engineers twenty minutes to kill these. Now For our plan to work we've got to think of somewhere suitable for you to hide. You know this place well Sandy any suggestions?"

Sandy took a moment to ponder her answer, but she struggled to imagine anywhere at first, as she didn't get to see any of the nice parts, only the seedy ones behind the scenes. A notion then came into her mind which brought a smile to her face when she shared it. "I've thought of a place which will be easy for us to blend in, the props room. It's ideal. Bill can get back into his gimp suit, and most of my outfits are in there anyway, therefore I'll put one on, and if anybody enters, we won't look out of place standing amongst all of the other life like statues." Marvin approved, as did Bill, even though he wasn't looking forward to seeing his suit again. However, he knew it was his only option and asked the new love of his life to give him a hand. Once he was aptly dressed Marvin had figured out the rest of his proposal and he shared it. "You two wait in the props room until you hear someone shouting, 'all clear' and the corridor lights go out. Then it'll take the agents about five minutes to exit the venue; at this point the countdown will commence. Now for the next part of my project you need to listen carefully, and to succeed you must be quick and precise. Wait five minutes once the building has darkened then make your way to the nearest emergency exit, then preciously thirteen minutes later when you open it, you'll enter the street. Now, this is the tricky part of the plan! I won't know which exit you've used, so I'll make sure I'm present when the building is secured. This will give me eighteen minutes to find the nearest hire car shop and secure some transport. Once I've succeeded, I'll race back to the venue and start circling the block until I find you. While you're standing at the exit try not to do anything that will make you stand out please."

Bill couldn't believe what he'd just heard, he thought he'd been rescued from his nightmare, but by the sounds of what Marvin had just told him, he was far from being out of the woods. With this thought sprinting through his mind he started to point out what he thought was potentially a big flaw in his idea. "Marvin what do you propose a man dressed in a bright red gimp suit and a woman dressed similar, should do to prevent standing out?" Both Marvin and Sandy blasted into laughter at Bill's flaw, before Sandy taught him the beauty of the plan; being in Vegas and dressed as they were, they'd blend in perfectly. Not looking forward to being spotted in public dressed as a gimp, Bill told Marvin his even bigger shortcoming. "You know how the plan has to be precise and we have to open the door after exactly eighteen minutes?" Marvin didn't say yes, unsure as to what Bill was leading to, he simply shook his head in agreement and allowed him to continue. "I haven't got a watch and neither has Sandy." Marvin recognised the problem and was in the process of taking his off to provide it to Bill, when it dawned on him how he'd require it to implement his accuracy. Sandy chipped in with her two-penny's worth by advising Marvin that giving his watch wasn't such a good idea, seeing as a gimp wearing a watch is bang on top and would definitely attract attention, especially in Vegas. Agreeing with what Sandy had just pointed out Marvin had no choice but to keep his watch, and he instructed both Bill and Sandy that they'd have to make do with counting hippopotamuses instead.

Bill, redressed in his gimp suit by now, didn't fancy the plans chances, especially counting hippos, hence he decided it was time to break some bad news to his fellow escapees. "Marvin and Sandy. I'm a little worried and confused about the proposals chances and also about both of your real intentions." Marvin tried to butt in, unsuccessfully, Bill wasn't stopping. "Ever since I met you both yesterday my life has been on a roller coaster full of unbelievable events. Marvin you've told me only to trust you, as has Sandy, but neither of you have answered my question about Conner, and he can't because you say that he's dead. So it looks like I'll never find out, and on that basis, I've decided the that safest thing for me to do, is to go and spend the rest of my days happily with my remarkable wife. If I don't testify against Vincent, he'll know I can keep a secret and hopefully let me live. With Conner out of the way Shelly and I can work on our relationship and get it back to how it was in the good old days. I'm sorry and I'd like to thank you both for all that you've done, but my decision is set in stone. So Marvin please take me to her?" His fellow escapees were shocked by Bill's wishes. Sandy burst into tears with the thought of losing her ideal man, and she begged for him to reconsider as she gave him a warm comforting hug, whilst making sure her monsters pushed firmly against his chest. Marvin asked if he understood the danger he'd be in for the rest of his life, by having to constantly watch over his shoulder, whilst continuously trying to prevent himself from accidentally bumping into his projectile. Bill didn't respond at first, his mind was fixed firmly on Sandy's assets while they were trying their best to make him reconsider. It didn't work, he was adamant and wanted his simple life of normality back. When he invited Marvin to take him back to Shelly, he refused before clarifying that he'd have to make it there by himself, as his number one priority now was Sandy's safety.

The room fell mute, apart from Sandy's weeping and she begged Bill to re-evaluate the situation one last time with the knowledge that he'd break her heart if he absconded. Bill's mind wasn't up for persuasion; hence he gave Sandy a final kiss, prior to grabbing Marvin's right hand and shaking it firmly whilst he inquired for directions. Sandy had vacated the room before Marvin had chance to provide them. "Turn right out of the door and keep going down until you get to the cash office on the very bottom floor, you'll recognise it by the big steel door with the keypad on it. Enter the code, 682034 and you'll view a door on the wall directly in front of you. Go through it, turn left and if you enter the third door on your right, that will bring you out directly on the stage, in the safety of being in plain view of everyone. You can go first. Sandy and I will have to modify my plan now it's only for two. A word of warning though, make sure you're not seen by anyone. You won't know if they're friend or foe, so it's not worth the risk of revealing your true identity until you're backed by safety in numbers. Now go my partner, look after yourself and I hope you find what you're looking for with Shelly." Confident he'd made the right selection, he entered the other room to say goodbye one final time, but all he got in return was. "Just go, you've ruined me enough already." With that he looked Marvin in the eyes while he passed him by, on his way back to normality.

Bill was anxious with the uncertainty of what lay ahead, when he cautiously departed the safety of the bosses office and entered the long corridor. Turning right as instructed, he found himself ambling down a wide walkway when his thoughts switched to what lay behind the numerous doors which he had passed. His reflections where disrupted by the ping of an elevator door and he hastily tried to open his nearest entrance, but sadly it was locked. In a panic and unsure what to do, he had a eureka moment and decided to stand faultlessly motionless and pretend to be a life like statue, whilst guaranteeing the door was in perfect sight. A man and a woman appeared from it, along with a pooch, then his heart sank to the floor with what happened next. "Freeze and put your hands in the air or I'll release the beast!" Somehow Bill managed to remain lifeless despite his racing pulse, and just as the man was about to carry out his threat, the lady saved his skin with what she indicated. "It's all right it's one of those sex bots, my friends got one and she swears by hers. It acts like her servant during the day and lover of a night. She especially likes the fact it doesn't answer back and never rolls over once it's had enough. It keeps going until she has. The man tittered with the thought of her sick friend's behaviour, while disbelieving its authenticity, so he probed her further. "It will do anything that you say, OK prove it and make it do something. I'll bet you fifty dollars that you can't." Whilst grinning the woman agreed but only if he made it a buck.

The man nodded, consequently the woman shouted. "Hey gimp, raise your right hand in the air." Bill was crapping himself; he knew if he didn't get this right, then he had a fifty-fifty chance of being the dogs next titbit. Very slowly he did as instructed, before having to query what mistake he'd made when the man cocked his gun and educated his partner how, with such a realistic arm movement, the gimp was a real person. The woman laughed once more before she ordered him to lower his

243

weapon while she explained about the advances in sex
bot technology, and how the cult were market leaders in
their development. She advised him not to worry if they
see any more as the building will be littered with them.
Still not convinced he let the canine loose and whilst
racing towards Bill, it barked and showed him its teeth.
He didn't know what to do for the best, stand still and get
eaten alive, or surrender with the possibility of having a
rapid demise. However, he wasn't beaten yet and started
to whistle strange noises very quietly in a high-pitched
tone, the sort of pitch that's undetectable to most human
lobes. Happily, it worked, and the mutts barking ceased
when his teeth went into hiding, whilst it continued to
curiously approach. The woman asked for her winnings
now that she'd proven its authenticity. Still unsatisfied,
the man refused until she'd given him additional proof
that it would obey ANY command, so she yelled
"Digby" and ordered it to sit, before directing Bill. "Hey
gimp, stroke the dog's ear with your right hand." The
gimp did as instructed, Digby loved it, and it's tail
wagged ferociously from side to side whilst Bill stroked.
Digby then pushed his head towards Bill's hand whilst
striving to obtain a sweet spot stroke. It worked, and
before long Digby was enjoying it so much, he rolled
over onto his back and gestured for the gimp to give its
belly a quick rub. Mercifully, he resisted and returned to
his lifeless pose. The woman demanded again for her
buck by clarifying how she's just given him his proof; if
the Gimp were a real person their natural instinct would
have been to stroke Digby's underside. As the man
handed over his dollar, he started hooting hysterically

with what had caught his eye. Digby, who didn't seem happy with the gimps refusal to rub, was taking his revenge by cocking his leg and using Bill's left one as a lamppost. Satisfied the woman was right, he settled his debt before calling Digby back and restraining him before all three headed in Bill's direction. His heartbeat was constant as fear rushed through his body. He'd managed to fool them from a distance but wasn't feeling very confident about doing so whilst they were close-by. The two officials were chatting between themselves while walking towards him. Then suddenly, and without warning, the man stopped debating and approached for a closer inspection of the gimp, thus enabling precise scrutinization for any signs of life. Bill's body remained motionless; his chest didn't move for fear that his breath would give the game away, then after what seemed like an eternity to him, but was realistically no lengthier than thirty seconds, the man turned away, and when he started walking Bill thought he was out of the woods. He wasn't, and the man unexpectedly turned around and shouted BOO!

Chapter 20

The luckiest man alive

Fortuitously he didn't get to witness Bill's reaction, the man's attention had been drawn to the big black man in the distance who was marching his way, inviting him over for a little chat. The man yanked on his weapon, and whilst struggling to contain Digby, he strode towards him and questioned who he was and what was he doing out of bounds. "I'm one of you and I need your help." The man didn't trust him and queried if he was new seeing as he hadn't recognised him. The big man then educated him how he wasn't allowed to raise any issues and instructed him to call his boss who would verify his tale when he found out it was agent 777. The man kept his hound and warhead trained on the suspect while the woman placed her radio between her lips prior to chatting. "Control, it's 369. I've got an unidentified who says I'm not allowed to ask him questions and that the boss will verify him." "That's strange I've never heard that one before, OK what's their number?" The voice responded into her ear, "777" she countered. There was a brief pause then control asked for the first and fourth digit of their pin. The woman repeated the request to the big man, who did what everybody body does when they find themselves faced in the same situation; they count on their fingers while reciting it in their head. "Nine and six," he responded before the woman repeated it through her receiver. Her face dropped when she heard what the

246

controller had to say once his history had been accessed. "Holy shit! I've never seen one like this before! It says nothing apart from, do not interfere in this man's business, give him free movement, ask no questions, do exactly as he instructs and give whatever assistance he requires. It's authorised by the boss himself, fuck me he's genuine, just do as he says!" The voice in the woman's ear fell silent and she advised the man to re-sheath his weapon seeing as the unidentified man's story stacked. The big man took total control of the situation and ordered them to bring the hound and follow him whilst he enlightened them with the very important job that they now had to complete.

Bill was relieved when he couldn't hear any voices or footsteps anymore, so very slowly, he rotated his head towards the direction in which he'd listened to them a moment earlier, and when he couldn't see anybody, he started his journey once again to the safety of the stage. Deciding not to take the elevator, he set off in search of the stairs, and it wasn't long before he found them. However, once he peered over the rail and realised he was a good fifty stories up, he dreaded the thought of the challenge ahead. Undeterred, he very quietly and carefully started his descent. The first ten or twelve floors were uneventful apart from Bill swimming in his own sweat. As he descended to the next one, he became startled by the sound of an opening door, and not knowing which door it was, he found himself stranded between floors. Uncertain whether safety was up or down, he decided to do nothing hastily, so he stood motionless whilst eavesdropping for any sounds of movement. He did but to him they sounded like they were several floors away. Another door opening then grabbed his attention, but this time it echoed from above, and it was followed by the sound of another set of footsteps. His racing heart forced his decision to go down and seek safety outside of the stairs. Fortunately, he managed to make it to the safety of the corridor, however, unconfident that he'd managed to avoid detection, he sought sanctuary in the nearest unlocked room, where he waited and listened for any noises associated with the activities of people or dogs. After what must have been ten minutes or more without any sounds, Bill plucked up the courage to enter the corridor once more, only this time he opted to take the quicker and more direct root. He was comforted when the door opened to reveal an empty elevator, then when he got in, he noticed he was on the sixty ninth floor and ever so pleased that he'd not persevered with the stairs. Bill found himself staring at the buttons unsure which one to press, 'G or LG'. Marvin had told him to go all the way to the bottom floor, which to him meant 'LG', but in his mind he was sure that the main arena would be on the ground floor and not in the basement. Selecting to follow Marvin's instructions he pressed the button, and when the door closed, Bill felt himself gliding towards safety. Finding himself staring at the display above the door, he consequently counted down with it while each floor passed, and when It came to an abrupt halt at the forty first, he panicked at first with the thought of not knowing who'd pushed the button, prior to calmly standing perfectly lifeless in the corner. His pulse raced when the elevator pinged, and the door opened. Luckily, it slowed right down when it closed without anyone appearing. Bill's descent commenced once again, and his thoughts turned to Shelly and how glad he'll be once he's swathed his arms around his beautiful wife and given her a comforting hug.

Bill's thoughts were disturbed at the twenty first when the elevators movement stopped, and he heard the same ping as before. Then he froze in the corner as the doors opened, while praying that it was another false alarm. It was, and his journey continued. Bill focussed on the countdown and was willing for it to display 'LG', and he was nearly there when, frustratingly for him, it stopped at the ground floor. Bill was hesitant with what to do, his body now trembling from all the various emotions which he'd experienced in his short elevator ride. Knowing he wouldn't be able to keep still, he decided that if anyone came in, then he'd surrender. The elevator pinged and the doors opened, Bill had his short surrender speech ready, a simple 'don't shoot' with raised hands in the air. Bill really is the luckiest man alive because unbeknown to him, when the doors closed and nobody exited, all the trigger happy heavily armed men standing in the lobby outside, lowered their weapons. Bill felt joyous that his journey was nearing its end whilst thinking only one more floor, a keypad and a few doors separated him from Shelly's limbs. On hearing the ping for the fourth time the doors opened and to his relief he entered an empty corridor. Now all that remained was to find the keypad once he'd decided whether to go left or right. He chose the latter, which was the correct choice, and a short while later, he found what he'd been looking for.

Whilst stood in front of the big steel door, Bill was trying his best to remember the secret code; he could think of the first five digits but struggled to recall the last. Unfazed by this small obstacle after coming so far, he decided to start at one and work his way up. When he tapped his first attempt 682031, the keypad made a funny noise and 'entry denied' flashed upon it. When he tried again, 682032 he was distraught to hear the same noise repeated. Bill commenced his next effort, 68203 but just as his finger hovered above the number 3, he suddenly had the thought to bypass it, because three's unlucky for some, and going by how his luck had been this weekend, he wasn't prepared to take the risk, therefore he pressed number 4, when to his delight, the keypad displayed 'enter' while it produced an unusual sound. The door that Bill needed next was easily identifiable by its sign, 'Backstage and Arena'. With the thought of soon being reunited with Shelly in his mind, he opened it and proceeded towards the third room on the right. While he passed the first one, he paid attention to what the sign said, 'Make up', absorbing this he knew he was on the right track. The next door exhibited 'Hair', and Bill's heart was pounding by now, knowing that the love of his life was waiting for him through the next door. When he put his right hand on the handle to turn, he noticed how it had no sign, only four screw holes where it once did. Brushing this aside, he rotated his hand and pushed the door to be greeted by a darkened room. As he stepped inside it illuminated when the motion detectors sensed his movement and Bill couldn't believe what it contained, oodles of statue's dressed exactly like him, along with woman, whips, and dildo's to name a few of the items that were in his sight. With everything inside tidied away neatly in its own place, Bill searched for the stage door, and while he was fumbling near the woman, he could have sworn he heard someone faintly call out his name. Dismissing this, he resumed his search, then when he received it again, he glanced in the direction from where it came, and to his surprise caught sight of Sandy stood dressed just how she was for their very first encounter.

"Oh Bill, you've changed your mind, you don't know how happy I am to see you," Sandy conveyed with an emotional voice before she hurried towards him and wrapped her arms around him tightly while she positioned his lips on hers. Bill couldn't understand how he'd taken a wrong turn after following Marvin's directions to the letter and thought he was supposed to be in his wife's arms. "Where's Marvin?" he queried the woman who he didn't know whether to trust. "I'm not sure, the last I saw of him, he was in the corridor distracting two agents; enabling me to make my escape. I'm so glad you chose me; I'm looking forward to feeling

your skin next to mine for the rest of my life." Once
Sandy had solved Bill's problem, he enquired what
modifications had been made to Marvin's plan, if any.
Sandy clarified how it was exactly the same apart from
the addition of a back-up plan just in case time went
against them. Bill then asked Sandy the killer question.
"So how do I get to the stage from here?" Her face
dropped with the discontent she felt, now knowing that
Bill hadn't changed his mind. She thought for a flash
about what answer to give, the truth, or deny all
knowledge of knowing the way in the hope that he'd
persist with her. Sandy's emotions got the better of her
and she decided that she didn't want to be with a man
whose feelings weren't reciprocal. Reluctantly she told
him before they gave each other a great big kiss and said
goodbye for the final time. Again! Bill could hear
Sandy's frenzied weeping as he walked towards the door,
feeling slightly guilty, he turned around to see her face
for the final time before the door shut behind him. Whilst
making his way back towards the cash office he abruptly
turned around as fast as he could and sprinted back to the
sobbing Sandy. As he opened the door the room
illuminated, and he was greeted by the sound of Sandy's
singing. Overjoyed that Bill had changed his mind once
again, she threw herself towards him, and they met right
in front of the sex bots display, where Sandy smothered
him with affection and didn't let him escape for air. Bill
was struggling to rebuff her advances, but to no avail;
she'd already said farewell forever to her man twice in
one day, and she was determined it wasn't happening for

a third. Just as he managed to break free the pair froze when they witnessed the sound of an opening door.

Sandy didn't observe the movement, she was standing with her back to the door. However Bill did and got gravely concerned when he saw a man dressed in a red gimp suit just like his enter, only his displayed a number. This man was swiftly followed by another identical one, apart from his suit showing a different digit. The Gimp train kept on coming and Bill counted them all in, nine in total. The men were yakking amongst themselves, whilst complimenting each other on their successful escape from the authority's. Number seven wasn't pleased and pointed out how they were now trapped in the props room of a building which was swarming with FBI agents striving to hunt them down. The penny dropped with Bill when he realised, he hadn't taken a wrong turn, Marvin had deliberately sent him there, for what reason he didn't know, but he was determined to find out. Then the room unexpectedly darkened, before illuminating again with the movement from one of Bill's fellow clan. The nine Gimps were all gossiping amongst themselves when from outside came a large bang. They fell silent upon catching sight of the opening door and two agents, a man, and a woman, striding in with a canine. Bill watched in horror while he listened to the beast's resonating bark, swiftly followed by the female unsheathing her weapon prior to pointing at number seven and yelling, "Freeze or I'll let the dog go." The mongrel was enthusiastic to get off his restraint and sink his teeth into the suspect. Fortunately for number seven, he did the sensible thing and gave himself up, along with the other eight. The agents couldn't believe what they'd found, the nine suspects they'd been sent to seize dressed like they were, so the woman instructed the man to radio for back up and another seven sets of cuffs. He didn't get chance to, upon hearing the woman's voice number seven recognised it instantly and introduced himself. "Gail, it's me Brian from Dallas, one of your bosses." The lady ignored his comment and told him to shut his mouth before he got it whilst waving her firearm in his mush. The male agent calmed the tension, by insisting his partner lower her warhead now he'd realised who the real Brian was. "Sorry Brian, I didn't recognise you, I haven't seen you in ages. I'm regretful for not travelling to the store for a while. I've been busy, and I promise I'll be in soon to pay my debt, it's just money's been a bit tight lately." He then addressed his female colleague and educated her how Brian runs the chat lines that she moonlights for. Hostility's over, and all eleven shook hands like they were the best friends in the world.

A confused Bill remained motionless, petrified with the thought of seeing these two agents again, and he noticed how Digby was sitting down, staring the man in his eyes, with a wagging tail and a shaking back end while he obediently awaited his reward for sniffing out Brian. The man took his toy from his pocket and threw it right in Bill's direction. It landed at his feet and his heart toppled while he hoped and prayed that Digby didn't howl whilst retrieving it. Luckily, Digby didn't and picked it up, but before returning to his master something caught his attention. The smell on Bill's left leg. This really fascinated Digby, who pushed his nose as hard as he could into Bill's shin, ensuring he got a good whiff, before marking his spot. On Bill's other lamppost. Once Digby had turned around, Bill's ears switched to what the others were chattering, and he heard Brian requesting help in finding a way out; in return the woman would get a hefty bonus and pay rise, and a lifetime of credit for the man, along with the quashing of his debt. The two agents glanced at each other, keen to help after hearing the rewards that were on offer. However, they knew there was only one way that they could; inside knowledge. The man then started to divulge. "Brian, you're a wanted man, along with your partners, and the whole venue is being swept from top to bottom searching for you. Therefore what I'm about to tell you is your only choice."

Brian didn't adore what he was hearing, but knew it was the only option, so he listened wisely as the agent continued. "When we leave here now, we'll give control the all clear, turn off the corridor lights and the lock down procedure will initiate. Once we've done this, it's imperative that you **DO NOT** switch the lights back on; they might detect this from their sensors. After we've given the all clear and it's gone dark, give it about five minutes and the main power will be switched off. However, the emergency generators will kick in to power the emergency exits. You'll then have ten minutes maximum to make your way to the nearest emergency exit and enjoy your freedom. You'd normally have a bit longer, but the engineers are already on site to cripple the generators; the authorities are keen to preserve the crime scene quickly after catching their mister mammoth. Well, that's the official version anyway. The word on the grapevine supposes that during this time, the dollar will be emptied before a mysterious blaze engulfs the building. If you're not out after ten minutes, then I'm sorry but you'll be frazzled." Upon hearing this, and knowing they clearly didn't have eighteen minutes, Bill trusted that the knowledgeable Marvin had modified his plan. He sought to grab Sandy's attention with the twinkle in his eyes, but sadly, they didn't sparkle enough to connect. The agents then shook every Gimps hand and wished them the best of luck with their escape, prior to concluding with a promise to visit Dallas soon. The door closed behind them and Bill overheard one of the Gimps ask, "who's wearing a watch," no one was, so he followed his question with a query, "who's good at counting hippos." Then a tone from outside shouted "all clear" and the room descended into darkness.

Chapter 21

We need a good plan

"Hippopotamus, hippopotamus, hippopotamus." "Kevin will you shut up I'm trying to think." Brian yelled in a stern voice, before Kevin reacted. "But I'm counting Hippo's so that we know when five minutes is up, then we can scarper to safety. Bloody hell you've made me lose count now, I'll have to start again." Brian didn't take kindly to Kevin's response, and unable to see him in the dark, he waved his hand to strike out towards the direction of his voice. However, that was a bad mistake as his movement was picked up by the motion sensors and the room suddenly illuminated. "Fucking hell Brian, you were specifically told not to move until five minutes was up. Now the FBI will know that we're here and they'll come in force to investigate." Kevin stated in a worried tone. Brian then realised the error of his ways, and he started to panic, whilst looking around the room for somewhere suitable to hide. The other eight men dressed as gimps all stared at Brian, and Cecil pointed out that seeing as Vincent had been captured, it was now down to Brian his deputy, to come up with a way of getting them all out to safety. Otherwise a long stretch in the clink would be waiting for them. Brian didn't take kindly to the pressure of being responsible for everyone presents liberty and shouted out. "Come on my fellow Gimps lets hide amongst the sexbots and keep still until the FBI arrive. Then once they're satisfied it was a false

alarm, they'll start the lockdown procedure again."
Abruptly, the room was full of movement as all of the
sexbots which were present started to move around in
circles whilst trying to do exactly as Brian had
commanded. Bill, who'd been listening carefully to what
the others had been saying, seized on the opportunity and
started to do exactly as the others in order to blend in. As
he passed Sandy, he gave her a nudge and encouraged
her to do the same. Luckily, she followed suit and soon
the two hundred plus sexbots dressed in Gimp suits, took
it in turn to try and hide behind each other.

"Gimps fall in line and stand still!" Brian ordered, and
they did exactly as they'd been commanded, just as Bill
was taking his turn at the front. So they all formed neat
rows of ten behind him, like an army does when they fall
in on parade behind their lone officer. Apart from the
nine bosses who hadn't moved an inch, thus enabling
Brian to think logically about the situation which they
now faced. He was doing this to the best of his ability
when Michael pitched in. "Brian, you know how we've
got to make it to the nearest emergency exit. Well that
means we've got to get past the cash office's electronic
door and seeing as the backup generators only power the
emergency exits, we're pretty screwed because there isn't
any exit's this side of that door. So you need to come up
with a good plan and quick." Brian recognised that what
Michael was stating was true, and you could see the
strain on his face as his brain worked tirelessly to figure
something suitable out. However, his thoughts were

interrupted by lots of commotion coming from the corridor outside, then he heard a man's deep voice shouting. "Don't worry about the movement which has set the sensors off it's probably a false alarm, but just in case, two of you stand guard at the door and shoot to kill anything that may attempt to walk through it. We've only got ten minutes to empty all of the cash out before the blaze is started." Bill didn't like what he'd just heard, and he prayed for a miracle. Luckily, his prayers were answered when Sandy's body sprang into life by showing off her assets as she moved towards Brian whilst saying. "Brian I'm so glad you're here to save me. I must have been drugged and placed in here with the rest of the sexbots by Bill. Please don't harm me. I tried my best to kill Bill as Vincent ordered, but I promise I'll find him and finish the job once I've tracked him down." Sandy's sudden appearance startled Brian, and he ordered her to cover up as this wasn't the correct time for nibbles. He then reassured her that if she came up with a suitable plan to get them all out alive, he would look past her failure, just this once, as long as she kept to her promise and made sure Bill didn't become the first contender to survive the wheel.

Somewhat relieved that her safety was secured for now, Sandy took firm control of the situation and whispered. "OK bosses, I think I've got a plan, but it's very risky and there could be a lot of bloodshed if it goes wrong. Nevertheless, from where I'm looking, it could be our only one, so please everyone be quiet and let me explain." The nine Gimp bosses all shook their heads simultaneously in disbelief that their life was now in the hands of a semi naked slut. But they had no choice other than to hear her out. "Now we know that they're currently stripping the cash from the building, so once they've finished doing that, the two guards outside will be ordered to vacate the premises. At that point you order the sexbots to charge the door and storm the guards, who will open fire and the leading sexbots will be mown down in a hail of bullets. Then once they've expended their first magazine, we overpower them, before we seize their weapons and hide behind the surviving sexbots so we can use them as a shield to ensure our escape via any exit possible. Only use your weapons if absolutely necessary, and hopefully the remaining agents will be distracted by the chaos of hundreds of sexbots charging at them, so we should be able to slip away unnoticed. Then with any luck enough of them will survive along with us, and when we're outside, you order them to start attacking anyone who gets in our way. Thus diverting any unwanted attention away from us whilst we make good our escape. What do you think to that?" Brian was a little bemused at what Sandy had just stated but he knew time was against them, and he decided to ask his partners if any of them had a better plan. Nobody uttered a word, so Brian agreed to it as long as Sandy took the lead while him and his partners remained hidden firmly to the rear.

Bill couldn't believe what he'd just heard, as if his nightmare of a weekend hadn't been bizarre enough already, his life now depended on him being able to pretend to be a sexbot once again. Only this time, he'd have to do it whilst dodging bullets. Now feeling extremely regretful at his choice of birthday gifts for Shelly, he was contemplating his surrender to a certain death, when suddenly a lady's voice shouted in the corridor. "It's OK you two, you can stand down and go and help move the cash while I send the hound in to give the room a once over." Bill's heart plummeted with the thought of his third encounter with Digby that day, and he quickly changed his mind about surrendering after realising that he'd probably meet his death when he became Digby's next meal. He recognised that all he could do to stay alive, was to stand perfectly still and if necessary, whistle like before. The door opened and Bill started his high-pitched shrill, but luckily for him he didn't have to do it for long, when he witnessed Gail enter alone after she'd instructed Digby to sit and stand guard. Once the door had closed behind her, she approached Brian and asked him what he was doing in the company of such an attractive female sexbot. Brian shook his head prior to explaining how it was actually one of his star employees who'd just come up with a plan to lead them all to safety. Gail chuckled for a short while before she told him how they might have to modify their plan, as she had some good and bad news for him, in advance of asking. "Which one would you like to hear first?" Brian didn't respond immediately; he was probably just as baffled as Bill was with how the evenings itinerary was altering minute by minute. However after a few seconds he gave his reply. "Hit me with the bad first." Gail duly obliged. "President Deer's on his way along with the secret service and their arrivals imminent. We don't officially know why he's coming, but the word on the grapevine is that Vincent asked for his right to make a phone call and he rang the President's personal mobile. Do you know if Vincent had his number?" Brian knew the answer but for a moment he was unsure whether he should enlighten Gail with it. Seeing as it would only be spread around the gossiping agents, the moment she left the room. However, Brian did love a good gossip and couldn't resist adding a bit of his own to the FBI's rumour mill. "Yes, he's got his number because the Presidents been a regular at the store for years, long before he came into office. But he only ever attends after hours when Vincent's the only person present. Now he's the big boss, even the Secret Service agents are ordered to remain outside while the two of them spend hours together inside alone before President Deer comes out with a big smile on his face. No one knows what they get up to, and to be honest I don't really want to find out either, as I'm sure the knowledge would almost certainly contribute to our extinction. Now for your own safety I strongly advise you to keep what I've just told you to yourself. Can I have the good news now please?" Gail didn't waste any time in spurting it out. "The buildings not getting torched anymore as a couple of the FBI bigwigs have found the title deeds to the complex, and they're going to get them transferred to their names so they can legally sell it on to the highest bidder. Thus helping to contribute to their children's college fund. Also the powers been turned back on, so you don't have to worry about triggering the lights when you move anymore. But try not to just in case it arouses any suspicions. I'll have to go now before someone comes in, although I'll tell them that Digby didn't detect anything out of the ordinary, and I'll tell the guards not to enter so that should buy you a bit of time to come up with a modified escape plan. I'll also see what else I can find out for you and try to keep you posted. Hopefully I'll be back soon." Gail then shook Brian's hand before she turned around and departed. Once she'd left, Brian rotated to his right towards Sandy and advised her to put her plan on hold. However shortly after he had, he heard Gail's voice shout from the corridor. "Hey, you two, this rooms all clear, so you come and stand guard as something very important that I've got to do has just come up. Now don't dare enter the room just stand outside and shoot if the door opens. I'll be back as quick as I can."

The room then descended into darkness once more, and all of the ten gimps including Sandy started to chat quietly amongst themselves whilst Bill was stood still, and as he listened, he pondered what other surprises were going to come his way. However, his thoughts were interrupted by the sound of Cecil pleading with Brian to allow them to surrender, as he too had secretly met with the President in the store before he came into office, and as a result, he owed him a big favour and he was confident that now was the time to ask for it to be repaid. Cecil's confession caught Brian off guard, and he curiously asked him what it was that he'd got up to with

President Deer that would ensure his safety. Cecil hesitated before answering, as he knew if he told everyone what he'd promised to keep a secret and the President found out, it would certainly lead to his extermination. So he quickly thought on his feet and came up with a made-up response instead. "It was a long time ago and I didn't recognise him at first. I was stood by the fetish outfits whilst choosing something suitable to wear for an upcoming bash that I was due to attend that night. He approached yours truly and advised me not to bother as the last time he'd attended such a party, he had a terrible experience when his body swelled, and he had to go into hiding for a few days to hide his embarrassment from being trapped inside his suit. Before he eventually plucked up the courage to ask one of his aides for their assistance in cutting him free. I laughed after he'd told me this and queried him whether he needed any help advising him on his next purchase. However, he told me that his terrifying experience cost him a lot in hush money and as a result, he found it cheaper not to attend any such parties in disguise anymore, and only ever carry out his improper antics safely in secret with only his partner in crimes company. Then, if they threatened to do a kiss and tell to the press, he could deny it strenuously and silence them with a payment from an unknown third party." Brian and the rest of his partners burst into laughter once Cecil had finished, and as soon as the laughter had stopped, Michael pitched in with his two-pennies worth. "That's not going to save us. That stories common knowledge amongst the fetish community, and I know because I read it in a magazine shortly before it's editor sadly died in an unexplained bizarre accident. So I wouldn't hold your horses on that one saving our bacon because we'll probably end up just like him." Feeling disappointed that his story was common knowledge and it hadn't convinced the others to surrender, Cecil's legs became weak and they buckled beneath him as he fainted before his body came crashing towards the floor. Thus causing the sensors to detect his sudden movement and illuminate the room once again. As his body made contact a loud thud echoed around the room, and a male voice shouted from outside. "What the fuck was that I'm going in to investigate." Luckily for everyone present, another deep voice reminded his partner how they'd been given strict instructions not to enter, and to only shoot to kill anything that emerged.

The corridor then fell silent once again, and after it had remained so for the time it took the room to fall into darkness, Sandy's voice broke out as she pleaded with Brian to reconsider his orders to put her plan on hold, as she didn't think it would stand a chance if they had to execute it once the Secret Service were in the building. Seeing as the whole complex and especially all emergency exits, would be ringfenced by them. Brian took on board Sandy's concerns and asked his fellow Gimps for their thoughts. His mind was made up for him, but not by his fellow partners, but when the sexbots enthusiastically whispered, "let's do it." However, Michael put a spanner in the works when he pointed out that they couldn't commence with it as Cecil was still unconscious on the floor, and how it would be unfair to let him miss out on all of the fun by leaving him behind. Brian must have agreed, because the room illuminated once again when his right leg kicked out and made a brash thud as it connected with Cecil's body as he muttered his command. "Get up you cissy, now's not the time to play your ridiculous attention seeking games, and if you don't, we'll dent the kids college fund when we arrange for you to have your own personal cremation here without any mourners." Cecil did exactly as he'd been instructed before he came up with a lame excuse about how he'd lost his balance while he was itching the back of his left leg with the inside of his right foot. Brian didn't believe him, but he knew now was not an appropriate time to question Cecil over it, as time was certainly not on their side. So instead, he advised everyone to gather round in a big circle away from any prying ears, as Sandy enlightened them with any modifications which she may have made to her plan, after taking into account what Gail had just said. Sandy didn't know how to respond, and as she saw it, it didn't matter who they faced because they'd still be heavily armed and dangerous. Eventually Sandy plucked up the courage to speak. "OK, I know time's against us, but for me to come up with a detailed proposition I need to know the exact number of reinforcements that we've got present, so I need a volunteer to go and count them for me please." Luckily, Kevin, who as we know from earlier was very good at counting, hastily moved towards the army of sexbots and stood right in front of Bill while he started to count them row by row.

Bill's body started to sweat heavily after only a few seconds, and he was becoming lightheaded from having to hold his breath to avoid detection from Kevin, who was well within striking distance. As Kevin continued his counting out aloud, Bill was getting desperate for breath and prayed that he was a fast counter. Fortunately for him he was, and before long he was up to twelve. However, by the time Kevin's counting had reached fifteen Bill couldn't resist any longer. Luckily just as he was about to admit defeat, Kevin's counting ceased when his head turned around as his attention was drawn to Gail's voice bellowing from outside, instructing the two guards to go and take a hike for five minutes. The door opened and in walked Gail alone, and once it had closed, Kevin made his way back towards his friends, eager to find out the grapevine's news. A relieved Bill somehow manged to catch his breath, undetected, as Gail gave everyone present an update on the President's visit. "Brian, It's not looking good I'm afraid. The Presidents arrived along with his entourage who are taking control of the proceeding's, and they're carrying out a sweep of the building for themselves to assess any potential hostile threat's which they might need to eliminate. You see, they know how corrupt the FBI are and they don't trust anyone. Well, that's the official word anyway, but someone on the grapevine says that they overheard the President asking Vincent whether any of his favourite

sexbots were on the premises, as he wouldn't mind a
little relaxation time to help take away the stress. Seeing
as he's had to be faithful lately, with the press stalking
his every move since the conniving slut's accusations.
So, I suspect that you may well be in for a Presidential
visit and as a result, I strongly recommend you think
about giving yourself up before they discover you.
They've been given strict instructions to shoot anyone
who's not supposed to be here, and if you make yourself
known before they find you; I can escort you to safety.
Then once word gets to Vincent that you're here safe and
alive, I'm sure he can persuade the President to let you
keep your liberty and brush this whole embarrassing
situation under the carpet. Bill couldn't believe what he'd
just heard, he'd always wanted to meet the President but
never in a million years would he have dreamt that he
would, and in such strange circumstances.

Brian's brain had hastily absorbed Gail's gossip, and
he'd managed to process it very quickly before he gave
the order for everyone human to follow Gail to safety.
Apart from Sandy that was, she was given strict
instructions to go and blend in with the sexbots and listen
very carefully to anything that was said by the President,
if the grapevine was correct. Brian also gave Sandy some
further instructions that once the Presidential visit had
ended, she was to somehow escape and make her way to
the local private airport where he'd arrange for suitable
transport to be laid on for her to get back to Dallas so she
could spill the beans. Sandy didn't take gladly to Brian's

instructions, but she knew that if she disobeyed him, then he'd almost certainly expose Gail's weapon and use it on her. Once she'd come to terms with what Brian was asking her to do, she queried. "What should I do if the grapevines wrong?" Quick as a flash, Brian sounded his reply. "Use your existing plan, it'll have a better chance of success if the sexbots only have to protect you." Once Brian had finished, he said his goodbyes to Sandy and wished her the best of luck, as did her other eight bosses along with Gail. Then, one by one, they made their way out of the room and into the corridor outside, were Gail announced to her fellow agents who'd just returned to their post, that she'd found some unidentified suspects and was taking them for interrogation. Once the door had fully closed Sandy raced over to Bill and gave him a big comforting embrace before she stepped back slightly whilst reassuringly telling him that despite all of the odds being stacked against them, she felt destiny was on their side, and somehow it would ensure that they pulled through safely so they could lead a long happy life together. Bill didn't know what to think, here he was trapped with a woman who he didn't trust and certainly didn't want to spend the rest of his life with. His mistrust had also been further compounded after hearing her earlier promise that she would personally track him down and kill him. However, Bill decided that he had no option but to go along with Sandy and pretend that he did trust her, whilst he prayed that her intentions were honourable. Bill's earlier frostiness suddenly changed to warmth as he placed his lips onto Sandy's, and he started passionately kissing hers until he couldn't withstand the moistness anymore, and when they separated, he seized on the opportunity to probe her concerning them. "I'm so glad I chose you instead of Shelly, but I need you to promise me that what you told Brian about tracking me down and killing me was only a lie to save your own skin, and that I'm safe with you." Sandy chuckled with what she'd just heard before she grabbed Bill tightly in her arms and whispered in his ear. "I promise, and I never break mine. Anyway, why would I want to cause the man of my dreams any harm, when all I want to do to you is make you happy and ensure that we have a pleasurable life together. Don't worry, you're safe with me, and if in later years you suffer from brewers droop, I'll just have to ensure that we've always got a decent stock of Dallas Pill's. Now let's go and hide while we keep quiet as well as still just in case the word on the street is true, then if after an hour has passed and no one has entered, we'll reassess the situation and make any necessary modifications to my plan before we execute it." Once Sandy had finished speaking, she gave Bill one final embrace before they mingled into the Gimp army, and shortly after they'd fallen into position motionless side by side two rows from the front, the room descended into darkness once more.

Chapter 22

Let me tell you a little secret

Due to the lack of a suitable timepiece, Bill could only presume about fifteen minutes had elapsed since he last heard a sound, and he asked Sandy whether she thought they should take their chances and make an early break for it now. Sandy pondered her decision for a short while before she agreed to give it another fifteen minutes, and then if the President hadn't visited, they'd put her plan into action. Bill was a bit disappointed with the prospect of having to wait and he decided to kill the time by asking Sandy to educate him on her plan for once they'd safely escaped. Sandy didn't hesitate in giving Bill her good news. "That's the easy part. Luckily, Marvin had the foresight to cater for any hiccups in his original plan, and he told me where I could pick up a car easily without my identity papers or give a payment if my circumstances changed. He also told me how to hotwire one, just in case, and where to meet him once I had. He'll be waiting for me there for the next twelve hours, and if I arrive intact, he'll guide me safely to his safe house from there. However, Brian's put a spanner in the works as he's told me to make my way to the airport, as has Marvin, so I'm unsure how I'm going to pull that one off, but I'll cross that bridge when I need to. My main focus right now is getting us both outside alive."
Unfortunately, Bill didn't have the opportunity to quiz Sandy any further, as his attention was drawn to what

sounded like hundreds of troops stomping heavily down the corridor. His body trembled when he witnessed the door opening and it shook when he heard President Deer's unique voice command the Secret Service to stand guard outside whilst Vincent and himself went in. As the two men stepped inside the props room, it illuminated to reveal the Presidents distinct figure. Vincent then gave the door a helping hand shutting before they made their way towards the army of sexbots, and once they'd reached the centre of the front row, they stopped, and the President looked towards Vincent, who was stood by his side, as he started to talk.

"Vincent, if I'm going to get you and your partners out of this mess then I'm going to need a scapegoat, and I want to know that you categorically haven't told anyone about how I've been secretly funding your sexbot development programme. That's the last thing that I need right now with these bloody stupid accusations flying around. Now have you any suggestions for a scapegoat and is my secret still safe?" Vincent responded by giving President Deer a great big man hug and once he'd finished, he sounded his reply. "Don't worry Roland your secrets safe with me and thank you for getting my partners and Shelly out of here alive. Now I've got some very good news for you. Our programme has come on leaps and bounds since your last visit to the store and the modifications that you requested are now complete. So please let me demonstrate our Mark IV realistic breathing sexbots." Vincent then rotated his head to the left and commanded all of the sexbots to breath. The sexbots replied with a simultaneous, "yes," and their chests started to expand and contract, while a realistically sounding pump simulated the movement and sound of breath with perfect synchronisation. He then informed Roland that the bots hadn't been programmed with a command to stop breathing, so the only way to stop them now was to kill them just like you would a human. A grinning President Deer then rotated and moved towards the nearest female bot in the front row, and he placed his right hand on her chest to check for any signs of movement. There was, so he turned towards Vincent and held out his right hand. Vincent responded by grabbing it, then whilst he gripped it with all of his might, he shook it vigorously while the President congratulated him on his success.

Once the congratulations were over, Vincent decided it was time to probe the President and he quizzed him as to what his true intentions were regarding the Mark IV's. Roland hesitated for a short while before he raised his righthand, and with his index finger pointing skywards, he started waving it up and down as he spoke. "Vincent, what I'm about to tell you no one else on this planet knows, and I'm only telling you because I trust you, so you must keep it to yourself. Now when I've been attending the various boring summits that I have to, and while I've been having my private chats with different world leaders, I've been telling them all about my solution to their adultery problem. All 195 of them loved the sound of it and have placed orders, even the space man. Although he wants a backup one just in case he gets angry and kills it accidentally. So now they're ready they can be dispatched, and they can help me obtain my ultimate aim of world domination by recording their secret conversations undetected before they transmit them back for me to use against them when necessary, in order for me to get my own way. After all, knowledge is power. I'll be honest though, I was a bit worried about the buffoon in the UK not getting re-elected, he placed his order months ago. However, if the other bloke had of got in, then I don't think he'd have ordered one. If that had of happened, then my plan would have been ruined, as I need the UK firmly in my pocket for it to work perfectly. Vincent now that's out of the way, I really need you to come up with a credible scapegoat so that we can make tonight disappear and you can carry on secretly working for me. Any ideas?"

Once Roland had finished, and while he was waiting for Vincent's reply, he moved towards the female sexbot whose chest he'd felt earlier, and he placed his right hand under her nostrils to check for any signs of breath. There was, so he enthusiastically started to unzip her suit in order to allow him to pay closer attention to her chest movement. However, his inspection was cut short by Vincent shouting out. "I've got it. I know who we can use as a scapegoat. Bill. He's married to our newly crowned queen of the cult. He should already be dead as I ordered his destruction earlier so we can pin it all on

274

him. When I get back to the store I'll be able to give you his membership card which has a picture of him that you'll be able to circulate, and then if Sandy has failed in her mission, I'll never have to worry about him turning up and ruining mine and Shelly's plans together because he'll be one of America's most wanted, and he'll have to stay in hiding for the rest of his life. Will he do Roland?" "He sounds perfect to me Vincent," the President responded before he resumed his close inspection of the sexbots chest, and once he'd carried out a few tests to increase her breathing and satisfy himself that it would pass as real, he instructed Vincent to be quiet while he came up with a good plan to get all of the bots safely back to Deer Offices without drawing any attention to them. Then once they're safely there, he could pick a male one as a gift for his wife and a female one for him, before his people took over the delivery arrangements. Vincent did exactly as instructed, and the room fell silent apart from the sound of Roland's footsteps as he paced up and down the front row, while his Brain worked overtime whilst trying to come up with a credible plan.

By now a mystified Bill, who was stood motionless in his row four bots from the right with Sandy stood to his left, couldn't believe what he'd just heard, and after he had, he instantly changed his mind about ever returning to Shelly. His allegiance turned swiftly to Sandy, whilst he prayed that she had a good plan to get them out of their current predicament, so that they could live the long happy life together which she had planned for them. His thoughts then turned to what the President had said about his plan for world domination, and once he'd imagined how horrible a place the world would be to live in if he succeeded, his conscience got the better of him, and his mind filled with the thought of killing the President whilst he could in order to save the world. However, he was a man of peace and hated confrontation and he knew that if he broke his cover and attempted to harm the President, then Vincent would raise the alarm and his life would probably be cut short before he could succeed. Bill's thoughts ended when the Presidents footsteps also ceased before he started to enlighten Vincent with how he'd come up with a viable solution to his problem. "Ok Vincent, I've got it. I think I've come up with a plan which will sort your shit out and get the bots to my offices safely. But it will cost you a lot in hush money, probably about thirty percent of the cults revenue in fact, and here it is. We use this Bill bloke as a scapegoat, and I'll arrange for an Interpol red notice to be issued so that it looks like he got away. Then once I've had a little recreation time whilst testing out how realistic these bots are, I'll order the building to be secured before I send my team in to smuggle the bots out at a later date. You and your partners will be escorted safely back to Dallas, but they must never know that I've had anything to do with getting you off the hook. Now I'm also going to need you to carry out my dirty work for me so I'm appointing you as my head of the world domination programme. You'll need to carry on development as I want the Mark V's to be indestructible so that I can use them as a mass army, and secretly invade any country who disobeys me before they eliminate the entire population of it by spreading a disease onto everyone who has sex with them. Then once this is complete, I will officially be the world's most powerful man, and you'll be my deputy. Is that OK with you Vincent?" It didn't take long for Vincent to agree with a simple bowing of his head, and once he had, President Deer's inspection of the bots continued whilst he decided which one he liked most to enjoy his recreation with. As he was inspecting the front row from right to left, Bill's body filled with anger at what he'd just overheard, and his anger turned to fear when the President turned his attentions towards the second row. As the Presidents inspection continued, and for some strange reason, he thought it funny to man handle each bot as he passed them; females got either a slap on the backside or a groping of the breast. Whereas the males got a swift punch to the goolies, in order to gauge their reactions. Bill didn't know what to do, he knew that if the President did the same to him, he wouldn't be able to act lifeless like all of the real bots were, and his movement would almost certainly lead to his immediate extermination once the President realised that somebody else knew his plans.

As the President was only two bots away from him, Bill's heart was pounding and his body heavily sweating, this increased significantly as he moved closer. Then when the President was stood right in front of Bill, he changed his greeting, and he raised his right knee as he grabbed hold of the back of Bills head before he pulled it down to make contact with his raised knee. Bill couldn't contain himself any longer and before his head made contact, he grabbed hold of the Presidents leg prior to pulling it from underneath him and swiftly knocked him to the ground. A bemused President grabbed hold of Bill's leg and started to wrestle him to the floor as he screamed out for assistance from the guards outside. Vincent and Sandy didn't know what to do, this was the last thing either of them had been expecting. Sandy managed to remain motionless and prevent her cover from being blown. Vincent however, showed what a shitbag he was, and ran as fast as he could towards the door in order to escape what he thought was a malfunctioning sexbot. Bill was knocking ten bells out of his opponent, who was giving as good as he got, when the room erupted with the sound of dozens of heavily armed Secret Service agents bounding in brandishing their weapons, as they instructed the intruder to "Freeze! Put your hands in the air!" Bill didn't. He recognised that he was a dead man anyway and his life wasn't worth living, as he grabbed the President in a headlock before he twisted his neck just like he did when he was killing a chicken back home. However, just as he was about to finish the President off, his body was suddenly covered in a mass of tiny red dots before his body twitched uncontrollably as each one of the Secret Service agents emptied their magazines into Bill one after the other. He'd failed to destroy the President and his plan for world domination but had given his life in a valiant attempt. Bill was lying lifeless on the floor as he was taking his final breath, and all he could hear was the

Secret Service asking if the President was ok. He was, and after he stood up and dusted himself off, he raised his right foot high in the air before stamping it down hard on Bill's head, and Bill's world went blank.

Bill's body had been lying lifeless for about forty-five seconds when it suddenly started to twitch. Slowly at first, before the spasms started becoming more frequent. Then Bill could hear what sounded like Shelly's voice whilst she was crying. He couldn't make out what she was saying at first, then he opened his eyes a little and thought he could see her standing above him whilst she gazed down in his direction, and that Conner was stood next to her. As Bill opened his eyes fully, Shelly grabbed him in her arms whilst sobbing uncontrollably as she stated. "Oh Bill, I'm so sorry. I thought I'd lost you forever once the Doctors had turned off your life support machine. I'm so glad you've pulled through." A bemused Bill was completely baffled by now. Only seconds ago he'd attempted to assassinate the President before being exterminated by hundreds of his bodyguards rounds exploding in him, and now he's found himself alive and awake in his loving wife's arms. Witnessing what a confused state her husband was in; Shelly didn't waste any time in explaining. "You've been in a coma for the past two years ever since you gave me pans for a present, and I lost my temper when I clobbered you with them. Then two days ago I had to make the horrible decision to turn your life support machine off and let the doctors use you as a trial, as they repeatedly poked and prodded your lifeless body with needles as they dosed you up with an experimental concoction of new mind-bending drugs to stimulate your brain back into life, and give you a chance of pulling through. I promise I'll learn to control my anger issues and never be so unappreciative towards you ever again. Please forgive me." Relieved that his nightmare weekend had in fact been just that, Bill cuddled his beloved Shelly as tight as he could in his arms as he apologised for being such a boring husband. Before he informed her that he was fed up with being an uninteresting country bumpkin and seeing as they were both not getting any younger, he wanted to waste no time whatsoever in selling the ranch so they could move somewhere where they could both live a much more exciting life. Shelly's eyes lit up as she expressed how she'd love to experience some excitement whilst she was still young enough, before she inquired whether Bill had anywhere specific in mind. Wasting no time at all Bill responded. "Honey, I want to move to Vegas."

Conner then piped in with his two pennies worth. "That's a great idea, you'll love it there. I got involved with a lovely crowd when I lived nearby a while back, and their antics certainly opened my eyes into what city folk really do for entertainment. I'll buy your ranch off you if you'd like, but only on one condition. I can come and stay as often as I like because what happens in Vegas, stays in Vegas." Bill stared at Shelly, who nodded her head in agreement, so he held out his hand towards Conner as he stated. "I'll give you five percent discount on the

Ranches going rate for a quick sale." Conner grabbed it and shook it enthusiastically as he shouted, "deal." With that, the doctor approached Bill and told him that before he went anywhere, he'd need to check him out for any long-lasting signs of brain damage first.

The End

Printed in Great Britain
by Amazon

79574261R00161